OWNER OF A
BROKEN HEART

OWNER OF A
BROKEN HEART

CHERIS HODGES

THORNDIKE PRESS
A part of Gale, a Cengage Company

Copyright © 2020 by Cheris Hodges.
Richardson Sisters.
Thorndike Press, a part of Gale, a Cengage Company.

LIBRARY OF CONGRESS CIP DATA ON FILE.
CATALOGUING IN PUBLICATION FOR THIS BOOK
IS AVAILABLE FROM THE LIBRARY OF CONGRESS

ISBN-13: 978-1-4328-7986-0 (hardcover alk. paper)

Published in 2020 by arrangement with Dafina Books, an imprint of Kensington Publishing Corp.

Printed in Mexico
Print Number: 01   Print Year: 2020

OWNER OF A
BROKEN HEART

CHAPTER 1

Nina Richardson was pissed. The sportswriter had never felt more disrespected or more angry in her career. Did this quarterback just call her *sweetheart* in the middle of a press conference? Her male colleagues chuckled and tried to hide it behind coughs. Nina gritted her teeth and fought the urge to roll her eyes.

Be the professional, she told herself as she looked at his garish outfit. They weren't in some nightclub; she was doing her damned job and he dismissed her question about his poor play and three interceptions with a sexist quip.

"Sweetheart, I'm going to get a suggestion box and put it outside this door and I want your suggestions about my route accuracy to be in there."

Nina's mouth dropped. *Oh, I have a suggestion. You might consider not mixing plaids and stripes, because not only do you look like*

a clown, your current QB passer rating sug-
gests you have the brains of one as well. And
I don't give a damn that it's preseason.

"Any other questions?" the media relations representative asked, then ushered the
quarterback from behind the podium. Nina
seethed as she and the other reporters
headed out of the meeting room. Part of
her wished she could've said everything on
her mind about that overgrown child.
August was too soon for the bull. There was
a lot of football to get through before the
Super Bowl and Pro Bowl.

And she needed her job as a freelance
sportswriter. She'd thought the days of
women journalists being disrespected by the
men they covered were over; obviously not
in Charlotte, North Carolina. Nina enjoyed
her freedom and flexible schedule. So, she'd
be damned if she'd let Cody Cameron put
that in jeopardy.

"Son of a bitch," she muttered as she
waited for the elevator. The local sports
columnist touched her elbow. Nina glanced
at him and he pulled his hand back quickly.

"He's young. Probably didn't mean anything by it."

"Thanks for mansplaining that." Nina
took a deep breath and counted to ten in
her head.

"It could've been worse, you know."

"Oh really. Please tell me more about how you've been through the same thing." Nina clasped her hands together. "We're not running the same race, Mel. I have to be twice as good as you guys in there. And I am."

"Point taken. Maybe this could be a teachable moment for Cody."

Nina rolled her eyes when Mel walked away. She couldn't wait to call her boyfriend — well, that wasn't the best way to describe Coach Lamar Geddings. Though they had spent the last year hanging out, watching football, and having sex. They just hadn't labeled their relationship. Nina wanted more, but she hadn't been brave enough to say so. Still, she played the girlfriend role, cooking for him, which wasn't in her wheelhouse, and rocking his world every chance she got.

That had to mean something, right? And then there was the fact that she had been pitching his story to every editor she knew. Lamar had taken over a high school football program with a state record for losing. He'd turned things around in his first season as head coach. The school had even made it to the playoffs. Unfortunately, there was a high school across town, which had a different record. They'd won over two hundred games in a row. One of Nina's assignments had been to cover their historic season.

But she saw the human-interest quality in Lamar's story. One she had no intentions of writing, because how could she write about the man she loved and be objective? Nina smiled as she stepped off the elevator and headed for the parking lot of Bank of America Stadium. She reached into her purse and pulled out her phone. When she dialed Lamar's number, she was perplexed when his voice mail picked up.

It was Thursday and their usual meeting date. Of course, the night game had changed the normal time they'd meet for a drink and dinner. Also, why was her phone vibrating so much?

Nina clicked on her Twitter app and to her horror she'd gone viral. Why did the world have to be so connected?

"Fuck!" she muttered as she sprinted to her ruby red Mustang GT. Tossing her phone on the passenger seat, the only thing Nina wanted was a thick vanilla milkshake and some fries to dip in it. She didn't want to read the tweets about her encounter with the popular quarterback. She'd already made up in her mind that everyone was on his side.

Okay, she was going to take one quick look.

How rude! Cody Cameron is a jackass for calling that female reporter sweetheart. She was doing her job! #Respect

Nina pumped her fist and muttered "thank you."

What is this 1960? Really, we're calling women sweetheart in the workplace?

It wasn't long before she found Cody defenders.

Sports reporting is a man's game, she ought to cover something else if she can't take a joke. #Damnfeminists

Nina dropped her phone and said a few curse words. Yep. It was time for a milkshake. She tore out of the parking lot headed for her favorite diner. When she pulled up to a stoplight, Nina called Lamar again.

Voice mail.

Where is he? She pulled into the parking lot and picked up her phone again. Obviously, she was a glutton for punishment.

Why do they let women in the locker room anyway? I bet that reporter wants to date Cody and he turned her down. #Thirstybroads

Nina grunted as she closed the app. She didn't date professional athletes. And before

Lamar, Nina never mixed business with pleasure. She hadn't wanted to be *that* sportswriter. She didn't flirt with players, though sometimes in the locker room she'd get comments on her ass. Nina ignored them, pretending she was unbothered, like her older sister Alexandria would be.

Other times, Nina would ask a question about the stupidest thing the player did on the field, just to let him know that she was serious about her job. Until Cody, she thought she'd had the respect of the players she covered.

Maybe that's why all of the tweets about her being a jealous groupie pissed her off. She didn't want Cody Cameron or anybody else in the locker room. Nina just prayed no one would dig up anything about her relationship with Lamar. But how could they? They'd never posted anything on social media. They rarely hung out in public and despite pitching his story to almost every editor she knew, the only high school she'd covered regularly was the record-breaking Independence High.

Besides, though things were a little on the gray side, seeing Lamar wasn't technically wrong because he wasn't officially a part of her beat. Sighing, she pulled into the parking lot of the diner and smiled. But as she walked into the diner, her smile quickly faded.

Was that Lamar sitting in the corner wrapped around some other chick? Nina took a breath and shook her head. There had to be a logical explanation for this. She couldn't think of one.

"Just one?" the hostess asked, breaking into Nina's murderous thought.

"Yes. Can I get a table back there?" She pointed to the empty one next to Lamar and his tart. She knew calling the woman names in her head wasn't right. Lamar was the liar — that chick owed her nothing. But Lamar had some explaining to do.

The hostess nodded and led her to her selected seat. Nina sat down and faced Lamar. She'd wanted to toss something at him, but she waited until he made eye contact with her. She raised her eyebrow and pursed her lips. Inside her blood boiled.

"Hello, Lamar."

"Nina. Hi." He nudged his date. "This is Nina Richardson, she's a reporter."

The woman nodded, then turned back to Lamar. "I'm going to the bathroom. Be right back."

Once they were alone, Nina tossed a sugar package at him. "What the hell?"

"Don't make a scene. You know we're not

a couple so . . ."

"Fuck you."

"Nina, I never made any promises to you about us being exclusive, so I can see other people." He spoke as if he was explaining the four-three defense to a freshman linebacker.

"Is that right? How long have you been seeing her? Were you sleeping with both of us at the same time? You bastard."

Lamar rose to his feet. "We're just friends, right? I don't see what the big deal is here."

Nina gritted her teeth and glared at him. This was the cherry on top of a trash-ass night. Just as she was about to launch into a tirade, the girl returned with a smile on her face.

"Bae, are you ready to go? We need to work off this dinner." She reached out for Lamar's arm and glanced at Nina. "Nice to meet you, ma'am."

Lamar took her hand and they headed out the door. Nina started to go after them when her phone rang. It was her editor calling and she wondered what else could make this night even worse. The only time she got calls from her editor was when something was wrong.

"This is Nina."

"You're trending on social media. I can't

believe Cody called you sweetheart in the press conference."

"Are you serious? I really thought this would've gone away by now." Nina groaned and shook her head.

"Number one trending topic on social media. I even got a few calls from folks asking for your cell phone number. Puts me in a pickle here, Nina."

"What do you mean?"

"I can't run your story."

"Why? I didn't do anything wrong, I didn't even respond on Twitter."

"Decision came from up top. They don't want our objectivity questioned because of the exchange and —"

"This is bullshit. So am I off the Panthers for the season?"

The editor sighed. "At least until the playoffs."

"If they make the playoffs. Okay, I'm a freelance writer. I turned down other gigs to take this job and now —"

"Nina, you're a great writer and I want to keep you working with us. Your work with Independence is extraordinary. You don't have to stop covering that. Just take a few days and let this die down."

"Fine."

"I still need you for the Dallas game, I

mean you're already on the list. And since it's preseason, you don't have to do a Cody-focused story."

"Wow, thanks." Her voice was draped in sarcasm.

"I hate this as much as you do, but I'm still going to pay you for your work tonight."

As if you had a fucking choice, she thought, then ended the call. Yep. This was one of the worst nights of her life, professionally and personally.

CHAPTER 2

Two days into her *suspension,* Nina knew one thing for sure: If she didn't get out of her house, she was going to lose her mind. Lamar had texted her and asked about the incident in the locker room. Her reply had been a middle finger emoji.

Then her sister Yolanda had called her and asked why she hadn't cussed Cody Cameron out for being a disrespectful ass.

"Because I want to keep my job," she'd told her. "And from the way things are looking, I'm hanging on by a thread."

"You can do better than writing for some local rag anyway. Why aren't people jumping on your side like they do when a white girl gets treated like this?"

"Because I'm not a white girl and obviously I'm in the wrong. Look, Yolanda, I got to go. I'm tired of talking about this and everything else." Nina had been asked to appear on a local newscast, but she covered stories and she wasn't going to become one.

"What else is going on? Spill it, Nina."

Nina had broken down and told her about Lamar and the woman he'd been with at the diner.

"Oh, girl, I'm —"

"We'll talk later." Nina had hung up on her sister and forced herself not to cry.

She needed to get away from Charlotte and the best place for her to go was home. She could spend some time hanging out at her father's bed-and-breakfast in Charleston, South Carolina. Then she could ignore the dull pain thudding in her heart and fight the urge to call Lamar. Nina knew she wouldn't get the apology or explanation she wanted or deserved.

Sheldon Richardson would be happy to have his baby girl come home. Her oldest sister, Alexandria, might not be so inviting though. She'd want to know why she was making this impromptu visit and ask too many questions. Then she'd probably try to put her to work. Alex was more like a mother to Nina than a sister. When Nina had been two years old, her mother died and Alex, who was ten years old at the time, became Little Mama. Alex took responsibility for her little sister and mothered her — sometimes smothered her. She'd been thankful that Alex wasn't on social media enough to know about the hoopla surrounding her and Cody.

Her father had called and told her he'd be happy to teach that smart-mouth quarterback how to respect women with his leather belt. Nina couldn't love her father any more if she tried.

Despite her viral encounter in the locker room, Nina had done quite well for herself as a sportswriter. Her career was thriving with her work appearing in several regional and national magazines and newspapers. She was set to have a spot on one of ESPN's broadcasts of *SportsCenter* at the start of basketball season, but she was hired by three magazines to cover Independence High School's historic winning streak and turned the ESPN job down because writing was her true passion.

If she was going to do TV, Nina wanted a spot on *NFL Live,* though she didn't see that happening anytime soon. Nina had heard so many people say that real football fans wouldn't want to listen to a woman's opinion on the sport. And she wasn't blond enough for most networks. And with all of this unflattering press about her, she probably wouldn't be bankable enough for a network to take a chance on her.

What made things even worse was the fact that Lamar's presence loomed over her like foreboding storm clouds. It wasn't as if she'd be able to avoid Lamar all season. His school had a regular season game against the Patriots and there were the jamborees. As a matter of fact, she was supposed to cover one Friday. To make matters worse, she'd invited him to sit in the press box with her at the Carolina Panthers' Monday night game and she'd already given him the pass. Oh, how she wished she could've taken it back. If she were bolder, she would've done just that two days ago.

Cursing inwardly, Nina wondered why she'd tried to buy him with football games and promises of media coverage. Did she really think that doing all of that would make Lamar love her? She basically allowed him to use her for coverage and exclusive access to NFL games. Nina played along, hoping things would change and he'd see her as more than a sex partner. Clearly, nothing changed.

But he bugged her about media coverage. Always wanted to tag along to Panthers' games and celebrate afterward.

Nina couldn't sell his story to anyone she worked for. No one cared because the story about Independence was bigger. At one time she'd hoped that his school would knock the Patriots off their throne. Now she just prayed Independence would keep West Meck from scoring a point and Lamar would get fired. A public firing that she would love to write about — for free.

Despite how much she wanted to, Nina couldn't totally blame Lamar. She made it easy to be used. Easy to be thought of as a fool.

Nina carefully set her laptop on the coffee table and picked up her cell phone. She couldn't face this right now. She was going to leave, even if it was going to cost her money. She dialed her father's number. She couldn't wait to tell her Daddy that she was coming home for a visit.

Charleston, South Carolina
Sheldon Richardson was a formidable man, Clinton Jefferson surmised as the older man shook his hand. Before Clinton could say a word, Sheldon spoke in a booming voice that reminded him of thunder and made him cringe like a sharp bolt of electricity had struck him.

"I know why you're here and the answer is no."

"Mr. Richardson." His voice didn't convey the nervousness that flowed through his

21

body like his own blood. He actually sounded confident, but that couldn't have been further from the truth. Clinton was damn near petrified as he prepared to do the unthinkable.

"No. I'm not selling, no matter how much Birmingham is offering. I don't want to be a part of a chain. You see, what I offer isn't something you can get from any hotel and you can say that nothing will change, but it will. I've been around the block and know how these things work. Hell, you're not even representing one of the best chains. So go back to Randall Birmingham and tell him Sheldon Richardson said hell no."

"Sir, I didn't come with another buyout offer." Clinton reached into his briefcase, pulled out his résumé, and handed it to Sheldon. "I'm looking for a job."

Sheldon laughed and his round belly shook like jelly. Clinton wondered if he could talk the older man into dressing up like Santa for the holidays. Before they'd have that conversation, Clinton would have to get the job first.

"A job? Why would you want to work for a family-owned company when you're hot shit at Randall's Fortune 500 company? I can tell you right now I won't pay what they were paying you." Sheldon took the résumé and looked over it. He nodded, impressed with the young man's credentials.

Clinton Jefferson didn't have many heroes growing up in North Charleston, but Sheldon Richardson had always been one of his. Every time he saw him in the newspaper, Clinton swelled with pride. Here was a man who looked like him making headlines for positive reasons. It was because of Sheldon that Clinton had studied hospitality in college. He also majored in marketing because he wanted to work in upper management and not the day-to-day running of the property. He'd been working with Randall Birmingham's company since he landed a paid internship there his junior year of college. But deep down, he'd always wondered what working for Sheldon Richardson would've taught him.

The day he walked into the Richardson Bed and Breakfast with an offer from Birmingham Properties to purchase the historic and picturesque hotel, he'd never been more nervous in his life. But Sheldon had made such an impression on him that he wanted to work for him and learn everything he could about the hospitality industry. It wasn't as if he was coming into the company empty-handed. With his marketing expertise, he could get nationwide recognition for the bed-and-breakfast and help Sheldon make more money than he'd ever dreamed of without having to sell to anyone.

"Sir," Clinton said. "If I wanted to keep making the same salary, I wouldn't have quit. I want to brand your business and make this bed-and-breakfast the premier destination in the Southeast. When people think of Charleston, this should be the first place they think about. I have media contacts and the know-how to get the job done. When I analyzed your company for Birmingham, the only weakness I saw was in your marketing. You don't do a lot of it and in this media-driven marketplace, you're going to need to do more if you want to keep the Randall Birminghams of the world at bay."

Sheldon looked over Clinton's résumé again. "Why should I take a chance on you? You could come in here and take my secrets back to your old boss. I know how this game is played, son. One thing you don't want to do is cross me."

Nodding, Clinton understood the older man's apprehension. "Give me a ninety-day trial period, have me sign a confidentiality agreement or whatever. Mr. Richardson, I've always admired you. When I was growing up in North Charleston, you were a legend. You came downtown in a time of segregation and opened this luxurious property and thrived. I'd never dream of doing something underhanded to take away what you've worked so hard for."

Sheldon smiled and pointed to a picture of an older white man hanging behind his vast oak desk. "*Mr. Richardson* is the reason a lot of racist white folk stayed here in the days of segregation. People assumed he owned this place and I was just the hired help. I made up so many excuses as to why he was never on the property. Would've paid a lot of money to see the look on their faces when they found out I was the real owner." Sheldon chuckled, then leaned into Clinton. "I'll let you in on a little secret. That's just an old picture I found at a yard sale in 1963. I don't even know who that man is. It was my wife Nora's idea to create the persona of Mr. Richardson being white. She was right, too."

"What you've done with this place is admirable. It's certainly understandable why you wouldn't want to sell. But I know I can make this place even more well-known than it is now with social media and —"

"Why are you here *again*?" an angry female voice boomed from the doorway of Sheldon's office.

"Alex, meet your new marketing manager, Clinton Jefferson."

"Daddy," she said as she breezed into the office like a hurricane. "You can't be serious. Isn't this Randall's stooge?"

"I still own the place, so I'm serious. The decision has been made. Clinton has something we need. He's a helluva salesman because I just bought his pitch, hook, line, and sinker."

Anger shadowed Alex's comely features as she glared at Clinton. A lesser man would've been intimidated by the Amazonian beauty. She was tall, nearly six feet. Her eyes were black as coal — just like Sheldon's but lacking warmth. With her straight black hair pulled back in a conservative bun, she looked like the grade school teacher who you didn't want to piss off.

But he didn't appreciate being called a stooge. Clinton was his own man, no one owned him — especially Randall Birmingham.

"Well, Mr. Jefferson, welcome to the company. But keep in mind that I handle the day-to-day running of this business. You will answer directly to me." Alex folded her arms across her chest and gave him a slow once-over.

"Yes, ma'am. I'm here to assist." The way

Alexandria spoke, Clinton had no doubt that this woman ruled with an iron fist.

Before Alex could say anything else, her father's private line rang.

"Hello, it's Sheldon," he drawled. "Baby girl. It's good to hear from you. How are you holding up? They did what? Now, that is some bullshit. If I ever meet that quarterback, he's going to have a really short career. Why are you being punished? Darling, I am calm. Okay. I'll be glad to see you. What about the Dallas game?" Sheldon laughed. "I hope the Dallas defense slams him to the ground and knocks some sense in his head."

Sheldon hung up the phone and turned to his eldest daughter and Clinton with a bright smile on his face. "That was Nina. She's coming home."

Alex smiled and scratched her head. "Doesn't she have to cover some sort of sporting events? How can she take off at the beginning of football season?"

Sheldon shrugged. "You clearly haven't been watching ESPN. She needs a break and she got suspended for a couple of days."

"Suspended? Why?"

"She'll be here soon and I'm sure you'll drag it out of her."

Clinton felt as if a family argument was

brewing and he figured he should leave. But go where? He didn't have an employment start date or an office. He couldn't help but wonder if Nina was anything like her older sister. He had to admit: Alexandria Richardson was one scary woman even if she was pretty. To remind father and daughter that he was still in the room, Clinton cleared his throat loudly.

All eyes focused on him and Sheldon smiled again. "Monday would be a good day for you to start. I'd like for you and Alexandria to go over a marketing plan that fits our company and for you to meet the entire staff — from the housekeepers to our cooks and the other managers. Get a feel for how we work. All of us are family," he said. "You know what? Why don't you get started tomorrow? Alexandria will show you around today so that you can get your feet wet."

Alex didn't look happy and Clinton got the feeling that he'd never view her as a sister or cousin — no matter how distant. "Let me show you to your office and it's not going to be big."

"As long as it's not a broom closet I'll be happy," Clinton said with a forced smile on his lips.

Once they were out of Sheldon's earshot,

Alex whirled around and focused an evil sneer on Clinton. "I don't know what your game is or why all of a sudden you want to work here. Know this: If you try anything underhanded to wrest control of this property from my family, there will be hell to pay."

"Alex —"

"Miss Richardson," she snapped.

"My apologies. Miss Richardson, your father has been one of my heroes for a long time and I would never do anything to try and take this company from him. When I came here two months ago, I was working for someone else who conducts business in a way that I don't want to be associated with. I chose to come here and offer my —"

"How are we to know that you're not still working for Randall Birmingham? I know his style and he doesn't give up when he wants something. For all I know, this could be a new ploy," Alex hissed.

"Because I quit and I suggest you call and make sure I did."

"Don't think for a second that I won't and you better be everything you say you are." Alex spun on her heels and stalked down the hall with Clinton struggling to keep up.

His office may not have been an actual broom closet, but it was close. There were no windows, just room for a desk, chair, and nothing else. The walls were the blandest shade of beige he'd ever seen and with the overhead fluorescent light on, the room looked as if it has been bleached. Sitting his briefcase on the desk, Clinton forced himself to pretend he liked the space.

"I'm right across the hall from you and I *will* be keeping my eye on you," Alex spat.

"Never doubted that you would," he mumbled as she walked across the hall to her lavish office with a view of the Charleston Harbor.

CHAPTER 3

The next day, Nina pulled into the parking lot of the Richardson Bed and Breakfast and smiled as memories of her childhood came rushing back. She, Yolanda, and Robin had spent mornings in the summer running around the property and splashing in the pool until Alex would call them inside and force them to do chores. Nina had gotten out of doing her work by cozying up to her father and asking him a million questions about the business or watching a football game with him. By the time he'd answered all of her questions or the game ended, the cleaning and other chores had been done. Her sisters used to get so mad that they would leave her alone in her room when they'd go to the mall.

But guilt would get the best of them and they'd come back with a brand-new Barbie doll for her or when she was older, a book or magazine because she loved to read.

31

Parking next to her father's Lincoln MKC, she smiled knowing that Alex was going to blow a gasket when she returned and found someone parked in her reserved spot. She left her bags in the car and dashed toward the front door, she couldn't wait to fling herself into her father's arms. Nina needed to mask the main reason why she'd come home.

Lamar.

She'd told her sisters so many things about him. Yolanda, with whom she was closest because they were only four years apart, knew what an exciting and gentle lover he was.

Robin, the hopeless romantic, knew how he made her heart flutter every time she heard his voice.

Alex, the mother hen, knew that he had a good job and his own house and always held the door for her when they went out to dinner at *his* favorite restaurant.

But she never told her father about Lamar, though she had planned to introduce the two of them at Monday night's game. It's not that he wouldn't have approved, but he would've wanted to meet him and interrogate him. *Maybe I should've let him do it because he could've told me Lamar was a no-good son of a bitch,* she thought as she walked into the lobby. How was it possible that she'd imagined a whole relationship in her head? *You didn't, you simply got played.*

Nina shook her head and focused on the changes in the bed-and-breakfast. She was really impressed with the new look.

The lobby looked like a slice of *Better Homes & Gardens* magazine with the deep brown overstuffed sofas decorated by bright orange throw pillows, and a heavy oak coffee table that was polished at least three times a day so that it was always shining. The walls were adorned with gold-framed paintings by local artists, which guests could purchase if they wanted to take them home. Nina's feet sank into the plushest caramel carpet that made it feel as if you were walking on marshmallow clouds. She wanted to kick off her knee-high sandals and walk around barefoot like she was ten years old again. She hadn't realized how long she'd been standing there drinking up the surroundings until a man approached her. "Excuse me, is there anything I can help you with?" His voice was more melodic than any smooth jazz song.

Turning around, she looked at the reincarnation of a young Denzel Washington — smooth brown skin, a dazzling smile, and eyes that seemed to pierce her soul. Inhaling sharply, Nina tried to tell him she was Sheldon's daughter, but she stammered incoherently. "Um, I, ah."

He placed his hand on her shoulder. "Miss, are you all right?"

"I'm looking for my father. Who are you?"

"I'm the marketing manager here, Clinton Jefferson. What's his room number, I can point you in the right direction."

Nina raised her eyebrow. "Since when did Daddy hire a marketing manager?"

"Daddy? As in Mr. Richardson is your father?"

Proudly she nodded and extended her hand. "Nina Richardson, my father's favorite daughter."

"Who obviously can't read," Alex quipped from behind her. "You're lucky I recognized those North Carolina license plates or else your little red Mustang would've been towed away."

Nina turned around and hugged her sister tightly. "Who is this guy?" she whispered.

Alex pouted as she released her sister and gave her a look. Nina recognized the scowl and knew Alex wasn't happy Clinton Jefferson was a part of the company.

"Have you seen Dad?" Alex asked.

Clinton smiled and folded his arms, feeling like the invisible man. Nina caught his tense expression and smiled at him. "It was nice to meet you, Mr. Jefferson."

"Please, call me Clinton, and it was nice to meet you too. Miss Richardson, I'm going to lunch if that's all right."

"That's fine, but please be back in an hour. We need to go over what your duties will entail and how we can implement any of your suggestions that I approve."

Nina shivered at the chill in her sister's voice. What had a man that fine done to Alex to make her treat him so coldly? Shaking her head, Nina figured he was a man and he'd probably lied or done something to get under Alex's skin. As sexy as Clinton was, he had to be cocky, probably challenged Alex's authority, and no one did that and lived to tell the story about it.

"You don't like him much, do you?" Nina asked when he was gone.

"I don't trust him and I don't know why Daddy hired him." Alex shook her head as she and Nina walked. "Just a few months ago he was here trying to buy this place out from under us, then he comes in looking for a job. The messed up thing is, Daddy hired him without question."

"And you think that there's something fishy going on?"

"I don't buy that he isn't still scheming

with his old boss. He's out of here in three months, though. I'm going to see to that."

"Daddy must like him if he hired him. And he wouldn't have given a job to someone he didn't trust." Nina wondered if he was really a likable type of guy. He certainly wasn't hard on the eyes.

Alex shrugged, then placed her arm around her sister's shoulder. "Forget him, let's talk about why you're here. I can't believe you got suspended from your job because of what that meathead said."

"Neither can I. Such bullshit."

"I'm glad you didn't respond. I saw a little bit of the controversy on ESPN. They could've used a better picture of you." Alex playfully tugged on her sister's ponytail. "And I'm glad that moron lost his endorsement of that yogurt."

"Well, don't go on social media and look at any of the memes." Nina shook her head, thinking of the cruelty she'd faced online.

"How's Lamar? I hope he's been helping you through this." Alex raised her eyebrow at Nina.

"Who?"

Slapping her hand against her thigh, Alex exclaimed, "I knew it. This is about a man — again. You made it seem as if this one was different. I thought he was the love of your life."

Sighing, Nina wanted to tell her sister that she had been fooled, but she didn't say anything because she didn't want to be judged by Almighty Alex, who would say something along the lines of *you're not the only woman who's been unlucky in love.*

"Can we just go see Daddy?" Nina asked.

"What did he do? And you know it was probably a bad idea to be personally involved with a coach when you cover sports. How would that look?"

"Just stop it. I made a mistake. I'll deal with it."

Alex stopped and placed her hand on her shoulder. "But you keep making the same mistake. Some man is always breaking your heart."

Nina narrowed her eyes at Alex. Mad that her sister was right, but she wasn't going to admit that right now. "I tell you what, when you stop sleeping alone in that big cold bed of yours, then I'll take your advice on men."

Alex inhaled sharply as she strode off to the elevator. Nina nearly had to run to catch up with her sister. "Alex, I'm sorry." Nina grasped her sister's elbow. Alex whirled around and focused a cold stare on her little sister.

"You, Yo-Yo, and Robin have run off and

lived your dreams, but I stayed here to help Daddy, so excuse me if I don't have a full social calendar. Maybe if you'd clear yours, you'd go further as a journalist."

"I'm paying my own way, aren't I? You've always wanted to mold me as a little Alex. I'm my own woman and maybe if you had a man in your life you'd feel more like a woman instead of a businessman."

"How's that working out for you and Lamar?"

Nina glared at Alex as they stepped on the elevator. "I deserved that, but let's not tell Daddy about any of this."

"I try to keep the tawdry details about your life away from Daddy. He worries about you enough as it is."

Nina pressed the emergency stop button on the elevator. "You got one more insult before I run out of here and throw eggs on your precious Mercedes."

Alex pulled the button to start the elevator moving again. "Grow up, Nina."

"Keep playing with me."

The sisters broke out laughing and hugged each other. "I'm not judging you," Alex said. "I just want the best for you. If I ever meet this Lamar person, I'm going to tell him a thing or two."

"That's all right, Lamar and I are over."

"Until you have to cover one of his games. Why would you get involved with someone you work so closely with? That's not a judgment, it's just a question. Wasn't that whole relationship unethical?"

"Maybe I'll come back here and cover sports here," Nina said in a small voice.

Alex shook her head. "Richardsons don't run. You won't be the first to be a coward. Do you think you're the only woman who's had her heart broken? Besides, one thing I know for sure is that you love Charlotte. Are you going to let that fool run you out of town? And there isn't a professional football team here."

"You're right. I bow to you, ma'am."

Alex narrowed her eyes at her sister. "I'm not that old."

I can't tell, Nina thought but didn't dare say. "I know."

Alex knocked softly on her father's office door.

"Come in," he growled. Nina smiled. Her daddy always pretended to be in a bad mood to keep salesmen away.

Alex opened the door. "Look what I found in the lobby," she said, then stepped aside to let Nina come into view.

Sheldon leapt to his feet and rushed from behind his big oak desk to embrace his youngest daughter. "I'm so happy to see you," he said as he swept Nina up into his arms. "And this mess will blow over. Don't worry about what Internet trolls say. Everybody is brave behind a computer screen."

Nina waved her hand. "Definitely not worried about that. Next week they will be on to something else that doesn't involve me." Her phone buzzed and she inwardly hoped it was Lamar texting to apologize. Instead it was her editor from *Sports Illustrated.* Her new assignment was going to be on the Dallas Cowboys' defensive shortcomings, particularly their star cornerback. Though she hoped during the Monday night game the defense would pound Cody Cameron into the turf. She shot her editor a quick reply, letting him know that she'd received the assignment.

She looked up at her dad and smiled. "At least I won't have to talk to Cameron on Monday. My story is going to be about the Cowboys' defense."

"Good. That'll be a better story anyway. When I told the boys at the barbershop that my baby wrote the *Sports Illustrated* cover story on the Carolina Panthers, you should've seen their faces," he said proudly. "They always tease me because Nora and I ended up with a houseful of girls and I never had a son to cheer for on the football field. Those players don't try to put their grubby hands on you, do they?"

"No, most try to run away when they see me coming," Nina said. "But Daddy, enough about me, how's business and who's Clinton Jefferson?"

Lunch wasn't fun for Clinton. He'd dropped mustard on his red silk tie and poured his cola on an elderly woman who'd bumped into him as he tried to rush back to his car. He was off his game because he'd never seen a woman more beautiful than Nina Richardson. Her black eyes sparkled like rare diamonds, she had the perfect button nose and thick pouty lips. But it was her body that made his tongue thick and words fail him. She was shaped like an old-school glass Coca-Cola bottle with curves that went on for days and days. Nina and Alexandria could not be related, one of them had to be adopted. Nina had a smile that brightened rooms and Alex just scowled as if she tasted sour milk.

Nina was tall, not as tall as her sister, but still a brick house Amazon.

Wonder Woman, Clinton thought as he got into his 1969 baby blue Ford Mustang. Looking down at his watch, he realized that he was going to be running five minutes late and Alex was going to have an attitude. He didn't care, though. She was his boss but she needed to treat him with a little more respect. Today was his first day, and he thought she'd be impressed with the amount of work that he had done. Instead, he was greeted with nit-picking and complaints. He had to wonder how much she really knew about marketing, since the plan that they had been using was older than either of them.

Then Nina walked in and he couldn't help but smile. Was she going to work at the bed-and-breakfast too? He pulled into the parking lot and dashed inside the building. Luckily, Alex wasn't in her office and she didn't know he was late returning from lunch. Taking his seat at his desk, Clinton pulled up his marketing and publicity plan to review it before Alex arrived for their meeting. He knew that she was going to rip it apart no matter how brilliant it was. As a safeguard, he e-mailed a copy of his plan to Sheldon; after all, it was his company. Though Alex liked to consider herself the queen bee, he knew all final decisions rested with Sheldon Richardson.

The sound of heels clicking across the marble floor caused him to look up from the computer screen. He'd expected to see Alex, but to his surprise and delight, Nina was standing in his doorway looking sexy and innocent at the same time.

"She's really not that bad," Nina said. Her voice had a singsong quality that Clinton could feel himself being hypnotized by. Then he imagined her whispering his name while lying across his bed.

What am I thinking? Clinton blinked, forcing himself to focus on Nina's conversation. "Are you talking about Miss Richardson?" His mouth felt as if it had been packed with cotton as he eyed Nina's physique. He couldn't help but wonder if she had on bikinis or a thong underneath her skinny jeans.

Nina walked into his office and took a seat on the edge of his uncluttered desk. "Alex, and please call her Alex, is territorial. She doesn't want other people to come in and take her shine away. She's in the office with Daddy right now talking about how she thinks you're going to fit in well here. That means he wants you here and she's going to have to deal with it."

"Has she always been so . . ."

"Bossy, pigheaded, and demanding?" Nina finished. She ran her tongue over those ripe lips and so many erotic thoughts ran through his mind. "Well, she's the oldest so, yes. Just let her get her way every now and then. If she thinks she's the boss, she'll calm down a bit. Also, prove her wrong."

"Meaning?"

"She doesn't trust you. Make sure she can." Nina crossed and uncrossed her legs as she smiled at him.

Clinton couldn't take his eyes off the leggy beauty. *Thank God she has on jeans, because if she had on a skirt, I would be tempted to touch,* he thought as he smiled tightly. "Thanks for the insight."

Nina bounced off the desk. "Don't mention it."

"So, will you be working here as well?"

Nina threw her head back and laughed. "God, no," she said. "I'm a writer. Working here would drive me absolutely crazy. Alex has always thought she was the boss of me."

It would drive me crazy to see you walking in here every day, especially if all of your clothing fit as well as those jeans. "A writer, huh?"

"Maybe you've read some of my stuff. Do you subscribe to *Sports Illustrated* or *ESPN the Magazine*?"

"I'm not a big sports fan," he said.

She raised her perfectly arched eyebrow.

"Really? Why not, if you don't mind me asking."

"Watching grown men run around and play with balls has never done anything for me. At my last job, people went crazy over fantasy football leagues and whatnot."

"I can respect that. Just for the record, you'd better hop on the football bandwagon if you want to make it around here. My father, my sisters, and I love football and we have a huge Super Bowl party every year. The whole staff comes and we have a great time. And even better food."

"I'll keep that in mind," he said. *And if you're going to be there, count me in.*

Nina headed for the door, giving him a bird's-eye view of her shapely hips and ass. She turned around before leaving. "Don't tell Alex I gave you the skinny on her, she'll accuse me of flirting and that's the last thing that I'm doing."

"All right, young Miss Richardson."

"Please call me Nina," she said, then smiled at him so brightly he thought she'd swallowed the sun.

"Nina, it was great meeting you. I hope to see you again."

She waved and sauntered down the hall. The next time he looked up, he saw Alex standing there. "Have you forgotten about

45

our meeting?" she asked like a schoolteacher demanding an overdue assignment.

"No, Alex, I haven't forgotten. I was just sending some documents to your father and printing my plan out for you."

She snarled at him, then beckoned him into her office. "Do yourself a favor, remember that Nina doesn't work here nor does she make employment decisions."

Just let her get her way every now and then, echoed in his head before he said, "Yes, Miss Richardson."

CHAPTER 4

Nina sat in her old room in the family section of the B&B, which was a four-room house behind the main building, and smiled as she thought about Clinton. So, she had been flirting with him. And maybe it wasn't her best idea right now. As much as she hated to admit it, Alex had a point about her choice in men. Lamar was just another loser in a list of heartbreaks. First there had been her high school sweetheart, Marvin Ware, who'd promised her devotion if she made love to him on their prom night.

She hadn't been ready for sex at age sixteen and turned him down. He'd left her standing outside of the Charleston Harbor Resort and Marina in the pouring rain. She'd never been more embarrassed to call her sister Yolanda to pick her up and take her home. Alex had been ready to find Marvin and beat him to a bloody pulp.

"No one treats my little sister that way,"

Alex had proclaimed that night.

When she'd gone off to Clark Atlanta University, a charming junior football player, Chad Allen, wooed her during freshman orientation and this time, Nina thought she had been ready to give up her heart and her virginity. Little did she know, Chad had a girlfriend who was due to return to school a week later when the upperclassmen moved back to campus. As quickly as he'd wooed her, he'd dumped her in favor of Diamond Turner. Nina had vowed to give up on men after that experience.

Robin had been the one who'd told her not to give up on love and that her time for romance was coming, but she needed to focus on her studies. That's what she'd done, carving a reputation as a smart student and talented writer. She had been such a star on the student newspaper staff that she'd had no problems getting an internship at the *Atlanta Journal-Constitution* newspaper where she'd covered the Atlanta Falcons and the Atlanta Hawks, the first female intern to ever do so. Nina's editors had admired her maturity and offered her a job when she graduated. But after a few years at the newspaper, Nina decided she wanted a change and wanted to work for herself. She spent the next few years building her reputation as a freelance sports journalist. She'd had the opportunity to cover several Super Bowls and NCAA Final Fours. She made Charlotte her home base because she was close enough to most major sports towns and not that far from her family in Charleston.

She'd done a great job of focusing on her career until she met Lamar. Thinking that she had learned her lessons in love, she'd given Lamar a chance. They hadn't rushed into sex and she'd thought they'd gotten to know each other pretty well. When things did turn physical, Nina believed that he was the one and he'd love her the way she deserved to be loved. Maybe, she'd thought, he'd fall in love with her over a plate of baked chicken and macaroni and cheese. Or maybe, she'd dreamed, he'd fall head over heels for her as they cheered on the Dallas Cowboys together.

Am I really that stupid? she thought as she hugged a pillow against her chest. *I was a booty call and a free meal. How could I allow myself to be used that way? It's like I keep making the same mistakes over and over again when it comes to men. Here I am thinking about him and he hasn't even bothered to call me and apologize for hurting me.*

Nina didn't want to become bitter, but

she was starting to feel that way. Stretching out on her bed, she felt the sting of tears in her eyes, but she was tired of crying. She knew that she couldn't make anyone love her and she knew she was a damned good catch. All she wanted was someone to hold her on rainy nights, someone to snuggle with on a rare Carolina snow day, and someone she could share her life with. Was that too much to ask?

Just as she was about to drift off to sleep, her cell phone rang.

"Hello?"

"Nina, where are you?" Yolanda Richardson asked. "I hope you reconsidered doing *SportsCenter.* I've been out here trying to fight these Internet trolls. Hell, I even called a local radio station to cuss —"

"I'm in Charleston. Stand down with the cussing people out on the radio."

"What? Why? Is Daddy okay?" Her voice was frantic with concern.

"I needed a break from . . . everything."

"I'm surprised you're not relaxing with Lamar."

Unable to hold back her tears and hurt feelings, Nina began to sob and told her sister the story that sent her running home to their father like a little baby.

"Damn. So, he just sat there with another

woman and said you should be cool with it? He's lucky you didn't stab his ass with a steak knife."

"Yeah, because what I needed that night was more attention. I was already trending on Twitter. Do you think I wanted to add a mug shot?"

"I guess you're right. Do I need to drive down to Charlotte and stick a banana in his tailpipe? Slash his tires? Throw a brick through his living room window?"

"No, that's childish and he lives in a gated community."

Yolanda laughed. "Thought about doing it yourself, huh?"

"Only every hour on the hour." Nina wiped her tears with the back of her hand.

"How long are you going to be in Charleston?"

"I don't know."

"Why don't I take a few days off and we can terrorize Alex like we did when we were younger. That should lift your spirits a little."

"Alex has her own problems, mainly Clinton Jefferson." Nina closed her eyes and envisioned the sexy Denzel look-alike sitting across from her, whispering all the right things in her ear. *Bring it down.*

"The ice princess has a man?" Yolanda

51

asked incredulously. "You've got to be kidding me. Now I know I'm coming down to see this."

"No, he's not her man. Just a new employee. I get the feeling that he's not bowing to her every demand and that's not sitting well with her."

"I will be there this weekend, for sure."

"How are you going to leave your boutique when it's back to school time and then the holidays?"

"Because I got it like that, baby. I'm the boss. And, I miss my jet-setting little sister. Nobody ever sees you anymore, Nina. This is a rare opportunity."

"I miss you too, Yo-Yo. Daddy's going to be too happy to see all of us."

"Not all of us. Robin probably won't be able to come down from Richmond. I think she and Logan are having some problems, but don't tell her I said anything."

Nina didn't want to hear that her sister, the only Richardson sister who'd gotten married, was having problems. If Robin couldn't make love last, then what chance did she have of finding Mr. Right? "I won't say a word. But why do you think something's wrong?"

"Well, Robin hasn't been her usual perky self and every time I ask about Logan, she changes the subject. Logan's putting in more hours at the hospital and he's rarely around when I talk to her. That's not like him."

"That's terrible. She was my relationship role model."

Yolanda sighed. "And that's probably why she isn't telling us what's going on. Besides, Robin has always tried to be Little Miss Perfect. She'll talk when she wants to. Listen, don't tell Alex I'm coming. I want to surprise her."

As close as the four Richardson sisters were, Alex and Yolanda fought like cats and dogs most of the time. Nina knew it was because they both wanted to be in charge of everything. When it really counted, though, no bond was stronger. If you messed with one of them, then you messed with all of them.

"Promise me that you will be nice to Alex. I don't want to play referee between you two all weekend."

"I'll be on my best behavior," Yolanda said. Nina didn't buy a word of it.

It was after seven before Clinton finished up his work. As he was about leave, he spotted Sheldon, Nina, and Alex heading out.

"Clinton," Sheldon called out. "You're still here?"

"Yes, sir. I'm getting ready to leave, though."

"Why don't you join us for dinner? We're going to the restaurant down the street. You can tell me all about your first day on the job."

"I don't want to impose." Clinton noticed the scowl on Alex's face.

"It's no imposition," Sheldon said. "I told you, we're all family here."

Clinton smiled and glanced over at Nina, who returned his smile. He noticed that she'd changed her clothes; opting for a knee-skimming brown skirt, a pair of nude heels, and a snug-fitting and low-cut white top. Her breasts looked ripe for kissing. Shaking his head, he turned away from her. She was his boss's daughter. Besides, the way she looked, there was no way Nina Richardson was single. Clinton knew there was a man somewhere waiting for Nina to return to him.

"Mr. Richardson, thank you for the invitation, but . . ."

"No buts. You're dining with us, no more arguments." Sheldon shot Alex a stern look as if he knew she'd have something to say.

Clinton smiled in defeat. One thing he

knew for sure: If Sheldon knew what he was thinking as she stared at Nina, he'd rescind that invitation quickly.

"All right," he said, tearing his eyes away from Nina and focusing on Sheldon. He couldn't help but wonder what his life would've been like with a father like Sheldon Richardson, who obviously loved his daughters. He noticed how he held their hands as they walked. Sheldon listened intently as Nina told a story about a funny interview she had with a Carolina Panthers wide receiver and smiled as Alex talked about mundane business issues.

Clinton Jefferson Sr. never showed an interest in anything other than football and basketball. When he saw that his son would rather read a book than tackle or dunk, he stopped showing an interest in him as well. It didn't matter that Clinton had been a star student at North Charleston High School. It also didn't matter that Clinton had received full scholarship offers from Duke University, Howard University, and the University of South Carolina as a junior in high school because of his academic achievements. Clinton Sr. thought his son was soft and he didn't have anything to brag about when other men talked about how their kids made the papers for some heroic deed under the Friday night lights on the football field.

Had it not been for his mother, Eliza Jefferson, Clinton would've never had the desire to do anything positive with his life. Eliza had always told him how proud she was of him and praised him for his good grades and gave him treats when Clinton Sr. wasn't looking. Clinton tried not to harbor bitter feelings toward his father, but that was hard because when he'd graduated from Howard with the highest honors, his father hadn't bothered to show up.

Looking at the Richardsons, Clinton longed to be a part of a loving family just as if he were still a twelve-year-old boy.

Once they arrived at the Blakemore Carriage House and Restaurant, Clinton did feel like a member of the family. Sheldon included him in their conversation, complimented him on his first day of work, and even joked that Alex wasn't as mean as she pretended to be.

"I'll do anything to protect my family," she said as they took a seat.

"And that's why we love you," Nina said. Clinton felt as if Nina was struggling to keep her eyes off him. *Nah,* he thought. *There's no way she's checking me out.* He glanced at Alex and the scowl on her face told him that she'd noticed the same thing.

"Nina, has that hotshot school in Charlotte lost a game yet?"

"No. And they should easily beat their next opponent."

"You cover all sports, huh?" Clinton asked.

Nodding as she sipped her water, Nina said, "I don't see why people make such a big deal about high school football. Those players are just kids and they try to elevate them to a celebrity status. Sure, it sells magazines and newspapers, but just think what it does to these kids mentally. We create the arrogant athlete and then tear them down once they act as if the world revolves around them."

And the kids who don't even play sports feel even worse, he thought bitterly. "Then why do you write about it?" Clinton asked.

Nina shrugged. "I like sports, it was how Daddy and I bonded."

"It was how she got out of cleaning up with the rest of us on Sunday afternoons," Alex said. "You weren't even slick."

"I did my fair share of work." Nina poked her lip out and Clinton's cock throbbed with desire.

Too sexy.

"No, you didn't," Sheldon said with a

laugh. "I'll freely admit that now. I feel so used. The only reason you watched football with me was so you wouldn't have to mop."

"Daddy, just think about it, had you made me mop, I wouldn't be able to get you those Dallas Cowboys tickets."

"You let her get away with it," Alex said, joining in the laughter. "That's it, I'm never cleaning another thing and Nina, you need to stay for at least six months to put a dent in all the work you got out of as a child."

"Oh please," Nina said. "When you went away to college, I more than made up for it."

Sheldon nodded. "Because Robin and Yolanda weren't as protective of their baby sister as you were, Alexandria. They made her do more than her fair share and I let them get away with it."

Alex laughed and for the first time, Clinton saw her as human. *She might not be that bad,* he thought. *Then again, Nina can make anyone smile.* He watched her as she toyed with her jet-black ponytail. He knew that her hair was silky and wondered if he'd ever get a chance to run his fingers through it or feel it fanning across his face as they woke up in the morning after a night of passionate lovemaking. It had been a long time since a woman enthralled him. She had a light that made him want to know everything about her. Then again, it could be the forbidden fruit thing too.

"Did you play any sports?" Nina asked Clinton. "Oh, I forgot, you're not into sports."

"I run and that's as sporty as I get," Clinton said. "Running clears my mind."

"Maybe we can run together before I go back to Charlotte. Charleston has the best running trails ever."

Alex cleared her throat. "When are you going to have time to run? Nina, you're not going to be here that long, are you?"

Nina narrowed her eyes at her sister as if Alex was on the verge of telling some secret. "I work for myself and I can stay as long as I want."

"Girls, you know the rules. No arguing at the dinner table."

"Yes, sir," they said, sounding as if they were young children.

Clinton fought back his laugh, unable to believe that Alex could act so humbly when she treated him as if she was the queen of Charleston and he should bow when she walked into the room. Then again, she was showing the proper respect to her father. Clinton wished he had a father he could respect.

Nina leaned in to Clinton. "I hope we're not scaring you. We're not crazy. And if you're around this weekend you'll get to meet my sister Yolanda."

"Really," he said.

"But it's a surprise, so don't let Evilene know." Nina nodded toward her sister.

Alex rolled her eyes at Nina as she whispered to Clinton.

"I won't," he replied, smiling at Nina and enjoying seeing a different side of his boss.

Sheldon yawned and rose to his feet. "I'm going to leave you all to have dessert without this old man." He dropped enough money on the table to cover the dinners and a tip. Moments later, Alex got a call about a problem back at the property.

Begrudgingly she left the restaurant and Nina and Clinton were left alone.

"So, what's good here for dessert?" Clinton looked over the dessert menu the waiter had dropped off at the table.

"Anything chocolate." Nina waved for the waiter and when he approached the table, she ordered a molten chocolate cake with a scoop of vanilla ice cream. "We're going to need two spoons, if you don't mind."

Clinton was charmed by her genteel way with the waiter and was still trying to figure out how she and Alex were related.

"All right," she said, meeting his stare. "Tell me the truth, how was your first day?"

"Well, your sister is something else. A taskmaster is the nicest thing I can say. If she had a whip, I really think she would have beat me."

Nina smiled. "She will grow on you, trust me. Just think of it as corporate hazing. You and my daddy seem to get along great, though."

I wonder how well we would get along if he knew the thoughts I was having about his youngest daughter right now. He'd probably fire me in two seconds flat.

"Your father is a very special man. I've admired him for a long time. What he's done with his property is legendary."

"Then you should've known he'd never sell his business," Nina said as she smiled at him. "Tell the truth. You're here to cause trouble, aren't you?"

"Nina, I don't cause trouble and I'm not trying to take anything from your father."

"Really? But you did work for his competition?"

"Your dad has no competition. I worked for Randall Birmingham because I didn't know any better."

She folded her arms across her chest and Clinton's eyes fell to her perky breasts. Why

61

did she have to be so sexy?

"What's with the silence?" Nina asked after a beat passed.

"Nothing, just thinking about dessert."

"So, you're saying my breasts look like cake? Because you've been staring all night."

Clinton laughed. Busted. "You have to know you're a beautiful woman."

Nina shrugged. "I'll take your word for it." She offered him a sly smile.

Clinton licked his lips, wondering if Nina's lips were as soft as they looked. "You're something special, Nina Richardson."

"That's because you've only met Alex."

He leaned across the table and placed his hand on top of hers. "No, I'm saying that because I've met you."

Nina trembled and inched closer to him. "You're one of those guys who always know the right thing to say, huh?"

"I'm a man who tells the truth. And if I'm being honest, I haven't been able to get you off my mind all day."

"Really? Glad to know that it wasn't a one-sided thing."

Clinton smiled. "Have you had a chance to look at yourself in the mirror lately? You're kind of a big deal."

Nina was closer to him, their faces inches

apart. "Don't say it if you don't mean it."

"Definitely not the guy who says things he doesn't mean." There was no way he could be this close to those lips and not get the answer to a burning question. Were her lips soft?

Lifting his head slightly, Clinton brushed his lips against Nina's. With the lightning-quick reflexes, Clinton brought his lips down on top of hers, sucking on her lips, tasting their succulence and forgetting she was Sheldon's daughter or they were in a crowded restaurant. Her lips were so soft he wouldn't have been able to pull away from her if Jesus himself walked into the restaurant and commanded it.

Nina, on the other hand, didn't feel that way. She yanked away from him and slapped hard enough to nearly knock him off his chair. "Are you crazy?" she snapped as she rose to her feet. Her eyes flashed anger as she glared at him.

"I'm sorry, I don't know why I did that," Clinton stammered. Had he misread her signals? He could've sworn she'd been flirting with him, but that blow to his jaw told another story.

Dropping into her chair with tears in her eyes, Nina turned away from him. "I'm sorry, this wasn't about you."

"I'm confused," he said, furrowing his brow. Wasn't he the one who'd been kissing her?

CHAPTER 5

Nina wiped her eyes with her napkin. "I'm going through something and I don't want my father to know about it. Why I kissed you, I don't know." What Nina didn't tell him was how good the kiss felt and if the situation was different, she would have been flattered by the kiss and even would've enjoyed it.

"Are you in serious trouble?"

"Not really, I just fell for the wrong man and got my heart trampled," Nina said as more tears spilled down her cheeks.

"I would've thought you'd be the one out here breaking hearts, as cliché as that sounds." Clinton found that hard to believe. On the outside, Nina looked like the perfect woman. And with a smile as warm as hers, there was no way a sane man would want to run away from her. But experience taught him to never judge a book by its cover, no matter how sexy and alluring it was.

na paused, looked at Clinton as if she was sizing him up to see if he was trustworthy enough to tell him her sad story. "I know I don't know you and after what you just did, I shouldn't even be talking to you. I was with this guy for a year. I thought we were developing something real, but it turned out he was just a user. He got all the sex, free dinners, and just about anything else he wanted from me. All I wanted in return was for him to love me. But, he was out there with another woman. And I'm looking like boo-boo the fool."

Clinton placed his hand on top of Nina's. "You gave way too much to someone who didn't deserve it. Sometimes, men don't realize a diamond when they see one." Part of him wanted to kiss her again, but not passionately, just soft enough to let her know that he cared and that all men weren't like the jerk that she was describing.

"Well, I'm done. With men, with love, with all of it. Maybe Alex has the right idea, all work and no play."

"I can't let you do that. You can't give up or turn bitter because one man hurt you," Clinton said.

"Whatever."

Clinton didn't mean to laugh, but in her indignant anger, she was cute as a button and funnier than an improv comic. He struggled to control his laughter before he said, "Maybe it's the kind of men who you date. Most men would look at you and see a young, sexy woman who has it together and think, I want her."

"Is that why you kissed me? You want me, Clinton?"

"Yes. But we're not talking about me."

"You're a man, aren't you?" Nina folded her arms underneath her bosom, drawing Clinton's attention to her chest again. Licking his lips, he turned away from her chest because he found himself wondering about her nipples.

"If you have to ask then I didn't kiss you right." A slow smile spread across his face. "Do we need to try again?"

Nina laughed despite herself. "So, Clinton, what do I need to do to make myself irresistible to the right man?"

Just walk in a room like you walked in my office earlier, he thought. "To the right man or to the man who you claim to love?"

Nina sucked her teeth. "Just answer the question."

"Nina, if you want that clown back, then you need to make him see that you've moved on. Men, at least the immature ones, hate to think that someone else has taken their place. The old adage is true: Success is the best revenge. Calling him and asking him to explain his actions is going to show him you still care. Even make you look a little too desperate."

"Really?"

"Yes. If he had any feelings for you at all, it would burn him up to see you've moved forward and are enjoying your life."

Nina bit her bottom lip. "What are you doing Monday night?"

"Working."

She shook her head. "You're coming to Charlotte for the Panthers game. Think of it as a way to bond with my father and to help me test your theory. So, do we have a date?"

"I can't let you use me to get back with or at this knucklehead. Why not just move on for real instead of playing games?" Suddenly, he felt jealous and didn't want to see another man look at her with lust in his eyes, the way he'd been looking at her all night.

"Help me with Lamar and I'll get Alex off your back," Nina bargained. "Besides, watching him squirm will make me feel better."

"Your sister really hates me that much?"

Nina nodded. "It's more like mistrust. But I can help you with that and you can help me with my issue. It's a win-win for everybody."

"Lamont doesn't deserve you," Clinton said.

"Lamar," Nina corrected. "And you may be right, but my heart isn't listening at the moment. If he doesn't mind seeing us together, then I'll know I need to move on and I'll do it."

Clinton held his right hand out to Nina. "All right, you have a deal." With those words, he knew that his fate was sealed because there was no way he'd be able to resist the charms of Nina Richardson.

One day soon, he was going to brand her his and have her in his bed. That is, if he could get her to stop thinking about this Lamar person and make their ruse real.

By the time the weekend rolled around, Nina's sad thoughts of Lamar had been replaced by the memory of Clinton's kiss and her plan to take him to the game on Monday night. What was going to happen after the game gave her more pause than what Lamar's reaction would be to seeing the couple. *What if Clinton wants to come back to my place for a nightcap and if he kisses me again? I won't be pushing him away,* Nina thought as she flipped over on her stomach. *If he kisses like that, I wonder what else those sexy lips can do. This is crazy. I don't know this man. So why does he keep invading my head?*

"I know someone in this family better welcome me," Yolanda called out, interrupting Nina's lustful thoughts.

Alex and Nina rushed into the sitting area and engulfed their sister in a group hug. "What are you doing here? Are you two dying and just don't want to tell me?" Alex asked excitedly. "Is Robin going to jump out of a corner too?"

Yolanda Richardson was the shortest of the four sisters at five foot five, but what she lacked in height, she made up for in personality. Her hair changed like the wind. One day she'd have long, silky black tresses and the next she'd be sporting a blond Afro. This day, she was wearing her hair cropped and slicked back like a 1920s glamour goddess. She concealed her petite figure underneath a pair of baggy jeans and an oversized Spelman College sweatshirt.

"Alex, just be happy to see us, you know it isn't often that we get a chance to be together." Yolanda turned her attention to Nina. "You look better than I thought you would."

Alex folded her arms across her chest.

"That's because she's found a new man to target."

"Shut up, Alex, you don't know what you're talking about."

Yolanda assumed the role of the peace-maker and said, "Let's not argue. Nina is still young and if she has gotten over old bucket head, then I'm happy. Alex, you on the other hand, aren't getting any younger and if you don't start using what you got, it's going to dry up and blow away."

Alex narrowed her eyes at her sister and shook her head. "Daddy spent all that money to send you to Spelman and you still don't have any manners. You two don't know what I do."

Nina and Yolanda looked at each other and laughed. "We certainly know what you don't do," Yolanda said. "Where's my daddy?"

"Golfing," Alex replied. "Why don't we surprise him with lunch? Does he know you're here, Yolanda?"

She shook her head. "I couldn't let Nina have all the fun."

Alex rolled her eyes. "Must be nice to be able to go and come without worrying about responsibilities."

"That's the difference between being a boss and a worker."

"And having Dad fund your little project doesn't hurt either, huh?" Alex said.

Yolanda curled her hand like a hissing cat's paw. "Testy, testy. And I'm turning a profit these days, so please stop it. You know what your problem is — you need a life. Actually, you probably need to get laid."

Alex smiled at her sisters and shook her head. "Whatever, Yolanda. I'm going to call over to the restaurant and have them fix Daddy's favorites and bring them over. He usually gets back at one thirty, so that should give you two time to catch up and do that giggly thing you two do. I'll be in my office — working."

"All that working is going to be the death of you," Yolanda called after Alex's retreating figure. "You need some fun in your life. Or a penis in your mouth, whichever comes first."

Alex turned around and flipped her sister off.

Once they were alone in the sitting area, Nina and Yolanda plopped down on the overstuffed sofa near the bay window overlooking the Cooper River and started dishing.

"Is there really a new guy this fast?" Yolanda asked.

"Not really. Daddy's new marketing manager is going to the game with us and Lamar is going to flip out —"

Yolanda held up her hand up. "Nina, stop. Just let that fool go. I hate that he hurt your feelings, but you can't make someone love you if they don't. He's a selfish bastard."

Nina sighed. "But he can't get away with what he did to me."

Yolanda rolled her eyes. "If you ask me, you have bigger problems. What about *sweetheart-gate*? Do you think that video is going to stop you from getting other jobs or covering the Panthers? You're an expert on that sorry-ass team."

"I hope not. My assignment for Monday night was changed, but I'm hoping it has more to do with the realization of the Panthers losing major players in training camp and not Cody Cameron."

"You're good at writing about sports. Hell, you should be, after all of the football you watched with Dad as a kid." Yolanda laughed. "Lamar is the least of your worries. Please tell me you're not trying to get back with that piece of shit."

"I don't want him back. I just . . . I don't know what I'm doing."

Yolanda placed her hand on Nina's shoulder. "The best thing to do is get a new hairdo, some sexy clothes, and enjoy life.

Everything else is just icing on the cupcake."

"You do have a point," Nina said. "I need to go shopping."

"So, tell me about this Clinton fellow."

Nina shrugged. "He's a good kisser."

"Wait. What? How in the hell do you know that?"

She told Yolanda about dinner.

"Slow down, Little Red Corvette," Yolanda cautioned. "You know mixing Daddy's business with pleasure isn't a good idea."

"Never said I was mixing anything. Clinton's cute but I'm trying to fix myself first. I can't bounce from man to man."

"I'm glad you know that." Yolanda stroked her chin. "But, a little rebound fling never hurt anyone. Just keep your feelings to yourself."

Nina nodded, silently promising herself that she'd never fall in love again.

"Maybe one good thing will come out of all of this," Yolanda said with a grin.

"What?"

"You'll get rid of that damned ponytail."

Nina tossed a pillow at her sister before taking off for her room. Even though she didn't appreciate her sister ragging on her ponytail, she couldn't wait to see her old hairstylist, Gisselle. After getting dressed, she headed for her shop in North Charleston. Nina didn't care that it was Saturday and she'd probably be in the shop for hours.

But when she walked in, it really felt as if she was home again.

"Hey dere, Nina chile," Gisselle said in her thick Gullah accent when she spotted Nina. "Hadn't seen you in a while. Where ya been?"

"I live in North Carolina now." Nina flipped her ponytail. "As you can see no one can do my hair quite like you did."

Gisselle beamed. "I know. You look like a tied-up mop."

"I know it's Saturday and you're busy, but do you think you can squeeze me in?"

Gisselle patted her leather chair and nodded for Nina to come over. "What ya wanna do to your hair?"

Closing her eyes, Nina said, "Make me somebody else."

CHAPTER 6

Clinton woke up Saturday morning with sweat dripping from his body because he'd spent the night dreaming of Nina. His thoughts of her naked body wrapped around him and those soft lips pressed against his neck were so vivid that he'd expected to find her sprawled beside him ready and waiting for him to make love to her. Why had he agreed to this stupid plan of hers when he was so attracted to her? Sure, he could try to win her over and show her that this Lamar character wasn't worth her time, but how could he convince her of that when she was so in love with him? Besides, if she didn't have the sense enough to know that she deserved better, he couldn't change her mind — even if he wanted to.

Women, he thought, *they always want the bad boy or the man that doesn't want them when they could have someone who would love and respect them if they looked right in front of them.*

Clinton decided that instead of sitting around his place all day thinking about Nina, he was going to go into work and set up that marketing plan that he told Mr. Richardson would push his business to the next level. Besides, sitting in his house would only give him more time to think about ways to make Nina forget that a man named Lamar ever existed. More time to think about tasting her all over and more time to dream up ways to make her scream with pleasure. *Yeah, I've got to get out of here,* he thought as the image of a naked Nina danced in his head.

After a quick shower, Clinton dressed and headed to the bed-and-breakfast. The last thing he'd expected to see was Nina walking into the lobby looking like a brand-new woman with a new hairdo and a leather dress that hugged every curve of her luscious body. Black was her color and the rich auburn hair color and close-cropped cut suited her very well, and brought out the sparkle in her eyes.

"Nina?" He struggled to hold back his drool.

"Clinton, what are you doing here?" Her face flushed slightly as he scrolled her tantalizing body with a slow, hot gaze.

77

"I decided to come in and do some work so that I wouldn't be behind if I went to Charlotte with you." He couldn't tear his eyes away from her breasts, which were even more perfect than he'd dreamed. "Um, what's with the transformation?"

"I was just trying something different. This dress is so not me," Nina said as she spun around. "Yolanda thought I should try the dominatrix look. I don't like it. What do you think?"

"The drool didn't give me away?" he asked with a nervous laugh. She was the boss's daughter, she was in love with another man, and she was the sexiest woman he'd ever laid eyes on. A smarter man would've walked away and forgotten all about Nina Richardson.

"Who would wear this outside of the house?" she said with a tense laugh. "If someone hadn't taken my purse with my keys in them, I wouldn't be out here." Nina looked over her shoulder at a woman who was laughing at her.

"Well." Clinton tugged at his collar. "Let me get to my office and get some work done." He silently prayed that she didn't see the effect she was having on him.

As he turned to walk away, he knew that he'd have another night of dreams about

Nina. This time he was certain that she would be carrying a whip.

When he walked into his office, he wasn't at all surprised to see Alex in hers working diligently. He waved to her, then started his own work. It wasn't long before Alex was standing in front of his desk.

"What's going on with you and my sister?" she asked, not bothering to say hello.

"Nothing."

"I find that hard to believe. Since that dinner a few days ago, your name stays in her mouth. And now you're going to Charlotte Monday night with her and my father."

"Alexandria, I think that your sister is a nice person with a beautiful soul. But if anything goes on between the two of us it's none of your concern as long as it doesn't interfere with my work here. But, there is nothing going on between the two of us, I mean, we just met."

Alex slammed her palm against the desk. "My family is always my concern and I don't want to see my sister hurt again. I don't trust you to work here, so do you really think that I'd trust you with my sister? A word to the wise, Clinton, stay away from Nina."

"And as I said, Alexandria, I don't know your sister like that, so how could I do

79

anything to hurt her? She's a nice person and that's where it ends."

"Make sure it stays that way. Because if you do anything to ever hurt my sister, you won't have to worry about what my father will do to you," Alex warned.

Clinton was getting sick and tired of her attitude. "I tell you what," he said. "Why don't you get a life of your own? Then you wouldn't have time to worry about what Nina's doing and who she's doing it with."

Alex rocked back on her heels. "How dare you? You don't know anything about me or my family and for you to sit there and judge me —"

Clinton raised his hands. "I'm sorry, I shouldn't have said that."

Alex stormed out of the office and Clinton couldn't help but wonder what he'd gotten himself in to.

Nina slapped Yolanda's shoulder once Clinton was tucked away in his office. "I can't believe you. Did you know he was out here?"

Yolanda smacked her lips and shook her head. "I can't believe that you're worrying about Lamar when a man who looks like *that* wants to lick you from head to toe."

"He does not. Clinton and I just met and

80

he's willing to help me —"

"Out of that dress, that's what he's willing to do," Yolanda shouted. "You're not dense, you had to see how that man was looking at you with fire in his eyes and it wasn't because you were half —"

Pressing her finger to her lips, Nina looked around to make sure her father wasn't in earshot. "Will you shut up?"

"As soon as you give up this silly little game of yours. When I talked to you earlier this week, I thought I was going to have to come here and talk you off the ledge. Let Lamar go and move the hell on. You're above this game-playing shit," Yolanda said. "It's stupid, childish, ridiculous, and did I mention stupid? Just be the bigger person."

"Why is it that the woman has to be the bigger person?" Nina whined. "Was he the bigger person when he said those things to me? Was he the bigger person when he was benefiting from all of my cooking, cleaning, and great — no — phenomenal sex?"

"What was that?" Sheldon asked as he approached his daughters. Neither of them had noticed him as he walked in.

Nina's face heated from embarrassment. "Um, I was talking about a book I'd just read by Bridget Midway."

"Well, there are a few things that a father

81

never wants to know about his daughters and I think this conversation is one of those. So, Yolanda, what do I owe the pleasure of your visit?"

"Can't I miss my father too?" she said as she hugged him.

Sheldon kissed Yolanda on the top of her head. "I guess you can. I hope you two haven't been giving Alex a fit."

Yolanda smiled slyly. "Would we do that?"

"Of course," he said with a laugh. Sheldon turned and looked at Nina. "Isn't it a little early for Halloween?"

"Oh, Daddy, I was just being silly and trying on something I would never wear outdoors." Nina looked pointedly at her sister and scowled. "Yolanda made me do it."

"Well, I hear that you all set up a luncheon for me. That was really nice. I can't remember the last time I got to eat with my girls."

Yolanda folded her arms across her chest. "We can't surprise you at all, can we?"

Sheldon shook his head and chuckled. "Not as late as you two sleep. You know you have to get up pretty early to put one over on me. I'm going to get cleaned up, I'll see you all in a few."

Yolanda patted her father on the shoulder. "That was super corny."

"I'm going to change my clothes, Daddy,"

Nina said. "I'll be in the dining room for lunch in a little bit."

"I do like the haircut," he said. "The older you get, the more you look like your mother." Sheldon's eyes shone with tears as he looked at his daughter. It seemed ironic that his youngest daughter was the one who looked the most like Nora Richardson, a woman she'd never gotten a chance to know.

Smiling at her father, Nina wished that she had memories of her mother and could remember how she looked and the feel of her arms around her. What would her mother think about this situation with Lamar? *Oh, Daddy, I bet you never disappointed Mama.* Tears sprang into her eyes as she thought about the fact that she couldn't attract a man who wanted to love her the way her father loved her mother.

"Are you all right?" Sheldon asked. "I didn't mean to upset you."

Yolanda stepped in and wrapped her arm around her father. "You know how she gets when we talk about Mom."

Nina nodded, but she knew her sister was aware of the real reasons for her tears. "I'll be down in a moment," she said as she turned to leave.

Alone in her room, Nina wiped her eyes and forced a smile on her lips. As she was about to change out of her leather outfit, her cell phone rang.

Looking down at the caller ID screen, she saw that it was Lamar. Of course, his name didn't come up since she'd deleted it the day after he'd smashed her heart. Despite herself, her heart fluttered as she picked up the phone. Had he finally come to his senses and called to apologize? *Why do I even care?*

"Hello."

"Hey, what's up?"

"Nothing. What do you want?" Nina tried to keep her voice angry and this conversation short. *When is he going to get to the "I'm sorry?"*

"Are you at home?"

"No, I'm out of town," she said. *Why do you want to know where I am?*

"Oh, I need you to look up something for me. You're on an assignment?"

He's asking me for an itinerary when he is out here sleeping around with half of Charlotte? Nina stared at the phone in disbelief. Could he really expect her to be civil and cordial to him after what he'd said to her? "No, I'm not." Normally, she would've told Lamar where she was and what she was doing, but not today.

"Well, call me when you get home," he said.

Nina snorted. "I don't think so. We don't have anything to talk about."

"What's with the attitude?"

"I'm busy and you're interrupting me."

"Guess we'll talk on Monday, then."

"Bye." She pressed the end button and tossed it across the room. *I should have let the voice mail pick up.*

Nina hated herself for wasting all of this energy on Lamar when he made his feelings clear. He was never going to be the man she wanted or deserved. Rubbing her hand across her face, she closed her eyes and expelled a frustrated breath. If she was hating herself for giving Lamar her energy, she really loathed the fact that she was now giving him her tears.

Before she got lost in her thoughts, there was a slight tapping at her door. Opening the door, she saw Yolanda standing there with a concerned look on her face. "Are you all right?"

"I'm fine," Nina replied.

Yolanda walked into the room and plopped down on the bed. "If you're so fine, why are you crying and what happened to your phone?"

Nina's cell phone was lying on the floor with a cracked screen. She crossed the room and picked it up. "It bounced off the wall.

85

Where's Daddy?"

"Alex pulled him into her office. Lunch is getting cold, so put some clothes on and let's go."

Nina quickly dressed in a pair of jeans and a form-fitting T-shirt and brushed a little foundation on her face. She didn't want her father to wonder why she looked like a sad sack. As she and Yolanda headed to the dining room, they ran into Clinton again. Her face grew hot when she looked at him, thinking about what she was wearing when they crossed paths in the lobby moments earlier.

"You're still here?"

He nodded. "Your dad saw me in my office and invited me to lunch."

"Nice," Yolanda said as they walked into the dining room.

"Did I tell you that I love your hair? It's very becoming." Clinton pulled out a chair for Nina and winked at her as she sat down.

She ran her hand through her freshly cropped hair. "Thank you. I thought I needed a change."

"Think Lamar's going to like it?" Clinton asked in a near whisper.

"I really don't care. I did this for me."

Yolanda cleared her throat and smiled at the duo when they looked at her. "You two want to share with the rest of the class?"

"Are all of your sisters like this?" Clinton asked.

Yolanda rolled her eyes. "Don't judge me by the actions of Alexandria the Great. I'm Yolanda, by the way."

As if she knew her sisters were talking about her, Alex appeared in the doorway. "Daddy sends his apologies, but he's doing an interview that Mr. Jefferson set up and didn't tell me about. He said he'll try to make it for dessert."

"Surely you can't be cross with Clinton for doing his job," Yolanda said with a fake British accent.

"Grow up," Alex snapped as she took a seat at the head of the table. She cast a contemptuous glance at Clinton and Nina.

"We're not talking about business at this lunch," Nina said when she caught her sister's eye.

"I had no intentions of doing so, especially since neither of you would know what I'm talking about anyway. I see you've taken a page from Yolanda's book and changed your hair. It's really cute, though."

Nina was surprised that Yolanda didn't have something smart to say. Could it be that the Richardson sisters were going to have a lunch without an argument?

"Maybe you should do the same," Yolanda said.

Oh well, Nina thought as she shook her head.

Alex flipped her shoulder-length hair and rolled her eyes. "My hair is fine."

"Whatever."

Nina pulled the top off one of the covered dishes. "Can we eat without an argument? Y'all know Daddy's rule. Clinton, would you like some shrimp and grits?"

"Sure," he said as he handed Nina his plate. She piled his plate with the low-country staple and smiled as she set it in front of him.

For a few moments everyone ate in silence and Nina stole glances at Clinton, taking in his milk chocolate complexion, long eyelashes, and perfect lips. She wished that she would've been in the right mindset to enjoy his kiss the other night. She wished that she could take the time to get to know him and see if he could be that guy who would bring her joy and smiles rather than heartbreak and tears. But now wasn't the time to get involved with another man when she was hardly over Lamar. But Clinton seemed different. His warm smile charmed her and his smooth skin made her want to taste him.

God, what is wrong with me? Physical at-

traction is why I'm in the mess I'm in now. For all I know, Clinton could have a wife or girlfriend tucked away somewhere and Alex isn't sure that he's not here to hurt Daddy.

"Nina, are you all right?" Yolanda asked. "You're quiet and that doesn't happen often."

Alex raised her eyebrow at Clinton as if to say he was the reason for Nina's sudden silence, when she was normally the family chatterbox.

"I was thinking about Monday's game," she said. "I have a big story to write. But Clinton and Daddy are coming up to Charlotte too. A friend of mine who works for the Panthers got me tickets in the owner's box because I told him about the B&B."

"Maybe you should be the marketing director," Clinton said.

"Oh, I don't think so. I'd go crazy sitting in an office all day," Nina said. "I love my freedom. I just get up and go when I get ready."

"Don't listen to her," Yolanda said. "She just doesn't want to work for Alex."

Nina laughed and silently prayed that Clinton wouldn't take Yolanda's bait.

"I love working with Alexandria," he said. "She's fair and stern. What more can you ask for in a supervisor?"

89

Yolanda stood up and clapped as if she'd just watched a Broadway play.

Alex scoffed at her sister and then reached for the food in the center of the table.

"So, Yolanda, right?" Clinton said. "What do you do?"

"I run a fashion boutique in Richmond. Next year I plan to expand into Atlanta or Charlotte." She popped a sauce-covered piece of shrimp in her mouth, then shrugged. "I might even come back to Charleston."

Alex coughed and shook her head.

"Y'all have such diverse interests," Clinton remarked.

"But there's one thing we have in common," Alex said. "We don't like people who try to mess with us and if you mess with one of us you mess with all of us."

With that comment, Alex sucked the fun out of lunch until Sheldon arrived, raving about the interview he'd had with *USA Today.*

"A photographer is coming Monday to shoot the place and me. So, baby girl, I can't go up to Charlotte for the game. Luckily, Clinton can go with you," he said as he sat down beside Alex. "Keeping my seat warm?" He kissed his oldest daughter on the cheek.

"Daddy, you know I always have your back," she said as she stood up so that he could take his seat at the head of the table.

Roberta, the bed and breakfast cook, walked into the dining room and placed a chocolate crème cake in the middle of the table. "Would you all like some coffee or anything?"

"I'll get it," Alex said. "Thank you for lunch, Roberta."

"You're welcome, it's so good to see all of you together again."

Nina smiled at the woman who'd been cooking for them since they were small children. "It's good to see you, Miss Roberta."

Shaking her finger at Nina, she said, "Don't stay away this long again, young lady."

"Yes, ma'am," Nina said. Seconds later, she and Clinton reached for the knife to cut the cake at the same time. When their hands touched, they exchanged fleeting looks.

"You're probably better at this than me," Nina said, allowing him to take the knife.

"I'm not trying to step out of bounds. But that cake looks delicious."

"So not out of bounds and the cake is more amazing than it looks," she said, then nibbled at her bottom lip.

Yolanda hid her grin behind her hand as if she could see what was going on between Clinton and Nina.

"Let's dig into this cake," Sheldon said. "And then my fashionista daughter can help me pick out a suit for Monday's photo shoot."

"I think I might stick around and make sure you don't mix your patterns and solids too much," Yolanda said. "Clinton, since you're going to Charlotte with my sister, do you think you can talk her into coming back after the game?"

"It's going to be too late to drive back after I do my post-game interviews and whatnot," Nina said. "And I'm not coming back because I have work to do."

Yolanda clasped her hands together and nodded. "And I hope you trip Cody Cameron on your way out of the locker room."

Clinton rose to his feet. "Then I'd better see about booking a hotel room."

Sheldon laughed as Clinton handed him a slice of cake. "You can do that after you eat Roberta's cake. Trust me, this is a treat not to be missed."

Nina couldn't help but wonder what kind of treat Clinton would be.

CHAPTER 7

Monday rolled around a little too quickly for Nina's tastes. After the quiet weekend she had, she certainly wasn't ready to see Lamar. But it was going to happen whether she wanted it to or not. She'd left early that morning so that she could meet with her editor and get more details on what her assignment was before the evening kickoff.

She made it home in record time because when it came to driving, Nina had never met a speed limit she didn't break. She'd checked her voice mail from the car as she sat in the parking lot, hoping that her editor hadn't called. More than anything, she prayed that Lamar had called to say he wasn't going to attend the game tonight. How could he show his face after she caught him with his *bae*?

But knowing what a fan of the game he was, that likely wasn't going to happen. He'd use the pass she'd given him because he was just that kind of asshole.

Then there was Clinton. Nina had been surprised that he'd agreed to come to the game and play her faux boyfriend. Now, she didn't want to play such a stupid game. Clinton deserved better than to be used as a pawn in a game Nina wouldn't win. And even if she did, Lamar was no prize. She knew that for sure. If he thought she was going to be one of his options, he was dead wrong.

In another world, Clinton would be the one. He was sweet, considerate, and had lips that were like sugar. Nina closed her eyes and relived that kiss — sweet and tender.

"Stop it," Nina said to herself as she dialed her editor's number. "You don't even know that man and he could be a bigger asshole than Lamar."

Nina talked to her editor, copying his instructions on her notepad, and tried to focus on her job and not the fact that she was going to be stuck in the press box with Lamar in a few hours.

Clinton sat in his office, scouring the Internet for a hotel room that didn't cost over two hundred dollars. He was only going to be in Charlotte for a few hours and he knew how these things worked. Because the big game was in town, hotel operators jacked up their prices and got away with it. After all, what was bigger than Monday Night Football and how many people would be sober enough to drive home? It was a marketer's dream.

But he wasn't going to fall victim to it yet, there was no way that he could ask Nina if he could crash at her place. They didn't know each other well enough and he could imagine the evil look Alex would give him if she had any idea that he and her little sister had spent the night together, no matter how innocent it would be.

Would it be innocent? Nina had been the star of Clinton's erotic dreams since the day that they'd met and he felt her lips against his. No matter how much self-control he had, he couldn't guarantee he'd resist temptation.

The phone rang as he surfed a hotel's website. "This is Clinton."

"This is Nina," she replied with a giggle. "You're still coming to the game tonight, right?"

"If I can find a hotel room," he said.

"You can stay with me. I have an extra room."

"No. I can't impose on you like that."

What Clinton really meant was that he couldn't be in her house and resist the urge to rip her clothes off and make love to her or walk in on her in the shower, accidentally on purpose, just to get a look at her naked body.

"It's not an imposition because I made the offer. And I know that the room rates are outrageous today. And what kind of Richardson would I be if I didn't provide my guest with a nice place to stay?"

This is about her childish scheme and as long as I remember that, then it will be fine and I won't get caught up.

"All right," he said. "Too bad Charlotte isn't close enough to Charleston so the B&B could get a piece of the action."

She gave him her uptown Charlotte address and told him he'd be better off using his GPS because she was horrible with directions.

"I should be leaving soon," Clinton said, looking around the corner to see if Alex was anywhere around. "Are you going to be at home?"

"Yes, I have the passes and I'm doing some research on this hotheaded Dallas receiver and his latest outburst for my sidebar," she said. "And I just got another assignment to interview the Cowboys' rookie quarterback. A few national outlets want a short Q&A with the superstar."

Clinton could feel her excitement through the phone. "Sounds like a lot of work to be done in a short amount of time."

"It is. But that's why I love what I do. I make diamonds under deadline pressure."

Clinton chuckled. "It's a great feeling when you do what you love, right?"

"It is. Thanks for coming with me. It'll be nice to have a friend with me tonight."

After hanging up with Nina, he wondered why she couldn't let this Lamar guy go. Rising from his desk, Clinton stood in the doorway and stole a glance from Alex's big window.

"Wishing that this is your office?" Alex asked as she appeared before him like a ghost.

"No, actually, I was about to leave for the day."

Alex sighed. "That's right, you're off to Charlotte. Clinton, I'm going to ask you to tread lightly with Nina. You may think I'm overbearing, but Nina is somewhat like a daughter to me. I don't want her hurt anymore and sometimes when it comes to men, she makes bad choices. Don't be another one."

He understood her concern for her sister

and actually respected her for having Nina's back. Clinton smiled at her. "Listen, Alexandria, I like your family. I like your sister, too, and I would never do anything to hurt her. We're just friends and getting to know each other better."

Alex nodded. "All right."

"I'll see you in the morning. By the way, how did Sheldon's interview go?"

Alex rolled her eyes. "The interview was fine until Yolanda and the photographer got into a little tiff. She wanted Daddy to be photographed from his right side and the photographer told her that this wasn't a *Cosmo* photo shoot. And wouldn't you know in the end, she and this photographer ended up setting up a date for dinner tonight."

"Your sisters are something else."

"And I guess you're wondering why I'm not like them?" Alex asked. "Since I'm the oldest, I have more responsibility than they do. Maybe I'm too serious, but this is who I am."

"I didn't say that. Alexandria —"

"You didn't have to. Your eyes said it all. Have fun tonight and remember what I said about Nina." Alex walked into her office and closed the door.

Clinton figured he'd better take advantage

of her good mood and hit the road.

Nina looked up at the clock and decided that she'd better shower quickly because Clinton would be there sooner rather than later. Rushing into the bathroom, she tore off her shorts and T-shirt and then jumped under the warm spray. She was looking forward to seeing Clinton again and not just to make Lamar jealous. He was charming and attractive. But he had to have some hidden flaw. *He probably has a stable of women at his beck and call,* she thought as the water beat down on her. Nina shook her head. Why was she even worrying about what Clinton did in his free time? The man was single.

Stepping out of the shower, she looked in the mirror and vowed that she would not under any circumstance allow her foolish heart to open up to Clinton Jefferson. As she wrapped a plush towel around her body, the doorbell rang. Nina searched for her robe while yelling, "Just a minute."

The chiming continued and Nina had no choice but to answer the door in her towel. As soon as she opened it, she was taken aback when she saw Clinton standing there in a pair of nicely fitting jeans, a muscle-hugging long-sleeve T-shirt, and a black baseball cap. "You — you're early."

Clinton tried not to stare, but seeing her damp body, her hair wet and wavy, and that towel barely covering her breasts made it impossible to look away. "Yeah. A little too early, huh?"

"Come in, I'll be dressed in a second." Nina dashed down the hall to her bedroom.

Quickly she dressed in what she'd dubbed her game gear — a pair of black jeans, a white oxford shirt that she buttoned nearly up to her neck, and black sneakers.

As one of the few women who covered the NFL, Nina was constantly trying to prove herself. She didn't want to be mistaken for a groupie, so she always took extra pains to keep her look professional. Reaching for her tennis shoes, Nina decided that tonight she could add a little extra to her outfit. She grabbed a pair of black leather pumps with a two-inch heel, then she undid a few of the buttons on her shirt and topped her look off with a black blazer with a huge pink rose pin on the lapel. Satisfied that she would catch Lamar's eye yet not raise the ire of her colleagues or the team staff, Nina headed to the living room where Clinton was waiting.

"We can grab something to eat unless you want to take a risk on the pregame meal," she said.

"It's up to you. I'm your puppet tonight."

Nina clicked her tongue against her teeth. "New plan. I'm not worrying about Lamar. You and Yolanda are right. I need to let this thing go and that's what I'm going to do. But it doesn't hurt to have a friend with me tonight."

Clinton smiled. "That's a plan I can get with. But what happens after tonight?"

She turned away from him because she didn't have an answer for that. As crazy as it was, she wondered what the next step would be with her and Clinton. Would their friendship develop into something more? Would this be a rebound fling? Because she wasn't ready for a new relationship. Nina scoffed inwardly. *New relationship? Clearly, you didn't have an old one with Lamar.*

"Not going to think about tomorrow until I meet my deadline. And honestly, I'm not giving him another chance to make a fool of me."

Clinton closed the space between them. "Smart move. Everyone doesn't deserve a second chance. When a person shows you their true colors, believe it."

"You talk as if you've been through this before? Who broke your heart?" Nina grabbed her purse from the edge of the sofa.

"I hate to tell you this, Miss Nina, but you don't have the market cornered on disappointment and heartbreak."

Nina looked at him with disbelief shining in her eyes. A man who looked like Clinton Jefferson didn't get his heart broken; he broke hearts. Men like Clinton didn't have to pin their hopes and dreams on one woman. She imagined he had a bevy of beauties vying for his attention.

"So, what happened?"

"Same old thing, boy meets girl, boy loses girl, boy buries himself in his work."

"Details, please."

Clinton sighed. "That's a story for another day."

"That's not fair," Nina said, pouting. "I spilled my guts to you and I can't even get a sneak peek into your world?"

"Her name was Ayesha Graham, a beautiful woman. Much like yourself. But she was just about her looks and nothing else. And I'm not going to lie, I was drawn in by her pretty eyes and —"

Nina threw up her hand. "I get it."

Clinton laughed. "I thought I had a prize, people envied me when they saw us together. But I wasn't enough for her."

Leaning against the wall, she watched him thoughtfully. "Not enough? Why not?"

"Because I'm just a regular guy."

"There's nothing regular about you," she said as she opened the door. "Let's go before we're stuck in traffic for an hour."

Clinton watched Nina as she drove. After the grilling she gave him in her place, he was sure that she was a great journalist. He hadn't thought about Ayesha since she broke up with him two years ago. She'd been the kind of woman who women envied and men wanted on their arm. Clinton thought he'd been lucky to have her.

Ayesha, on the other hand, didn't think she was lucky at all. Clinton wasn't enough for her: not rich or prestigious enough for what she wanted. So, the moment a man with the status and the money she wanted strolled into her life, she had dumped Clinton in a heartbeat.

Part of him wanted her back, but he realized Ayesha wasn't the one and no one would be good enough for her. And he wasn't going to try to make her see the light.

She wasn't worth it and the right woman would eventually walk into his life. Looking over at Nina, he had a feeling she could be the one. But falling for Nina Richardson would be like jumping into a powder keg with a lit match.

"What?" she asked when she noticed Clinton's stare.

"Nothing. Just wondering if you're going to turn me into a football fan."

"Maybe. There's nothing like watching the game live."

Clinton shrugged. "If anyone has a chance to do this, I'm sure it's you."

Nina laughed. "You're something else, Clinton."

He grinned. "What you see with me is what you get."

Nina quickly glanced at him. "And what a nice package you're wrapped up in."

"That's cute, but I have nothing on you. One day, you're going to meet the man who can't live without you."

"Is there another man out here like you? Honest and cute? Otherwise, I'm willing to live the single life forever. For some reason I'm attracted to emotionally unavailable men."

He laughed. "At least you're honest about it. They say that's the first step. But don't give up on love."

Nina snorted. "What are you, my life coach?"

Clinton grinned and nodded thoughtfully. "I could be. A brother needs a side hustle."

Nina pressed the brakes as the traffic in

front of her slowed. "You're funny. But I need a break. Tired of being lovesick."

"Sometimes love does seem like a sickness that makes you do crazy things. Trust me, you're not the only one who's done crazy shit for love."

"For Ayesha?"

Clinton smiled sardonically, thinking about all of the things he'd tried to do to show his father that he was a worthy son. He worked his tail off in college and it hadn't mattered. He worked hard with the hotel chain and became the youngest marketing manager in the Southeast. It hadn't mattered to his father either. Clinton Sr. had wanted to live his NFL dreams through his son. When Clinton showed no interest in sports, it was as if he'd died in his father's eyes. Still, he did the dutiful-son thing and sent his father one thousand dollars a month so that he could pay his bills that his social security didn't take care of. Did that matter to Clinton Sr.? Nope. Clinton never received a thank-you note, Christmas card, or birthday greeting.

"No," he finally said. "Not for her."

Nina shrugged as she pulled into the gravel parking lot marked for media. She reached into her computer case and handed Clinton his pass. "There's no cheering in the press box."

"Trust me, I won't be cheering unless you plan on standing up and doing a cheerleader routine."

Glaring at him, Nina pretended that she was offended. "See, that's the attitude I have to deal with day in and day out. You're lucky that I think you're cute or I'd leave you standing out here."

"Cute? That's all? Give me credit, I didn't use the *s* word," he joked as they headed for the stadium entrance.

CHAPTER 8

Nina and Clinton cleared the security checkpoint and rode the elevator up to the press box. She couldn't help but be impressed. Something about Clinton was calming. He seemed to have a beautiful spirit and wisdom that belied his age. Yeah, she wanted to get to know more about this sexy man. But she couldn't make the same mistake twice — or three times — in a row.

Nina always believed that men had it easier than women when it came to finding love. They had so many choices and a woman with standards didn't have many. Would Clinton be more of the same?

"What's going on in the pretty head of yours?" Clinton said, noting her silence.

"More than you want to know."

"Thinking about your cheerleader routine?"

Nina giggled. "You wish."

The elevator doors opened to the press

box, and Nina put her game face on. She stopped smiling and led Clinton to their seats above the fifty-yard line. From this vantage point, she could see everything on the field.

"This is the best way to watch football, inside and surrounded by free food," Clinton said as he helped Nina remove her jacket.

"Yeah. Unfortunately, it's not the same for all games. When I cover high school games, it always seems to be cold and raining. The press boxes at most high schools are the worst. Drafty, cold, and wet."

Clinton smiled, but Nina could tell he really didn't care to talk about sports and for some reason, she found that to be soothing. All she and Lamar talked about was sports and that got tiring. Especially when she wanted to talk about her growing feelings for him, but she'd always been afraid to bring it up. Looking over at Clinton, she vowed that she wouldn't think about Lamar for the rest of the game. She had a job to do.

"Hello, Nina," a familiar deep voice said from behind her.

She and Clinton turned around and looked into Lamar's smiling face.

■ ■ ■ ■

The half smile, half scowl on Nina's face alerted Clinton to the identity of the man standing behind them. Lamar wasn't what Clinton had expected. He figured that if a man was going to let someone as beautiful as Nina go, that man would look like a *GQ* model. That certainly wasn't the case with Lamar Geddings. He was average and that was being kind. He looked as if he spent a lot of time eating on the sidelines, rather than running up and down them. He reminded Clinton of the high school football star who never made it to the NFL after his college career ended, but never lost weight, either.

This man made you cry? He glanced over at Nina.

"Oh, you made it?" Nina rolled her eyes at Lamar before turning to Clinton.

"Come on, now," he said with a toothy grin. "I'm a Dallas Cowboys man, you know I couldn't miss this." Lamar looked at Clinton. "I think you're in my seat."

"No, I'm Nina's guest, so this is my seat."

"Really?" Lamar stated more than asked. He looked as if he was mad about Clinton being in such a prime seat.

Nina nodded. "There's a seat for you right behind us."

"Who is this guy?" Lamar asked.

"Clinton Jefferson. Nina and I go way back and she knows what a big Carolina Panthers fan I am, so she invited me." Clinton extended his hand to Lamar.

Lamar ignored Clinton's hand and Clinton turned to Nina, intimately touching her knee as if the two of them had more than a few days of history together.

"That's nice," he said, watching Nina and Clinton smile at each other. Lamar's face was emotionless.

Nina slowly rose to her feet. "I'm going to get some coffee. Clinton, you want anything?"

Loaded question. He shook his head and then Nina walked away.

While she was gone, Lamar and Clinton silently sized each other up.

"You and Nina go way back, huh?" Lamar asked.

"Yes, we're both from Charleston and I work for her father."

Lamar raised his eyebrow. "Is that so?"

He's fishing when he's the one who threw Nina away. What a damned loser.

"Did Nina tell you I would be here?"

Clinton shrugged. "Why would she? Who

are you, anyway?"

Lamar narrowed his eyes. "I guess you're right. Nina and I are just good friends and she's a *really good* friend."

Grinning, Clinton leaned back in his chair. "Friends come and go but what Nina and I have is forever." His tone was so convincing Clinton almost conjured memories of him and Nina hanging out together as teenagers in Charleston.

Lamar rolled his eyes. "So, you're sleeping with her?" His voice was a near whisper.

Clinton shook his head. "This isn't a conversation that we should be having and what Nina and I do is none of your business. After all, she's just your friend, right?"

Lamar hopped off his stool and headed toward Nina. Clinton smiled as he watched him approach her. *Nina is off-limits. I work for her father and we're just going to be friends.*

He started to stand up and walk over to them, but he saw Nina storming down the hall to what he assumed was the bathroom. Lamar looked as if he was going to go after her, but stopped and turned around to hop in the line for the pregame meal.

Draping his jacket over his seat, Clinton stood up and went looking for Nina. He met her as she walked up from the bathroom.

Her glassy eyes told him that she was holding back tears.

"Are you all right?" Clinton wanted to take her in his arms and kiss her cheek. But this wasn't the time or the place. Neither of them wanted to create a scene and Clinton knew his embrace would do just that.

"I'm fine."

"It doesn't seem that way to me." Clinton stepped closer to her so that no one could hear them. "What did he say to you?"

"Can't get into it right now. Game is about to start and I need to keep my eye on the action." She leaned against him briefly and Clinton saw from the corner of his eye that Lamar was watching their every move.

The game moved at a snail's pace. Nina felt as if the referees and the defensive linemen had conspired against her to keep her in Lamar's presence longer than she wanted.

When she'd offered him the pass, she had been looking forward to watching Monday Night Football with him and showing him what her job was really like. At the time, she had been excited about taking him into the locker room to meet his favorite players and the possibility of them spending the night together making love. Now, she didn't want him near her. But she felt his eyes bore into the back of her head as the game crawled along. Every time Clinton reached for her hand, Nina smiled slightly. But her mind went back to the conversation she and Lamar had had while she'd made her coffee.

"Why did you bring that dude here?" he asked as she stirred her coffee.

"Because I wanted to."

"Nina, I know what you're doing. You wanted my attention — you got it."

Nina rolled her eyes. "Go to hell. No one wants your attention."

He ran his index finger down her cheek. Nina jerked away from him.

"Don't fucking touch me." Her voice was a low hiss. "You just want me in your bed when you feel like giving me some. You want me to get you tickets to games and write about your football program. You want me to be your Internet researcher and . . . This isn't the time or place for this. Unlike you, I'm working."

Lamar smiled. "So, are we going to see each other tonight?"

"You have some nerve. Knowing how I felt about you, you think that I'm going to go back to being your booty call? Where's Bae?"

"Obviously, I didn't mean as much to you as you claimed that I did. How long was it before you hopped in bed with that square?"

113

Nina stormed away, for once not giving a damn about what the other reporters thought of her. Tears stung her eyes as she entered the bathroom. Why did I let him get to me like that? Lamar will say anything to get what he wants and the only reason he wants me now is because I'm sitting up here with Clinton.

Nina steeled herself and headed back to the media area. There was no way she was going to let Lamar see her sweat, and though she'd half expected to see him standing in the hallway waiting for her, Nina was glad to see Clinton there instead. It spoke volumes about Lamar and what she'd really meant to him: nothing.

Now turning to her left, she smiled at Clinton and it wasn't for Lamar's benefit. "Thank you for being here," she whispered.

"Thanks for the invite. And for the record, I'm still not a fan."

She giggled softly. "Whatever."

"What did he say to you?"

Before she could answer, a murmur rippled through the press box. The Carolina Panthers' star wide receiver had just caught a forty-two yard pass from the backup quarterback, which was heavily defended by two Dallas Cowboys' cornerbacks. This had been the spark the home team needed with their star quarterback sidelined with an ankle injury. Secretly, Nina was not sad that Cody Cameron had gone down in the first half.

Nina scribbled down some notes and mouthed *later* to Clinton.

At the end of the game, Nina bolted to the elevator to get to the locker room. Clinton told her that he'd wait for her in the press box, but much to her chagrin, Lamar followed her.

"I'm sorry," he whispered in her ear. "But I'm not the only one who was seeing other people."

"Whatever." Nina didn't look at him and she prayed that her heart would stop racing. Anger and reporting didn't mix.

"Listen, I didn't think we were serious like that. Clearly, you're making a point. I get it."

Rolling her eyes, she clutched her iPhone tightly. "I can't talk to you about this right now, and you've made it clear that you want to dip you dick around town, so let's stop pretending and stop the bullshit."

Before he could respond, the doors of the elevator opened. Nina jumped off quickly, pushing through a throng of her male colleagues. Lamar, close on her heels, grabbed her arm. "Listen," he said. "I never made you any promises and I never told you that we were going to be a couple. So I don't get why you're mad all of a sudden."

She nodded. "That's true. But I'm not doing this right now. I'm working and I know where we stand. Maybe you need to let go as well."

Lamar furrowed his brows. "We had a misunderstanding. But let's move on. I don't see why things have to change."

"Again, we're not doing this now or ever. It's over and I'm over it."

"Then meet me later and let me explain what . . ."

She shook her head as the media relations representative walked out of the locker room and beckoned the media inside. Nina tore away from Lamar, ready to do her job.

The entire time Nina worked the locker room, she felt Lamar watching her. When she talked to the star of the game, a rookie wide receiver who'd caught the winning touchdown, he was just inches from her. While she interviewed a talkative middle linebacker who'd sacked the quarterback three times, he was standing near the trainer's table watching her. Nina couldn't remember the last time that he'd shown this much interest in her. Hell, they hadn't been out on the town in months. Once she finished her interviews, Nina turned to leave the locker room.

"Nina," Lamar called as he jogged to catch up with her. "What time are you coming over?"

"Around never-thirty. I'm so much better than this. To hell with you." Stomping away, she smiled as she thought about the confused look Lamar had to have on his face.

CHAPTER 9

Clinton didn't quite know how to take Nina when she walked into the press box with a smile on her face. Had she and Lamar made up? She walked over to her chair, pulled out her laptop, and began typing.

"Is everything all right?" he asked.

"Yes," she said. "I've got to get these stories written." Nina started typing rapidly and ignored Clinton as she flipped through her notes. Then she slipped her earbuds in and replayed what he assumed was interviews with the players.

Clinton stood up and stretched. Figuring Nina needed to be left alone in order to meet her deadline, he walked over to the wall of televisions and watched the highlights of the football game. He still didn't understand the obsession with a child's game. To him most professional athletes were just overgrown kids who needed a good spanking. Anytime a pro team stayed in a hotel where he worked, the players acted as if the world revolved around them. He felt as if Lamar had that same attitude. There was no way that Lamar could do better than Nina. She was beautiful, smart, and sexy — the total package. He would be hard-pressed to find a better woman. But Nina could easily find a better man.

Clinton poured himself a cup of coffee and dumped in a few packets of sugar. Nina looked beautiful when she was focused.

Lamar walked up beside Clinton. "You're still here?"

"Why wouldn't I be? Nina and I rode together."

Shaking his head, Lamar smirked. "You do know that all of this is because of something I said that she didn't agree with. Once she decides to forgive me, you're back to the long-distance-friend zone."

"That's what you think?" Clinton laughed.

"What?"

"Nothing, but I think you ought to leave her alone," Clinton said. "She's over you and maybe you should try to get over her."

Lamar rolled his eyes. "Whatever. I can have her anytime I want."

"We'll see." Clinton walked away. Nina had gotten what she wanted, she knew that Lamar was still into her, and when he was back in Charleston, they would probably reconcile. Clinton hoped that Nina was smart enough to know Lamar wasn't into her, but didn't want her with anyone else. Typical male ego.

Walking over to Nina, he saw that she'd just finished her story and was packing up her computer and notepad. "That was quick," Clinton said.

"That's what deadline pressure does to you. Are you ready to go?"

Clinton smiled. "Absolutely."

Nina rose to her feet and pulled her jacket on. He noticed that she hadn't looked in Lamar's direction once.

"So what's next?"

Nina shrugged. "Let's just get out of here. And you were right, using you to make him jealous was a stupid idea. I'm glad I saw the light."

Clinton slipped his arm around her waist. "You're learning, grasshopper. I thought you were going to cook for me."

She shrugged her shoulders. "That's the last thing you want me to do. But I can take you to my favorite diner."

"Sounds like a plan."

Nina and Clinton headed for the elevator, not caring that Lamar was watching their every move.

■ ■ ■ ■

As they drove to the diner, she couldn't help but smile. She was having a good time with Clinton and it had nothing to do with making Lamar jealous. He was funny and sweet.

"What's that grin all about?" Clinton asked.

"Tonight turned out a lot better than I thought it was going to be. Thank you."

"You don't have to thank me. I actually learned something tonight."

"What's that?" Nina frowned as a car stopped in front of her for no apparent reason. "Oh, come on!" She leaned on the horn and fought the urge to scream profanities at the car. Glancing over at Clinton, she smiled. "Sorry, I have road rage pretty bad. But you were saying?"

"I see," he said with a smile. "Football isn't that bad. How much farther to the diner? I'm starting to fear for the safety of the other drivers."

Nina turned into a parking lot and brought the car to a stop. "We're here."

They walked into Midnight Diner and took a seat at a secluded table in the corner.

"Seeing him threw you for a loop, didn't it?" Clinton said.

"It did, even though I knew he was only paying attention to me because you were there. So childish. But it was nice to have you by my side." Nina toyed with the menu and averted her eyes from Clinton's gaze. "Sorry I tried to use you."

"I have an ulterior motive," he admitted.

"Really, and what would that be?" Nina lowered her menu. Was this the moment his true colors came out?

"I just wanted to get to know you better away from the watchful and suspicious eyes of your sister. I know you're having a hard time believing in a man because of Lamar. But believe me, we aren't all bad."

"I never thought that, it's just . . ."

Clinton reached across the table and took her hands into his. "You need a break."

"With football season about to start and all of the high schools looking to take down Independence? I can't take a break." Nina slid her hands from his. "Besides, Cody gave me one with sweetheart-gate. I have to regroup now."

"Can't or won't? Self-care is important and you need to take care of Nina."

"You're right, but the way my bills are set up, I have to work."

"Two days won't hurt you. Besides, after

seeing how hard you work, you deserve this."

"I won't argue that fact." She inched closer to him. "Night games are the best and the worst. You know everyone is going to read your stories and you will gain more social media followers. But the rush to get everything done" — she expelled a breath — "it can be hard."

"And that's why you deserve to relax."

His face was inches from hers and their lips brushed against each other's. Nina's cheeks flushed as he took her face into his hands. Clinton captured her lips so quickly that she couldn't protest, not that she wanted to. His kiss thrilled her, sent heated waves of lust through her body. Unlike their first kiss, she welcomed his tongue as he slipped it between her parted lips. He tasted rich like her favorite coffee. A soft moan escaped her throat as Clinton deepened his kiss. It was as if they were alone and not in the middle of a diner. As if they realized their surroundings, they broke off the kiss and stared into each other's eyes.

"We'd better stop. This is dangerous."

"How so?" He took her hand in his and wouldn't let her turn away from him.

"It's way too soon for me to get addicted to your kisses. And I'm —"

"You're right, but I'm the one with the addiction problem. I've been wanting to do that all night."

"Clinton," she murmured.

"Don't spend too much energy worrying about what you could've had with *him.* You're going to find a man who will adore you and you'll never have to question how he feels about you."

Nina opened her mouth to ask him when, but the waiter walked over to the table to take their drink orders.

"You know we're playing with fire," she said once the waiter left.

"You think? I didn't expect this to happen, but look at you. The minute I saw you, I knew I was going to be in trouble. Couldn't get you out of my mind."

"Then why did you agree to play this crazy game with me?"

"For selfish reasons. I knew I'd get to spend the evening with you. Though, I didn't think we'd be alone together."

"You knew what you were doing when you set up that interview. It all makes sense now." Nina laughed and tweaked his nose. Clinton took her hand and brought it to his lips.

"I really didn't do that. Your father's story is amazing and I think the world should know about it. And were it not for Yolanda, I would've been there to oversee the photo shoot and everything. She took the styling of your father very seriously."

Nina rolled her eyes. "I bet she did. There's no way Yolanda would've allowed you to step in and do your job today. So, I saved you."

"And for that, I'm forever in your debt."

"Be careful. I'm going to collect one day." She chewed her bottom lip as their eyes met and the air seemed to sizzle between them.

The waiter walked over to the table with their drinks and to take their food orders.

"Why do we like playing with fire so much?" Nina asked when the waiter left.

"Wish I had an answer. I'm not going to lie and say I don't want you, Nina, but you're going to have to want me, too."

"I do want . . . Clinton, you're a breath of fresh air and I want to get to know you more, but is this just a physical thing?"

"Nina, I'm in no hurry to take you to bed. But that doesn't mean that I don't want to. You're sexy as hell and —"

"Maybe that's the problem. I'm the girl everyone wants to take to bed."

"Stop, because that's not what I'm saying. There's so much more to you and I want to uncover every piece."

She smiled, wondering how she was going to keep her thighs together when they arrived at her place.

The waiter brought their food over before things went too far — burgers, fries, and chocolate milkshakes — and they dug in. As hard as Clinton tried not to focus on Nina's lips, he couldn't help it. Every sip she took from that straw made him hard as he imagined her treating him with the same slow suck.

"You don't like the food?" She glanced at Clinton's half-eaten burger.

"It's fine. I just got a little distracted." He popped a fry in his mouth.

Nina raised her right eyebrow and took another sip of her shake. There he was being distracted again. She leaned her cup toward him. "You know you can have it, if you want it that badly."

Clinton inhaled sharply, then wiped a bit of cream from her bottom lip. He felt Nina shiver and he knew it wasn't the coldness of the milkshake that caused it. Need, want, and desire had enveloped them both. "We'd better eat and get out of here. You have an early morning drive."

He nodded. "Yes, I do."

Nina laughed and sent his heart into overdrive. "And please don't be late for work. Alex punishes people for having fun."

They finished their meal in a comfortable silence. Clinton even allowed Nina to swipe his fries without comment and he was enjoying those salty fritters. But the taste didn't compare to watching Nina's lips. When the waiter returned to the table with the check, Clinton pulled out his credit card and slid it in the black billfold. "My treat."

"You don't have to do that." Nina reached for the check, but Clinton kept it out of her reach until the waiter returned to the table.

"I know, but I got this." He handed the waiter the check, then turned back to Nina. "It's the least I can do."

She smiled and reached for her jacket. "Well, let's go."

The ride to Nina's town house was much smoother because game traffic had died down. The duo rode in silence and when they arrived at Nina's, she couldn't help but think about what would happen when they got inside. Her mind wandered to what his lips would feel like between her thighs. *Stop it,* she thought. *This is why you're in the situation that you're in now.*

Nina dropped her keys as she attempted to unlock the front door.

"Are you all right?" He bent down and picked up the keys. Clinton unlocked the door and held it open for her.

"Too much caffeine." Nina smiled as she flipped the light on. "The perils of a late game."

"I hope you'll be able to get some sleep. I know I have to get an early start if I plan to avoid traffic."

She stepped back and nodded. "And the wrath of Alex. I put clean towels in the guest room and the sheets are fresh too," she said, her voice quivering with nervousness.

"And she's protective of her family. I'm going to have a long way to go to win her trust."

"It shouldn't be that hard. I feel like I can trust you," she admitted, which brought a smile to Clinton's face.

"Thank you for your hospitality," he said, closing the space between them. His lips were inches from hers. "And I really want to thank you for that kiss earlier."

Nina didn't want to speak because if she'd moved her head one inch, she and Clinton would've been locked in another passionate embrace. He lifted her chin and forced her to look into his eyes. He winked at her and Nina knew she wouldn't stop him from kissing her again. "Point me in the direction of the guest room."

"Umm, upstairs and to the left."

"Good night, Nina."

She watched him as he walked up the stairs, thinking that she had to thank his mama for an ass like that. *Go to bed, Nina!*

When she heard the guest room door close, Nina headed upstairs and straight for a cold shower.

Clinton couldn't sleep, despite how comfortable the full-sized bed was. All he could think about was Nina's lips. When he heard the shower start up, he imagined her stepping underneath the water, her nipples perking up as the tepid water hit her body. *Like you know how hot she likes her water. Just because you need a cold shower doesn't mean she does.* Clinton closed his eyes and her naked body flashed in his head again. He'd never been envious of a loofah before, but tonight was a different story. He imagined Nina soaping one up and rubbing it across her svelte body. He could see her hair curling up from the moisture as the water hit it. He wanted to run his fingers through her tresses as she wrapped her leg around his waist. The thought of her heat enveloping his hardness lit him up like a candle. Sighing, he cupped his hands behind his head and closed his eyes hoping to go to sleep. But as his erection made a tent in his boxers, Clinton wanted to head down the hall to the bathroom and make love to Nina in the shower. *The last thing I need to do is try to rush into something physical with her,* he thought. *Nina is more than that.*

Still, the image of a wet Nina wrapped in only a towel haunted Clinton until sleep finally grabbed him.

The next morning, Clinton climbed out of bed about five, grabbed his towel, and headed for the bathroom to take a quick shower before he drove back to Charleston. All night he'd dreamt of Nina, and walking into the bathroom made him want to make his dreams come true. Like he could go and wake her up after telling her that they needed to take things slow.

Looking around the bathroom, Clinton knew two things: Rose was Nina's signature scent and favorite flower. Her walls were covered with wallpaper decorated by roses, and she had three bottles of rose-scented perfume on the counter.

Turning the shower on, he stepped underneath the warm spray and closed his eyes. He couldn't help but hope Nina would join him underneath the water and make his dreams come true. *And if she does, there's no way you're going to make it back to Charleston.* Clinton dipped his head under the water, needing to wash his lustful thoughts away.

Following his shower, Clinton dashed into the room and dressed. Then he was faced with a dilemma: Wake Nina so that she could lock the door behind him or wait until she woke up and then leave. His overwhelming desire for her kept him from knocking on her door. Suppose she slept naked? That he wanted to see.

Clinton figured if he was going to wake her up that the least he could do was brew some coffee or cook breakfast for Nina. As he headed downstairs to the kitchen, he was met with the aroma of strong coffee, fried eggs, and buttery grits.

"And I was going to come down here and try to surprise you with breakfast," he said when he spotted Nina at the stove. She was dressed in a pair of black yoga pants, a cropped cotton T-shirt, and pink socks. And she looked absolutely amazing.

"My father always taught me to feed my guests before they leave," she said.

Clinton smiled. "Is that so they'll come back?"

Nina grinned as she spooned grits onto a plate and handed it to him. "Say that after you've tasted my cooking."

Glancing at the watery grits and rubbery-looking eggs, Clinton wondered if Nina was more of a protein smoothie type of breakfast person. "I take it that Alex did all the cooking when you guys were growing up?"

She folded her arms across her chest and smirked. "I never said cooking was one of my many talents. It's not going to kill you, it just may not taste good."

Clinton set his plate on the counter and gently pushed Nina aside. "Tell me where everything is and I'll cook a breakfast with some taste."

"Fine, and I'll check the coffee. I'm good at making coffee." Winking at him, she pointed him to where to find the ingredients. As Nina reached up in the cabinet to grab two mugs, Clinton watched her booty jiggle. Even first thing in the morning she looked like a goddess. He almost dropped a dozen eggs as he watched her make the coffee. One thing he could say was that she was serious about her java.

After Clinton made a simple breakfast of toast, creamy instant grits, and perfectly scrambled eggs, he was surprised Nina had been so impressed with his effort.

"I've never had a guy cook me breakfast before."

"What kind of men have you been dealing with?"

"The wrong kind, obviously," she replied as she spooned grits into her mouth. "There are several restaurants in town that claim to have Charleston cuisine, but these are the best grits I've had since I've been in North Carolina."

"It's nothing spectacular. I like to cook, though. Some of my best memories are of my mother and me cooking in the kitchen, much to my father's dismay."

Nina stared at him thoughtfully. "Why would your father be upset about you spending time with your mother? I wish I could've had a chance to know my mother. Maybe I'd be a better cook."

He reached over the table and grabbed her hand. "I'm sorry."

She shrugged, but her eyes glistened with tears. "I was so young when she passed away. That's the one thing I really envy about Alex and Robin, they have so many wonderful memories of our mother and all I have is their stories." She hugged herself, then dropped her hands and turned to Clinton.

"I don't know what I would've done without my mother. My father made no bones about it, I was a disappointment to him because I didn't run with a ball or shoot one." Clinton tried not to think bitter thoughts and ruin the moment he and Nina were sharing. But whenever he thought of the past and his father, he couldn't help but grow angry. Many of his classmates and former football players whom he'd gone to high school with were either in jail, dead, or stuck working a dead-end job in a factory. Clinton was successful, never been to jail or in any kind of trouble. Still it wasn't enough to please his father. In a way, he felt as if he and Nina were kindred spirits, trying to make the wrong man love them for all the right reasons.

"We've gotten really serious really fast," Nina said, breaking the uncomfortable silence that had fallen between them. "You'd better hit the road."

Clinton rose to his feet. "You're right, but before I go, I have to clean up. All good cooks clean up after themselves."

"You don't have to do that."

He winked at her as he took their plates to the kitchen sink. "I know. What are your plans for the rest of the day?"

"You mean after I go back to sleep?"

Clinton laughed. "Not a morning person?"

"Umm, after about three cups of coffee." Despite his objections, Nina helped him wash their dishes. Standing that close to her was almost unbearable.

And though he knew he should keep his lips to himself, Clinton leaned in and kissed her on the cheek. "Then I appreciate you allowing me to cook breakfast for you this early in the morning." He could've sworn he saw Nina blush. Looking back at her confirmed that he was right. Clinton wondered how she could be so sexy and so innocent at the same time.

CHAPTER 10

When Clinton left, Nina thought she'd be able to sleep, but her mind was filled with Clinton Jefferson. She'd spent half the night fighting the urge to creep into his room. Instead, she'd taken a cold shower. Acting on her lust would've been a mistake. But his kiss burned on her lips all night. Nina decided to clean her place and work on some story pitches. By noon, her body was ready to shut down. She stomped into her bedroom, kicking off her slippers and plopping down on her bed. Just as she was about to drift off to sleep, the phone rang, shattering the silence.

"Hello?"

"Is that guy still there?" Lamar demanded, without extending a greeting.

"What?"

"Have you gotten rid of my replacement?"

"You have a lot of nerve. Don't call me again." Nina ended the call and rolled over on her side. Closing her eyes, she hoped sleep would come quickly, but the phone rang again.

"What?"

"Is that any way to talk to your favorite sister?" Yolanda asked.

"I'm in the bed."

"Alone or is Clinton beside you?" Yolanda teased.

"Whatever, Yolanda. He left after we had breakfast." Nina couldn't help but smile as she thought about washing dishes side by side with him. They'd spent the morning flicking water on each other and flirting. She'd never had more fun washing dishes.

"Oh, no! Please tell me your non-cooking ass didn't poison that man with your so-called food. You know the last time you cooked, we could drink your grits through a straw." Yolanda laughed loudly.

"Ha, ha. I didn't cook, Clinton did. It was so sweet. And he's a good cook."

Yolanda stopped laughing. "Don't tell me you're jumping from heartache to love again. Be careful, Sis."

"I plan to. Clinton's a nice guy and all. But what do I know about him?" *That he can kiss you right out of your panties.*

"What did Lamar think when he saw y'all at the game? You're not going to keep play-

137

ing this game to get him back, are you?"

Nina sighed. "Lamar isn't worth my time. Not when someone like Clinton is out there and values me for more than a booty call. Someone who's concerned about how I feel and . . ."

"Yeah, you got it bad and you don't even know it yet. If you plan to get involved with Clinton, do me a favor, make sure he's what you think he is. I don't want to see you wallowing in self-pity in a few months. And since I can get my hands on this one, I will hurt him if he hurts you."

"Slow down, My Little Pony. Clinton and I just met. And he told me he's in no hurry to get in my drawers."

"Ooh, classy. Tell me he didn't use those words."

"No, he didn't." Nina closed her eyes and thought about their conversation at the diner. Just hearing him say he wasn't in a hurry to take her to bed made her want him even more. She stopped herself from moaning, remembering Yolanda was on the line. "Are you still in Charleston?"

"Yes, but I'm leaving today because your sister is getting on my last nerve with her bossy self. Alex needs to realize that we are all adults. That girl really needs to get some in the worst way. If she had a life of her own, then she could leave us the hell alone."

"Stop it. You know how Alex is. She wants the best for us and she knows what's best." Nina snorted. "But she's always been a control freak."

"Whatever. Anyway, I'm going to have lunch with Daddy. If I see your new beau before I leave, I'll tell him you said hello."

"You better not!" Nina exclaimed. "Besides, I'm sure that I'll talk to him before you will."

Nina could hear her sister's smile through the phone. "I bet you will."

Clinton arrived at the bed-and-breakfast five minutes before he was scheduled to begin his day. Still, he was met with an angry Alexandria as he entered his office.

"Good morning," he sang, trying not to let Alex's scowl spoil his mood.

"Despite your little vacation in your first week, the interview went well. In the future, you'll be here to supervise your projects. After all, that's what we're paying you to do."

Taking off his jacket and laying it across his chair, he looked up at Alex and smiled. "Absolutely. Do you have a copy of the paper?"

She hurled a copy of the paper at him.

"And we've gotten some website traffic from the article."

"Then what's the problem?" He collected the paper and glanced at the pictures. Clinton was satisfied to see Sheldon Richardson looking suave and important on the front of the travel section. "I can share it on our social media sites."

Alex rolled her eyes. "I've done that already. Keep your mind off my sister and on the job you were hired to do. I still don't trust you and if I find out that this is some ploy by your former employer to gain control of this place, I'll personally make you pay." Alex turned on her heels and stomped down the hall.

Clinton shook his head, wondering how Nina and Alex could be from the same gene pool. They were polar opposites and he couldn't be happier. Nina was sweet and light and Alex seemed to be doom and gloom. He dropped his head in his hands because he hadn't gotten Nina's number and he wanted to talk to her. Before he could berate himself, his desk phone rang.

"Clinton Jefferson."

"Nina Richardson."

"I was just thinking about you. An old wives' tale says that you're going to live a long life," he said, smiling.

"Good. I realize that I didn't give you my number. I'm glad you made it to work safely and on time. Have you seen Alex?"

"Yes, I did. How's your day going?"

"Eh, it's going. I finished up a few stories and got some assignments for the rest of the week. What are you doing this weekend?"

"I don't have any plans. What do you have in mind?"

"Well," she said, clicking her tongue against her teeth. "I'm covering a basketball tournament in Charleston. I know you aren't a sports fan, so why don't we meet for dinner after the game."

"That sounds great and I'll do you one better, I'll cook."

"If you're trying to spoil me, you're doing a good job of it. Where do you live?"

"Out in Summerville."

"That's a heck of a commute every day."

"I like it out there. It's quiet and it gives me a chance to de-stress," Clinton said.

Nina laughed. "I guess working with Alex would cause one to stress. Speaking of my illustrious sister, she didn't give you any grief today, did she?"

"No more than usual. I could talk to you for hours, but I'm sure if Alexandria catches me chatting away on the phone with you, she'll have my head. Check out your father's article in *USA Today* when you get a chance."

"I will do that and I'll see you on Friday night."

After hanging up the phone, Clinton was all smiles and couldn't wait for Friday.

"Knock, knock." Yolanda sauntered into Clinton's office with a bright smile on her face. "I just came to say good-bye. So, did you and my little sister have fun last night?"

"If by *fun,* you mean we enjoyed each other's company, then yes, we had a great time."

Yolanda perched herself on the edge of his desk. "Listen, I'm not Empress Alexandria. You can be real with me. You like Nina, don't you? And I'm talking about in a more-than-friends way."

Clinton leaned back in his chair and assessed Yolanda Richardson. She was definitely the wild one of the bunch. He could imagine her and Nina causing a lot of trouble together. "I do like her. She's a very nice —"

"Look, that's good and all, but you better treat her right or I'll make Alex look like a teddy bear. I don't get into Nina's business a lot, but I don't want to see my sister hurt. And if you're the one who causes her pain, you can get these hands."

He rose to his feet and scooted Yolanda off his desk. "What is it about the women in this family? This is the second time I've been told off by a Richardson woman today. But let me assure you, I'd never do anything to hurt Nina. I respect her and I can't wait to get to know her better."

Yolanda tweaked his nose. "I'm sure you do, but I wouldn't be on my job if I didn't warn you. I think I like you, Clinton Jefferson, and I hope you're just what my sister needs. Any more like you at home?"

He shook his head. "Sorry, I'm one of a kind."

She shrugged her shoulders. "Figures." Yolanda strolled out the door as if she had her own theme song playing in her head.

Clinton chuckled and dove into his work. He definitely liked Yolanda.

CHAPTER 11

Nina was floating as she went through her day. Just the thought of Clinton brought a smile to her lips and a fluttering in her chest. But all of that changed when she got a call from her editor.

"Nina, it's Johnny. I need you to do something for me."

"What's that?"

"An interview with Coach Geddings."

Hell no! she screamed inwardly. Johnny continued. "The turnaround at West Mecklenburg High is noteworthy. And we have a few parents who want to see the school in the paper."

You can't expect me to talk to this man after he trampled over my heart the way he did. "When do you want this interview?"

"Today. I was going to do it, but I'm tied up on several things. He's expecting me at three over at the school. Can you swing that?"

Say no, just say no. "Sure, Johnny."

"You've lobbied for this story for a while, so I hope you're happy I finally saw the light."

"Thrilled," she said flatly. "Let me get ready so that I can get out there."

"Thanks, Nina. You're the best. Sure that I can't interest you in a staff position?"

She laughed and said no before hanging up. Nina dashed into her bedroom and threw on a pair of jeans, an oxford shirt, and a pair of loafers. She ran her fingers through her hair and didn't bother to put on any makeup. The least she could do if she had to do this interview was to make sure she looked like she meant nothing but business.

I will treat Lamar like any other coach. He's not a part of my life anymore and I won't be sucked in again. Wrapping her jacket around her shoulders, she headed to her car and drove slowly for a change.

Nina hated that because she'd lobbied so hard for some editor to care about Lamar's story, now she had to pay for it because she had to write the story. As she drove into the school's parking lot, she shook her head solemnly wondering how she'd ever fooled herself into believing that what she and Lamar had was love. *Maybe I'm just in love with the idea of being in love,* she thought. *I'm old enough to know that sex and love are two different things. He was skilled at giving me orgasms and that's about it. Lamar's main concern has always been himself and that damned football team. Maybe that's why he wanted me, so he could get some media coverage.*

Nina sighed as she pulled into an empty parking spot near the coaches' offices. She realized that she allowed herself to be used because she'd built up this fantasy version of Lamar when reality was staring her in the face all the time.

She put on her game face as she headed into the office. For a moment, Nina stood in the doorway looking at Lamar as he spoke with a player. She couldn't deny that he was still attractive, his skin still looked like the smoothest chocolate and those curly eyelashes still framed his sexy brown bedroom eyes. Inhaling sharply, she tapped on the door. "Coach Geddings, Johnny sends his apologies and me to do the interview," Nina said.

Lamar's eyes lit up as he drank in her appearance. Nina figured he was thinking about the last time they were in the office together. Nina had shown up in a long leather coat, thigh-high red patent leather boots, and a red satin teddy. Lamar had been going over his playbook, but when Nina dropped her coat, he pushed everything on his desk to the floor so that he could have his way with her. It was exciting and fun to her at the time. Now she felt like a fool for stopping her work to drive all the way out to the school where she was to give him a cheap thrill.

"Chavious, we're done. We're going to have a good season," Lamar said, ushering the student out of his office. Then he turned to Nina. "Have a seat."

She took a seat across from his desk, reached into her purse, and retrieved her iPhone and notepad. "So, Coach," she said flatly, "to what do you attribute the turnaround in your team this season?"

"And how are you doing?"

"Doing my job, please answer my question."

Lamar reached over and pressed stop on the phone. "So, that's how it is?"

"How what is?" She folded her arms across her chest and rolled her eyes at him.

"You're just going to come in here and pretend I'm just another coach?" Lamar leaned forward and smiled seductively. "You know what happened the last time we were in here alone together?"

147

Nina threw her hand in his face. "And that's just what it was, the last time we will ever. Do you want this story written or not?"

"I want the story and I want you. Am I wrong for that?"

"Yes," she snapped. Nina leapt to her feet. "You want me and every other woman you can parade around town. Sweetie, I'm not a second-round draft pick. And I'm done being reduced to an option in the life of Lamar."

He stood and closed the space between them. "I want you and I want things to stay the same. When you add labels, everything changes." He tried to draw her into his arms, but Nina pushed against his chest.

"Are you going sit down and do this interview or continue to beat this dead horse?"

Lamar didn't answer, he just brought his lips on top of hers. The quickness of his kiss and the force of it didn't give Nina a chance to react, but her treacherous body responded to his kiss as if he hadn't broken her heart. It seemed second nature for her to wrap her arms around his neck and kiss him back. She was angry and showed it with her kiss, pressing her lips hard against his and digging her nails into his neck. Then, in an instant, Nina pulled back, pushing him away.

"I'm not doing this. You're insane. This can't happen, not after you flaunted your other woman in my damn face!"

Lamar reached out and grabbed her. "You want me, I could feel the fire in your lips. Whatever you and that cat did last night can't compare to what we have. You know that, otherwise you wouldn't have kissed me."

"We don't have anything!" Nina shook her head and narrowed her eyes at him. "You only want me because you saw me with Clinton. Negro, you told me to move on and when I do you want me? Grow up, Lamar."

Stepping back from her, he rested on the edge of his desk and cast a cold stare at her. "To say you claimed to love me, it didn't take you long to move on. So, that leads me to believe that you were playing games all along," he said. "Why would you have that guy at the game when you knew I was going to be there? Then you gave him my seat."

"Oh, go to hell," Nina screamed. "For the last year, all I did was fall in love with you. I gave my heart and soul to you like a damned fool and you want to sit there and accuse me of doing the same thing you did. We're just friends, remember? No commitment. Isn't that what you said? Or does that only work for you?"

"I'm just saying, how much love was there if you could replace me in five minutes?"

Nina slapped him as hard as she could. "You son of a bitch. You can't do what you want to do and get upset when I do the same thing."

Lamar rubbed his cheek and glared at her.

"Obviously, I'm not going to be able to do this interview with you." Nina snatched her jacket from the back of the chair and stormed toward the door.

Lamar crossed over to the door to block her exit. "Look, this wasn't the right time for this. I'm sorry. But seeing you with that other guy did something to me."

Nina pulled her jacket on. "I'm not a possession and you're not going to treat me like a discarded toy that you want back because another kid is playing with it."

Lamar stepped back from her. "So, you're saying you slept with him, huh?"

Nina narrowed her eyes and remained silent, then she took a step forward.

"Are we going to do this interview or what?" he asked.

Though she wanted to say no, Nina knew she had bills to pay and a deadline to meet.

Huffing, she walked to his desk and sat down. "Let's get this over with."

The interview went fast and Nina walked away as soon as she asked her last question, barely listening to his answer. Thank goodness for the electronic ear.

Lamar watched her as she slammed out his office. She was aware of his stare, but didn't look back. If she was truly going to put him behind her, this was the last time that she would ever speak to him.

As Tuesday turned to Friday, Clinton couldn't wait to see Nina. All week he'd put up with Alexandria's bad attitude with a smile on his face because he knew he had a special weekend planned. Thanks to the article in *USA Today,* the bed-and-breakfast was getting more reservations than ever during what was normally a slow period for the business. Sheldon Richardson was beside himself with joy.

Friday afternoon, he walked into Clinton's office smiling like the cat who had eaten the canary. "I should've hired someone like you twenty years ago," he said as he sat in the chair across from Clinton's desk. "I don't remember a busier winter. The reservations are through the roof. And we're booked for the rest of the summer."

151

"People like to get away in the winter and summer," Clinton replied, smiling at his boss.

"Did you and Nina enjoy the game?"

"It was very nice. I'm sure you hated not being there."

Sheldon fanned his hand. "There'll be other games. Besides, I think she had more fun with you than she would've had with her old man, anyway. Alex tells me that she's coming down here this weekend for some basketball event."

Clinton nodded.

Sheldon smiled, then grew serious in a split second. "Most fathers meddle in their daughters' love life. I don't. But if there is anything going on with you and Nina, make sure you treat her right. I love my daughters and each one of them is special. Nina's the youngest, she's the one who missed out on knowing her mother. I did what I could to make up for that. What I'm trying to say is that we're all a little overprotective of Nina. She hates it, but what I hate more than anything is seeing my little girl hurt."

"Sir," Clinton began. "I would never intentionally hurt Nina. I think she's a great person and we have fun together."

Sheldon held up his hand. "I don't need the details. Just make sure that you are what and who you say you are or you're not going to like the consequences." Sheldon rose to his feet and left the office with his warning lingering in the air.

Clinton didn't blame Sheldon one bit for looking out for his daughter, though he wondered how Nina would feel about it. Rising to his feet, he made a mental list of the things he needed to put together a special low-country meal. He planned to make shrimp and grits along with a corn soufflé. If his breakfast had impressed her, then this dinner would knock her off her feet.

As he was about to leave for the day, Alex entered his office and dropped a thick file folder on his desk. "I need you to contact these companies and tell them about our holiday promotion."

Clinton raised his eyebrow in aggravation. "You didn't tell me about a holiday promotion."

"It's your job to come up with one. I need your report and proposal Monday morning."

Instead of arguing with Alex, Clinton simply nodded. "Anything else?"

Alex pivoted out of the office without saying another word.

Now leaving early wasn't an option as he

had to come up with a holiday promotion and write a report for Alex. It was after six before he emerged from his office and ran into Nina as he crossed the lobby.

"Where's the fire?" she asked, touching his arm to slow him down.

"Hey, I didn't expect to see you here." Clinton leaned in and kissed her on the cheek. "I also didn't expect to work this late, but something came up."

Nina smiled. "Let me guess, Alex dumped work on you at the last minute?"

He nodded and returned her smile. "How ever did you figure that out?"

"I know my sister. She can't stand the idea of someone having fun. Why don't we just order takeout?"

"What time is your game over?"

Nina shrugged. "Barring overtime, I should be out of there by nine thirty," she said. "I just came to say hello to my daddy."

"All right, I'm going to see if I can pull together dinner for you so I don't have to subject you to takeout. If you liked my eggs, you'll love my dinner."

Nina grinned at him. "You don't have to go through all of that trouble for me."

Clinton stroked her cheek gently. "I like to cook, so it's no trouble. Trust me, you're never going to want to eat in a restaurant again after you taste this meal." He waved good-bye to Nina and dashed to his car. Hopefully, her game would go into overtime and he'd have time to prepare a special meal.

CHAPTER 12

Nina prayed as she sat on the sidelines that the game would end soon. Her prayers went unanswered. The referees seemed to see fouls that weren't there and sent players to the free throw line every fifteen seconds. Now the game was tied up with less than a minute to go. All she wanted was a miracle from one of the teams. She didn't care who won. Nina wanted to get out of the small gymnasium and head to Summerville.

There was something about knowing that Clinton was sitting at home waiting for her instead of the other way around. He made her feel so special and she couldn't wait to see him again. For all Nina cared, he could've made peanut butter and jelly sandwiches with apple slices and she would've been satisfied. It was nice to feel appreciated instead of used. Now that she had a chance to reflect on what she and Lamar had, she realized she had been used and tossed out like a rumpled tissue.

Clinton was different and she needed something like him right now in her life. The sound of the buzzer broke into her thoughts and she smiled as the home team scored the winning basket. Overtime was not in her future. She raced to the center of the floor to grab the head coach and the star players from the winning team so that she could do her postgame interviews and get out of there.

For once, when she didn't want to, she found a coach who was extremely talkative, along with players who didn't know when to shut up either. Nina spent over an hour interviewing the winners and she still had about a thirty-minute ride to Clinton's place in Summerville. When her interviews were finally over, she hopped into her car and headed back to the bed-and-breakfast to change her clothes. She had hoped to sneak in without running into Alex. Clearly, tonight wasn't her lucky night.

"Where are you off to?" Alex asked when she appeared in Nina's doorway.

Alex was already prepared for bed with her hair in rollers, a scarf wrapped around her head and a plush terry cloth robe covering her pajamas.

Nina had just slipped into a short-sleeve

black dress that skimmed the tops of her knees, and she was looking through her bag for a pair of pumps. "What makes you think I'm going somewhere?"

"Those don't look like pajamas to me. Please don't tell me it's another coach."

Nina sat on the edge of the bed and looked up at her sister. "If you must know, I'm going out with Clinton."

"What? I really wished that you wouldn't jump into something with this guy. I don't trust him, Nina."

"What's he done to you to make you not trust him?" Nina pulled her shoes from her bag and slipped them on her feet. "From what Daddy has said, he's doing a great job."

Alex tugged on her scarf, causing one of her rollers to slip from underneath it. "I'm not going to be fooled by this guy. He has an agenda, working with our family, trying to date you . . ."

"First of all, Clinton and I aren't dating. We're friends. I had a good time with him at the football game and he offered to cook me dinner tonight." Nina ran her fingers through her hair and turned to her sister. "You're way too suspicious."

"Sometimes I forget how young you really are," Alex said flippantly.

Nina reached for her purse and pushed past her sister. "On that note, I'm leaving."

Alex grabbed Nina's arm. "Please be careful. You don't know this guy and with your track record you need to exercise caution."

She pulled away from her sister. "Good night and don't wait up. I plan to come home very late, if at all." Nina hated how Alex made her feel like a silly child about to run into oncoming traffic. There was nothing wrong with her spending time with Clinton and there was no reason for anyone to mistrust him. As long as her father thought he was a good person, she didn't give a damn what Alexandria Richardson thought.

Clinton was on pins and needles waiting for Nina to arrive. He'd struggled with whether he should set the table with or without candles. This wasn't a night of seduction. He decided to dim the lights and keep the wine chilling until she showed up. He hoped that she didn't have trouble finding the place, since his home sat about a mile off the main road. Just as he was about to look out the window again, the doorbell rang.

When Clinton opened the door and saw Nina standing there, he was speechless. There was something about the black dress, her new hair color, and the glow of her skin that made him want to forget his promise to himself to take things slow with her. "You look amazing."

"Thanks," she said as she walked in. "I rarely get to dress like this."

Clinton looked down at his faded jeans and Rolling Stones T-shirt and felt incredibly underdressed. "I can change and we can go out if you want."

Nina shook her head as she slowly walked into the living room, drinking in the rich brown and maroon colors of the walls and the paintings he had decorating them. "No, I don't want to go anywhere. You have good taste. I like the art." She pointed to a bright blue painting of a man holding a woman emerging from a lake. "Is that a Celina Hart?"

He nodded. "Her work brightens my little hideaway."

"What do you have to hide from?" Nina placed her hand on her hip and smiled slyly at him.

"Alex, for one, and I like to get away from the city and the noise as much as possible. I hope you're hungry."

"I am, but not for dinner, right yet. I want to know more about you. It seems like since the moment we met I've been spilling my guts to you and I don't know anything about Clinton Jefferson," she said before sitting on the sofa and crossing her legs.

Inhaling sharply, Clinton smiled and sat beside her, trying to tell himself not to look at her shapely legs but into her beautiful eyes. "What do you want to know?"

"Everything. Does your family still live in Charleston? What made you decide to work at the B&B after you tried to get my dad to sell? How many other women come here on a weekly basis?"

He chuckled softly, wondering what he should tell her. "Well, I don't bring a lot of women here. Like I said, this is my hideaway, my fortress of solitude. As you can tell, I was a comic book nerd and Superman is still my favorite. My father lives in North Charleston but we don't talk much. My mother died two years ago and my dad and I ran out of things to talk about. Asking your father to sell his bed-and-breakfast was the hardest thing I had ever done at that time."

"At the time?" She raised her right eyebrow. "What was harder?"

Clinton shrugged, then looked away. There was no way he would tell her that the hardest thing he'd ever done was to not join her in the shower a few nights ago.

Noting his silence, Nina sucked her teeth.

"So, you're not going to tell me?"

"Nope."

Nina inched closer to him and placed her hand on his shoulder. "Not going to give me one little clue?"

"You're good, but no. I'll tell you something else, though. Your father inspired me even before I met him."

"Really?"

He nodded. "That's how I ended up in hospitality. I remember reading an article about your father. I must have been a sophomore in high school and I knew what I wanted to do when I grew up."

Nina laughed softly. "I'm still trying to figure out why my sister thinks you're some kind of spy."

Maybe it was the lighting or maybe it was the way her lips glistened that made him want to kiss her. Clinton cleared his throat. "I'm not a spy. I don't want to do anything but my job and learn more about the business so that I can run my own hotel one day."

Nina smiled and he couldn't resist stroking her cheek. "You know," she said, "I think you'd do very well with your own property."

"Have I told you enough about me now?" he asked.

Nina shook her head and folded her arms

across her firm bosom. Clinton had to look away. "So, Clinton, why in the world are you single?"

"You're a hell of a reporter, aren't you?"

"What do you mean?" She batted her eyelashes at him.

"You ask tough questions. But that answer is, I haven't met her yet."

Nina smiled. "And how will you know? What if you met her at the supermarket and just let her pass you by?"

"Here's what I know: It's time to eat."

When she licked her lips, Clinton prayed she wouldn't notice how she affected him as he stood up. He led her to the dining room. He pulled her chair out, glad the high-back chair blocked his crotch.

"Thanks," she replied.

"You're welcome. I hope you enjoy this meal," he said before heading into the kitchen to get the main course. If Clinton had his druthers, he'd feast on Nina all night long. But this wasn't the plan.

He took the shrimp dish out of the oven and headed for the dining room. "Dinner is served," Clinton said as he set the food in the middle of the table.

"It smells wonderful. What is it?"

"A secret family recipe. I wanted to make something a little more special, but I got a late start." Clinton spooned a bit of the casserole on Nina's plate. "I'll be right back with the salad." He headed back to the kitchen and returned with a wooden bowl filled with a fresh tossed salad in a balsamic dressing.

"Let me find out that you're an undercover chef." She watched him intently as he scooped salad on her plate.

"Now you know my secret. I want to beat Bobby Flay one day." He winked at her, then took his seat next to her.

She took a bite of the food. Closing her eyes, she moaned in pleasure. "This is good. I could get used to this, Mr. Jefferson. Don't start something you can't finish."

"I'm not that guy. I believe in marathons. So, get used to this."

"Be careful what you ask for. You might see me at your dinner table once a week."

Clinton filled his plate with salad and casserole. "You say that as if it's a bad thing."

Nina spooned more food in her mouth and Clinton was transfixed by her lips. Then she moaned again and he was hard as dry concrete. *Let it simmer,* he thought as he turned away from her and focused on his own meal. But what he wanted to taste was underneath the table.

A tense silence fell over the room as they

ate. Need and want filled the air.

"I wish I could cook like this," Nina said after eating her fill and leaning back in the chair.

"It's really easy. And I'm willing to teach you, if you want to learn," Clinton said as he inched his chair closer to hers.

"I might not be a good student," she said. "I don't have the patience to wait for dough to rise and whatnot."

"Maybe that's why you can't cook, you're too impatient. There's a lot to be said for taking things slowly."

Nina raised her eyebrow as she studied his face. "Are we still talking about cooking?"

He took her face into his hands. "You just have to let things marinate sometimes."

"Clinton."

"Just for the record, I didn't ask you to come here tonight to take you to bed."

"I know." She offered him a sly smile. "Maybe that's why I came to you." Nina leaned forward and brushed her lips across his.

Damn taking it slow. He swiftly brought his lips down on top of hers, kissing her until she was breathless.

Clinton hadn't expected Nina's response to be as passionate as it was. When he felt

165

her fingers dance on the back of his neck, he was done for. Nina's kiss set his soul ablaze. There was something different about this kiss. Hotter. Wetter. Filled with a burning passion. Sanity told him to live by the words he'd said to her. Take it slow.

Going slow was so damned overrated. He mustered up every ounce of self-control he had inside him and pulled back from her.

"Nina. This isn't why I invited you to dinner."

She ran her tongue across his bottom lip. "We're adults and no one is being forced into anything."

Clinton groaned. "Tonight, I just need to taste you." His voice was like a panther growl as he lifted her up on the table. Clinton pushed her dress up and smiled at the barely there lace thong. Placing his hot hands between her thighs, he stroked her wetness until she purred. Her wetness covered his fingers like honey as he pressed each digit deeper inside her. One. Two.

Nina gasped as she tightened herself around his fingers. "This. Is. Torture."

"Relax." Clinton dove between her thighs, pulling her thong to the side, then capturing her most sensitive spot with his mouth. He felt her shiver, felt her get wetter. He lapped her sweetness, sucked her throbbing clit, and licked circles inside her.

Nina breathlessly called out his name as she trembled. He pulled her closer, licking and sucking until she exploded. Clinton didn't stop. He couldn't because she was so sweet and delicious. A treat that he knew he'd never get enough of anytime soon. When his tongue lashed her pearl, Nina came like a raging river. Tearing his mouth away from her, Clinton drank in the sated look on her face.

"Now that I've had my dessert, what can I get you?"

Nina was breathless, satisfied and thankful that she and Clinton had stayed in.

"Water. I need some water." Sliding into the chair, she focused on Clinton's magical lips.

"Come here," he said, then lifted her from the chair. "You relax on the sofa and I'll bring you water." He carried her into the living room with ease. The heat of Clinton's body made her throb. He gently deposited her on the butter-soft leather sofa. "Be right back."

Sitting in the stillness, Nina closed her eyes, reliving every luscious moment on that table. Clinton proved he wasn't a selfish lover, making sure her needs were met and exceeded. Nina's body was still trembling — especially her thighs.

"Are you all right?" Clinton's voice was melodic and soothing.

"Mmm, I'm good. Really good." Nina took the glass of water from his outstretched hand. Clinton sat down beside her and stroked her arm.

"Want to watch a movie or . . ."

She tilted her head to the side and studied his face. She wanted more of his lips and his touch. "What kind of movie do you have in mind?"

"Not a sports one," he quipped. Clinton turned the smart TV on and clicked on a movie-streaming icon. "I have a thing for old-school seventies movies."

Nina's eyes lit up. "Like *Shaft* or *Cleopatra Jones*?"

"I'm impressed. What do you know about blaxploitation movies?"

Nina fanned her hand. "Please, my dad has the biggest crush on Pam Grier. We used to watch those movies all the time, once he thought I was old enough. That's where I learned my driving skills from, according to my sisters."

Clinton laughed. "So, *The Mack* or *Foxy Brown*?"

"Umm, why not *Coffy*?"

He pressed the search button on the remote. Nina smiled as the title came up on the screen.

"This is the only Pam Grier movie that Dad wouldn't let me watch back in the day. One of the first DVDs I bought in college was this one. Became one of my favorites."

"Why?"

"I just loved how strong Coffy was and she drove a Mustang. Beginning of my obsession with that car. I tried to grow my hair out into an Afro like Pam Grier, but the heat in Atlanta kept me in braids."

"It can't be hotter in Atlanta than it is in Charleston."

"There's also an ocean breeze in Charleston. I don't know why I decided to go somewhere with no access to water."

"Yet you live in Charlotte."

Nina shrugged. "Didn't want to be too far away from home." She leaned her head on his shoulder. "As much as I like my independence, I'm a true daddy's girl."

Clinton kissed her forehead. "I can understand why. Your dad is an amazing man."

"That he is."

"I'm going to get some wine and popcorn, then we can watch some jive turkeys get theirs." Clinton rose to his feet and headed for the kitchen. Nina tucked her feet underneath her thighs and relaxed. This felt so nice. But was Clinton everything she thought he was? Only time would tell and she'd make sure to take it slow with him just to be sure.

"I got Merlot and Chardonnay." He set the bottles on the table and the popcorn on the sofa next to Nina.

"Good taste in wine, great cook, and still single. You snore like a train, don't you?" She pointed to the Chardonnay. "I'll take the white."

As *Coffy* ended, they decided to watch *Shaft's Big Score!* and agreed that *Shaft in Africa* was a movie that never existed. Nina yawned and glanced at her watch.

"Wow, it's super late."

"I guess time got away from us. It's too late for you to drive home." He nodded toward the empty bottles of wine. "And I wouldn't feel comfortable with you getting behind the wheel, either."

"Yeah, not a good idea."

"I can sleep down here and you can have my bed if you like."

"Not going to put you out like that. I'll take the sofa and —"

Clinton shook his head. "What would I, a hospitality professional, look like making a beautiful guest sleep on a hot leather sofa?"

"You're just going to have to sleep with me, then."

Clinton raised his eyebrow. "Nina . . ."

"I said sleep. And I promise, I'll keep my hands to myself." She winked at him as they stood up.

"I hope I can do the same." Clinton led her upstairs to his bedroom. Nina looked around the room after he flipped the light on. Of course he had a king-size bed. And it looked so comfortable, covered in a tan and burgundy comforter. There was a world globe night-light in the corner that caught Nina's eye. "Part of your plan to take over the world?"

"Ha. World domination is everyone's goal, right?"

She crossed over to the light. "There has to be a story behind this."

"How about we save it for another day so you'll have a reason to come back."

Nina nodded as she ran her hand across the soft surface of the globe.

"Would you like a T-shirt to sleep in? And if you want to take a shower, I can get you a towel and —"

"Thanks, but a T-shirt is fine. I'd probably fall asleep and drown in the shower." Nina pulled her dress off and Clinton turned to his dresser to grab a shirt for her. Nina started to tell Clinton that she didn't need the shirt, but if she climbed into bed in just her underwear, they wouldn't get any sleep.

Clinton handed her his Howard University shirt as he stole a heated glance at her body. Nina smiled as she tugged the T-shirt over her head.

"That shirt never looks this good on me."

She looked down at the HU crest. "My Clark Atlanta peeps can never know about this."

"So, if I snap a picture, then I have some leverage over you, huh?"

Nina crossed her arms across her chest. "Don't you dare!"

"No cameras up here. I don't even bring my phone to bed with me at night."

"What happens if someone really needs you?" Nina wanted to ask him if he ignored booty calls in the middle of the night.

He nodded toward his watch. "Comes in handy in an emergency."

"Techie nerd."

"Please. I saw all of that fruit tech at your place."

Nina yawned. "That's for work and one nerd recognizes another nerd." She eased onto the bed and it was even more comfortable than it looked. She sank into the pillow top mattress and Nina was nearly asleep as soon as her head hit the pillow.

Clinton pulled a blanket up over Nina's sleeping figure. She was so beautiful. He had to remind himself that she was just going to sleep in his bed. Yawning, Clinton decided that he needed a shower before he could fall into his own slumber. Heading across the hall to the bathroom, he turned the cold water on and stepped under the shower spray. As the ice-cold water beat down on him, he prayed that he could climb into bed and sleep as soundly as Nina was. He wanted to be able to sleep against her delicious body and remember that he wasn't here to make love to her. She couldn't drive home because it was late and despite how sweet she tasted and how much he wanted to make love to her, he had to show her that he was different, cut from a cloth that didn't want to use that body for pleasure.

I got this. Clinton shut the water off and dried his body, then pulled on a pair of boxers and a white T-shirt. He headed into his bedroom and saw Nina was sound asleep. He got into bed and wrapped his arms around her slim waist. It didn't take long for him to drift off to sleep.

Clinton thought he was dreaming as he

brushed against Nina's slumbering body. But he knew it wasn't a dream when she arched into him and his body went rock hard. Then she moaned and rolled over. Her eyes fluttered open and Clinton smiled. She was beautiful in the morning, too.

"Good morning." He kissed her on the chin.

"Only this bed could make me a morning person."

"Really? So that means I don't have to make coffee?"

"Oh, you have to make coffee. You don't want to see me uncaffeinated."

Clinton shrugged. "You look pretty good to me."

"That's because you still have sleep in your eyes." She stroked his cheek. Clinton shook his head.

"I see your beauty quite clearly."

Nina smiled. "Whatever."

Clinton released her. "Come on, if I'm going to cook, then we're going to have to get out of this bed."

She pretended to pout as she and Clinton rose from the bed. "And still no pictures of me rocking the HU gear."

"Umm, there are cameras downstairs. You never know what might happen."

Nina watched him a little too closely as he

pulled on a pair of gray sweatpants. "So, what are you cooking up this morning?"

"You'll have to wait and see," he said as they headed for the kitchen. "And you're going to be my assistant, right?"

"You've seen my breakfast skills, why are you trying to ruin a good meal?"

Nina leaned against the countertop as Clinton grabbed two pans.

"What do you say to French toast, eggs, grits, and turkey bacon?" he asked as if he was reading the contents of his refrigerator.

She hopped up on the countertop, exposing part of her thigh. "That sounds good. But first, coffee."

Clinton strolled over to her, sliding in between her legs. "Then you're going to have to move your sexy self out of the way. Beans are behind you."

Nina hopped off the counter and reached for his coffee beans. She was surprised to see they were whole beans. "Okay, you take coffee even more seriously than I do."

He nodded. "These beans came from the Baltimore Coffee and Tea Company. I like to try a blend and see if I can get them into the hotels. The bed-and-breakfast has great coffee."

Nina held her hands up. "Hence my addiction. You're trying to make a lot of changes at the B&B, huh?"

"No, I just want to get some more eyes on the place and more reservations. People need to know what I know about the Richardson B&B."

"What's that?"

"How amazing and awesome it is year-round."

"Aren't you just creative. No wonder you and Alex bump heads."

"Maybe."

Nina nodded. "Alex is Ms. Law and Order. Well, maybe more My Way or the Highway Lady."

"I've noticed."

"Best thing you can do is ignore her."

"That's easier said than done, since she's my boss."

Nina shrugged. "Note taken. Just don't prove her right or me wrong."

He stroked her cheek. "That's the last thing you have to worry about. That and me calling you sweetheart."

She nudged him with her elbow. "Too soon. I still have Twitter trolls showing up in my mentions."

"Come on, let's get cooking."

With Clinton's guidance, Nina wasn't as hopeless in the kitchen as she said she was. Except there was a burnt omelet because

Clinton kissed her while her hand was on the dial for the burner.

"This is on me," he said as he scraped scorched eggs into the trash.

"I'm glad you know that."

"Just means we get to try again." Clinton dropped the pan in the sink. Nina crossed over to the mixing bowl and cracked two eggs. As she began whisking, Clinton crossed over to her and wrapped his arms around her waist.

"Whip it slowly." He placed his hand on her waist and Nina eased against him. The softness of her ass made his body hum with need. He was ready to end this cooking lesson and just feast on Nina. Just the thought of her sweetness from the night before made his mouth water.

"Oh." Nina felt his excitement and took a small step forward. "Cheese. This needs cheese." She whirled around and stared into his lust-filled eyes. "Why are we doing this?"

"Because we need to eat."

Nina shook her head. "That's not what I'm talking about. You and I are acting like there isn't something burning between us."

"Oh, I know it is." Clinton nodded toward the sink. "But you see what happens when things get too hot too fast."

She pressed her body against his. "So, I'm

supposed to believe you want to take it slow?"

Clinton couldn't deny his want any longer, but he had to. "I finish what I start and we started this cooking lesson."

He tried to put maximum effort into showing her how to make a fluffy cheese omelet, but his body couldn't resist Nina's sensual appeal. Reaching around her, he shut the stove off.

"I've always liked brunch better."

He pulled her against his chest; she was hotter than the eye on the stove had ever been.

"Clinton," she moaned as his fingertips danced across the small of her back.

"This shirt has to go."

Nina grinned. "Yours first."

Clinton pulled his shirt over his head and tossed it aside. She ran her hand across his chest, smooth as silk, tempting like the most decadent chocolate. He grabbed her hand and lowered it to his throbbing erection.

"Look what you did."

Nina licked her lips as she stroked him back and forth. "Sorry, not sorry?" With her free hand, she tugged at the waistband of his sweatpants. She worked them down his thighs and smiled as she dropped to her knees. "Shall I kiss it and make it better?"

Before Clinton could even take his next breath, Nina had taken him into her mouth, sucking and licking his shaft. The heat of her mouth nearly brought him to his knees. She locked eyes with him as she took him deeper into her mouth, sucking slow, then fast, then slow again.

"Nina, Nina, Nina!" He ran his fingers through her hair, trying not to climax. But she was making it harder and harder while her mouth grew wetter.

Then she ran her tongue from the tip of his dick to his balls. Clinton exploded and Nina slurped his pleasure, then smiled as she swallowed.

"Jesus!" Clinton gripped the counter as Nina rose to her feet.

"That's just how I felt last night." She winked at him. He swooped her up in his arms and rushed to his bedroom. He laid her on the bed and peeled her T-shirt off in one swoop. She wrapped her arms around his waist, silently telling him what she wanted.

But he wasn't going to rush anything else as he parted her legs and slipped his finger inside.

Nina moaned as he probed her hot body with his finger. It was as if he was on an expedition to discover what pleased her and how to make her revel in delight. Each touch made her hotter, wetter, and Clinton could barely contain his desire to melt with her.

"Clinton," she moaned as his tongue replaced his finger. He pressed her body closer to his lips so that he could taste every inch of her. Nina grasped the back of his neck as waves of pleasure washed over her. Clinton traveled up her body, spending time around her navel, before reaching her breasts and suckling them until they swelled against his lips. Easily, he could have taken her, his hardness pressed against her thighs and the heat radiating from her body making it difficult to control his desire. When she wrapped her legs around his waist, Clinton knew it was going to be hard to hold on to his restraint.

"Slow down, baby. We have all the time we need."

"I want you," Nina moaned. "Need you inside me."

"And you're going to have me. But remember, I like to take things slowly." Clinton took her breast back into his mouth as she ground against him.

Pulling back, he reached for a condom from his nightstand. Nina stroked his chest with her fingertips as he slid the sheath in place. He pulled her against his chest and their lips met. Her passion shook him, made all that talk of taking it slow float out of his head. He wanted to bury himself inside her. As they broke off their kiss, Clinton found his way into her moist pool of femininity. He felt as if he'd gone straight to heaven as her warmth enveloped him. She kneaded his back softly as they fell into a sensual dance, fueled by passion and desire. Nina matched Clinton thrust for thrust. He'd never felt like this before and when she took control, rolling over so that she was on top of him, his body went into overdrive.

She rode him fast then slow, then faster and then slower. She leaned forward and nibbled on his earlobe and Clinton lost it. He climaxed and gripped her hips tightly as he spent himself. She fell against his chest and kissed his smooth skin.

Nina glanced at the clock. "I guess we can try for lunch now?"

"I know a great Chinese joint that delivers and we can eat in bed."

"But first." Nina straddled him again and his body stood at attention. "We can work up an even bigger appetite."

CHAPTER 13

By the time the Chinese food arrived, Nina and Clinton were starving. True to his word, they had lunch in bed — naked. He fed her rice noodles with chopsticks as she allowed him to eat egg rolls from her fingertips.

Clinton chewed the crunchy roll and smiled as he swallowed. "I could do this all day."

"Wish I could." Nina sighed. "I have to get back to the B&B. I want to spend some time with Daddy before I go back to Charlotte." Nina kissed him on the tip of his nose. "Wanna come with me?"

Clinton laughed but declined her invitation. "I think I'll wait until Monday to see Alex. But if you want to come back for dinner or a midnight snack, I'll be waiting."

She nodded and expelled a resigned breath. "If I don't get dressed, I'm never going to leave."

"Won't get an argument from me if you

want to stay. But I know you need to spend time with your dad."

"Yep." She reached for her panties and slipped them on. Clinton watched her every move and his body responded. Though he wanted to pull her back into his arms and make love to her until it was time for dinner.

"Now, where is my dress?" Her voice broke into his lustful thoughts.

"I think it's underneath the bed." Clinton leaned down and picked up her dress. "You're sure you want to put it on?"

"Umm, I don't want to, but I have to." She took it from his hand and smiled. "Anyway. Thanks for everything."

Clinton pulled on his sweatpants and crossed over to Nina. "I should be thanking you. This has been an amazing weekend."

"And it isn't over." She winked at him and kissed him on the cheek. He walked her downstairs and when they reached the front door, she glanced toward the kitchen. "Maybe I'll come back for another cooking lesson."

"And if you do, we're really going to cook this time."

Nina tried to downplay what she was feeling as she pulled into the bed-and-breakfast's parking lot. This thing with Clinton felt right and fast. She didn't want to get hurt again.

Before Nina could cross the lobby and head to her room, Alex swooped down on her. "It took you long enough to get here."

"Alex, please calm down," she said through clenched teeth.

She shook her head as she eyed Nina in the same black dress she'd left in the night before.

Nina threw her hand up. "Whatever you're thinking keep it to yourself." She started walking toward her room and Alex shook her head in disgust.

"Fine, but the next time your heart gets broken, don't come crying to me."

"If it means having to listen to your judgmental ass, then trust me, I won't." Nina stomped away from her sister.

Once she reached her room, Alex's words sunk in and took some of the sheen off the night and afternoon she and Clinton had spent together. Nina plopped down on her bed and stared up at the ceiling. Before she got lost in her thoughts, there was a soft knock at the door. "Come in," Nina said as she sat up.

Sheldon walked in and smiled at his daughter. "So it is true, you are here."

"Not you too, Daddy," Nina groaned.

"I was just wondering why I didn't see you last night or this morning," he said as he took a seat on the edge of her bed.

"Well, the game that I was covering was over pretty late and I spent the night with a friend. You know I wouldn't have left without seeing you, though."

Sheldon gently patted his daughter's knee. "I know. What do you say you and I have dinner tonight and invite Clinton."

"Clinton?"

"I know that's the friend you spent the night with. Alex couldn't stop fussing about it this morning." Sheldon rose to his feet and headed for the door. "He's a good guy and I like him."

"Thanks, Daddy." She flung her arms around Sheldon's neck and kissed him on the cheek.

"You're welcome, baby." Sheldon winked at Nina as he walked out the door. "See you two at seven."

Once she was alone again, Nina thought about the things Alexandria had said. She didn't know Clinton, yet she'd shared something so passionate and tender with him. Heading for the bathroom, Nina decided that she'd let the chips fall where they may and ignore Alex and her cryptic words.

■ ■ ■ ■

After Nina left, Clinton couldn't get her off his mind. Her scent lingered and, when he closed his eyes, he felt her lips against his. As he cleaned the kitchen, he wondered what the future held for them. Was she truly over Lamar or had she used him as a substitute? Clinton wanted to call her and make sure that he was right. But before he could pick up the phone and dial the bed-and-breakfast, the phone rang.

"Hello."

"Clinton Jefferson, it's Randall Birmingham. How the hell are you?"

"Mr. Birmingham, how can I help you?" Clinton asked, surprised and dismayed to hear from his former boss.

"I must say that things have been different since you deserted us. Still, I believe you owe this company a great deal for your success."

"Okay, but what do you want from me since I don't work for you anymore?"

"I want what I've always wanted — Sheldon Richardson's bed-and-breakfast. That classic little property is in the right spot and I want it. It would behoove you to help me get it."

Though he recognized the threat, Clinton was unmoved. "No."

"No? After all that we've done for you? You have the nerve to tell me no?"

Clinton sighed. Randall Birmingham had given him his first job after he'd graduated college, and there were times when he hadn't been able to help his father pay the household bills and purchase his medicine and Randall had helped.

Still, Clinton didn't believe that he owed Birmingham anything other than the years of service he'd given his company. When he was Birmingham's employee, he worked damned hard for him.

"I appreciate all that you've done for me, but there's nothing I can do for you now. Mr. Richardson doesn't want to sell his company."

"Actually, there is," Birmingham said. "All I need is a little information. Since that *USA Today* article, everyone has been flocking to the Richardson Bed and Breakfast. Winter is hard enough for waterfront properties and you're turning that B&B into the go-to spot. You suggested that story, didn't you?"

"That's my job, something that you all didn't allow me to do," Clinton pointed out. "Remember all of the plans I suggested that you shot down to save money?"

"My bad. But I won't make the mistake of allowing this bed-and-breakfast to slip through my fingers. You have access to files, accounts that the property has. I need those things."

"What part of *no* don't you understand? I have too much respect for Sheldon Richardson to betray him. Why not work on the properties you already have and leave the Richardson Bed and Breakfast alone? The boutique hotel market is booming. You can convert one of your current properties and —"

"You have so much faith in this family and I know for a fact that his daughter, Alexandria, is looking for any excuse to fire you. With those people, you'll always be an outsider, an employee. But with me, you're like family. Just think about it. You've always wanted your own property; once we bankrupt the bed-and-breakfast, it will be yours. I'll make you the general manager when my company buys it."

Clinton ended the call. He wouldn't be seduced by promises of power and property.

When his phone rang again, he started to ignore it, but he answered without looking at the screen, "You can go straight to hell. I don't care what you think you've done for me in the past, I don't owe you a damned thing."

"Wow, um," Nina said. "All I want you to do is join my father and me for dinner."

"Sorry," Clinton said, his cheeks growing hot from embarrassment. "I thought you were someone else."

"That was pretty obvious. Ex-girlfriend giving you problems?"

"No. Just someone who doesn't realize that no means no. What time are you and your father having dinner?" Clinton needed to stop Nina's questions.

"Seven and Alex won't be joining us," she said.

Clinton laughed. "I can't wait to see you again."

"Neither can I." He could hear the smile in Nina's voice. "And I think Dad is onto us."

"Then I better be on my best behavior."

"Good idea. Well, I have to get ready. See you soon."

After hanging up with Nina, Clinton decided to head into the city early. He figured a leisurely drive would allow him to process Birmingham's bullshit. Did he really think that Clinton would sell out his boss? If Clinton had anything, it was integrity, and no amount of money was worth it.

Even if he hadn't been growing to care for Nina, he wouldn't help Randall with his vendetta. He didn't know how to tell Sheldon what Birmingham was trying to do without giving Alex the ammo she needed to kick him out of the company. She wouldn't believe that Clinton wasn't in on the scheme. And what would Nina think? He wouldn't say anything right now because he could handle Randall himself.

Since Clinton had no intention of giving Birmingham what he wanted, there would be no need to alarm anyone. He prayed that he was making the right decision.

Alex ignored Nina for most of the afternoon, which Nina didn't mind at all. Getting ready for dinner without Alex's scowling face was a blessing. She was excited about her dinner with Clinton and her dad. But she was concerned that her eyes would tell him what she and Clinton had done earlier.

I wonder if Clinton has said something to my father about us? Nina thought as she walked into the bathroom to soak in the tub. *Is there anything to tell? I hate to admit it, but Alex did have a point. I don't know much about Clinton. But he makes me feel good and that's all that matters right now.*

Nina pulled herself from the tub, dried off, and fingered some coconut oil through her hair.

After dressing in a semiconservative red dress that showed enough cleavage and thigh to tease but was decent enough to wear out to dinner with her father, Nina headed down to the lobby hoping to greet Clinton before Sheldon or Alex did. As she reached the lobby, she saw Clinton walking in the door and he took her breath away. He reminded her of a chocolate-dipped Cary Grant, suave and debonair in his black slacks, white shirt, and black sport coat. Though he had a casual look about him, he oozed sensuality. Then again, every time Nina looked at him, she thought about their lovemaking and it made her hot all over.

"Hi," he said.

"Hello." Her breath caught in her chest as they stared at each other.

"I thought black was your color, but you're working that red." He took Nina's hand in his and spun her around as if they were in the middle of a dance floor.

Nina blushed. "Thanks. I'm not sure where we're going."

"We're certainly going to be the best-dressed people at Emma's tonight," Sheldon said as he walked up behind the pair.

He was uncharacteristically dressed in jeans and a white button-down shirt. Sheldon had a green sport coat draped over his arm. "Let's go."

The trio headed out the door toward the Lincoln Town Car that was waiting for them. As they piled in the back seat, Nina's leg brushed against Clinton's knee and she shivered as if a current of electricity had flowed through her body. Nina turned her head and looked out the window, afraid that her father would see the lust in her eyes if she looked at Clinton too long.

"What's going on with you two?" Sheldon smiled and leaned back in his seat.

"Daddy!"

"Nina, I'm not blind and I knew the first time that you two met there was an attraction there. Clinton, are you serious about my daughter?"

Clinton faced his boss with a nervous smile. "I'm very serious about your daughter. Nina's special and I really like her."

"Nina, are you serious about Clinton?"

"Do we really have to talk about this?" Her cheeks were burning from embarrassment. "I mean —"

"Listen," Sheldon said. "I know how you young people fall in and out of love and lust. I want to make sure that whatever happens between the two of you doesn't affect my business and I don't want to see you hurt, Nina."

"Mr. Richardson —"

"Sheldon," he corrected.

"Sheldon, I don't have a crystal ball, but I know that I would never do anything to hurt Nina purposely."

God, let him mean what he's saying, Nina thought as she stared at Clinton, admiring the way he handled her father.

Sheldon nodded and turned to Nina. "Well."

"What, Daddy?" Nina's cheeks were on fire as she watched Clinton and her father stare at her. "It's just what Clinton said."

"I think a lot of Clinton and I wouldn't want you to hurt him, either," Sheldon said.

"I won't." She smiled at Clinton and squeezed her thighs tightly. Was it wrong to have these wanton thoughts about Clinton with her father sitting inches away from them?

Sheldon nodded. "Good, now that it's all cleared up let's all enjoy dinner."

They rode to Emma's Soul Food restaurant in a comfortable silence, with Clinton and Nina stealing glances at each other. At dinner, the trio shared laughs and at the end of the night, Sheldon suggested that

Nina and Clinton stick around Charleston Harbor and watch the stars, since it was a warm night. "I'll send the car back for you after I get dropped off," he said before kissing Nina's cheek. "Clinton, don't let her fall in the water."

"I won't."

After Sheldon left, Clinton turned to Nina. "You don't think your father's playing matchmaker, do you?"

"I've never seen him like this. I'm sorry if he embarrassed you."

Clinton chuckled. "It seems that you were the one blushing in the car."

Nina shook her head. "It wasn't because of what Daddy was saying. I was fighting the urge to lean over and have my way with you in the back seat. Daddy might have gotten upset." Nina linked arms with Clinton and they began walking down the boardwalk.

"At least he approves and I won't have a pink slip Monday morning. Because you know some fathers never think anyone is good enough for their little girls, even if she is all grown up."

"I know what we told my dad. But are we going too fast? Long-distance relationships don't work." Nina knew her trust issues would send her mind racing to dark places with one missed call. She also knew that she couldn't judge him by her past, but it was going to be hard.

Stroking her hair, Clinton sighed. "We're going to make it work, Nina. You're the only woman I want. I'm ready for this journey because I know you're taking it with me. If you're ready."

She eyed him thoughtfully. "I'm ready, but I'm going to be honest, that whole keeping your phone downstairs at night is going to have to change. I know my head will create all kinds of bad scenarios if I can't reach you."

He tapped his watch. "I'm always going be there for you."

She blushed. "Are you ready for all of this?"

"I am, because I care for you, Nina and I want to grow something real with you. Is it going to be easy? No. But I'm willing to work for it. For you."

She leaned her head against his chest. "So am I." Looking up at him, Nina smiled. "There is one thing that I want right now, though."

"Name it."

"I like that baby blue Mustang of yours and I've been dying to drive it since I saw it parked in your driveway. May I?" She batted her eyelashes.

Clinton placed his hand underneath his chin and pondered her request. "Do you think you can handle it?"

"There isn't much I can't handle when it comes to the pony car," she said confidently. "Let's ride."

"You're going to have to be careful, my car has real power, not all that digital stuff like you have now. Blue is a real pony," he said.

Nina winked at him. "I can handle it. Let's ride."

They took the car that Sheldon had arranged for them to the B&B, where his Mustang was parked. After Clinton tipped the driver, he handed his car keys to Nina.

"Be gentle," he said as they slid into the car.

Nina started up the engine and listened to the roar of the motor. "This sounds amazing."

"Wait until you see how she handles," Clinton said.

Nina backed out of the parking lot. "Why do men always refer to their cars as *she*?"

Clinton shrugged. "Because, other than a woman, what's more unpredictable than a car? What else will a man happily spend money on than a woman and a car?"

Nina giggled as she pressed the clutch down and shifted gears. "Never thought of it like that."

As they came up on a sharp curve, Clinton gripped the door handle. He glanced over at the speedometer and Nina was going about sixty-five miles an hour. "Think you want to slow down a bit?"

She downshifted and glanced at Clinton. "You're not afraid, are you?"

"Just a little."

She slowed down just a little. "Now that scene in *Bullitt* makes so much sense! I need a classic Mustang in my life."

"Hopefully, you will drive it a little slower than you do now. You need to enjoy the ride, let the engine sing to you," he said. "Pull over up here."

"Aw, do I have to?" Nina pretended to pout.

"It's going to be worth it."

She pulled over and discovered that Clinton had directed her to a secluded park. Trees surrounded the small park with a reflecting pool. They exited the car and walked over to the benches that surrounded the silver pond. "You were right," she said. "This was well worth the stop."

Clinton drew her into his arms. "It certainly was." He sought out Nina's lips with his, planting a soft kiss on her tender mouth. She returned his kiss, only with a little more fire. Clinton parted his lips, allowing Nina to take control with her tongue. She probed his mouth, reveling in his sweetness. He pulled her against his body, pressing her against his desire and showing her just what she'd done to him. Taking a cue from his erection, Nina took his hand and slid it between her thighs, also to show him what he'd done to her.

They broke the kiss and looked deeply into each other's eyes. "Thank God for global warming," he whispered. "Because if it were a regular fall night, I wouldn't dream of doing this." He unzipped the back of her dress, then slid it off her shoulders.

"And I wouldn't be able to do this," she said as she unbuttoned his shirt. Nina pressed the palms of her hands against his chest.

Clinton leaned in and kissed Nina's neck, causing her to melt against him. They fell back on the wooden bench and he completely undressed Nina. For a moment, he took a look at her reflection in the pool. The way the moonlight bounced off her made her look ethereal. Maybe Nina was an angel who had fallen into his life.

After a beat, she stroked his cheek.

"What's wrong?"

He shook his head. "Nothing's wrong. Everything seems so right," he whispered as he ran his finger down the valley of her breasts.

Nina reached up and unbuckled his belt. "I really hope no one sees us out here," she whispered as she unzipped his pants and pushed them down to his ankles. Clinton kicked out of his slacks and boxers in one swift motion. A slight breeze blew across them and caused the trees to sway. A few blue jays sang overhead as Clinton kissed her breasts until her nipples perked up. Moaning, she stroked the back of his head, urging him to continue. His erection pressed against her thighs and heat radiated from every pore in her body. "I want you," she moaned.

"You got me and you can have me any way you want," he said as he parted her legs. Clinton could feel how wet and ready she was even before he removed her lace panties. He slipped an index finger inside her, touching her sensitive bud. Nina arched her back, crying out in pleasure as Clinton replaced his finger with his tongue.

With his face buried between her thighs, Clinton lapped her womanly nectar as if she was the juiciest piece of fruit. She pressed her body against his lips as if to say, *More.* Clinton answered her silent plea, deepening his kiss and lashing her throbbing bud with his tongue.

Nina felt as if her pleasure was more important to Clinton than his own. That made her body tremble even more.

Clinton reversed the direction of his kiss, ending up at her lips. Nina gyrated her hips, wanting to feel his thick erection deep inside her wetness. He gave her what she wanted and plunged into her awaiting body. She called out his name as he dove deeper and deeper. He lifted her from the bench and onto his lap. Nina wrapped her arms around his neck and rocked back and forth as if she was riding a prized steed in the Kentucky Derby.

Clinton toyed with her nipples as she arched her back, jutting her ripe breasts upward. "Oh, Clinton," she called out as the waves of an orgasm washed over her.

Wrapping their arms around each other, Clinton buried his face in Nina's hair. "So, was it worth it?" he asked.

"Absolutely," she replied breathlessly. Nina ran her hand over her cropped hair. "This is something more than a physical thing, isn't it?"

"Of course," he said. "Look, I'm too old

to play games and you deserve a lot more than just sex. You're worth more than that." Clinton tugged at her chin. "Besides, I don't just let anyone drive my car."

Nina smiled. "So, are you going to let me finish driving to your place?"

"That would be a no," he said as he quickly snatched the keys from the ground. "You need to slow down. Ever think of driving in the Coca-Cola Six Hundred?"

"NASCAR isn't my thing. But if I could've taken on Jeff Gordon back in the day, I'd have a highway named after me." She smiled as she slipped her dress on.

"I don't doubt that." Clinton pulled his slacks on, then wrapped his arms around Nina's waist. "There probably isn't anything you can't do when you put your mind to it."

Turning around, she planted a soft kiss on his lips. "You're right about that."

CHAPTER 14

Over the next few weeks, Nina and Clinton spent more time together and slowly began to fall in love. He made her melt every time she heard his voice or saw his smile.

Since Clinton wasn't big into sports, he and Nina spent a lot of time going to concerts and roaming around their new favorite spot in Charlotte, the Bechtler Museum. She'd find herself going there just for a reminder of Clinton when she was having a bad day, when an interview went bad, or when she missed him.

Still, there was a part of Clinton she couldn't understand: his relationship with his father. Though she knew the two men didn't get along, Nina wondered if she would ever meet him. Did he have something to hide? Nina hated that she kept waiting for the other shoe to drop.

Closing the lid on her laptop, Nina stared off into the distance. *Maybe I'm just borrow-*

ing trouble. Nevertheless, she was going to surprise her man tonight, depending on how long the game ran, with a trip to Summerville.

Rising to her feet, she headed to the bathroom and started getting ready for the basketball game she was supposed to cover. Nina was able to breathe a lot easier now that she didn't have to worry about seeing Lamar while she was out on assignments. When Independence lost a game in the regular season, her season-long story ended. Thank God for basketball.

With the holidays around the corner, Nina couldn't say no to most assignments because she would be taking a few weeks off before jumping back into work in January. Besides, *sweetheart-gate* had caused her phone to ring less frequently. At least she got more respect in the NBA locker rooms.

After she'd gotten dressed, Nina headed outside to her car and was surprised to see a long-stemmed red rose underneath her windshield wiper. Nina looked over her shoulder, wondering if Clinton had beaten her at the surprise game. She didn't see him as she read the note.

Haven't heard from you in a while, wondered if you missed me — L.

Nina tossed the rose on the ground and stomped on it.

"That wasn't very nice," Lamar said, appearing out of what seemed to be thin air.

"Stalking doesn't become you."

"Well, you haven't called and I figured if I called you wouldn't answer." He stood next to the door with his hand on the window. "How have you been?"

"Busy. I have to go." Nina reached to close the door, but Lamar wouldn't let go. "Lamar."

"Nina, I miss you."

"Running out of warm bodies?"

He smiled suggestively. "Don't be like that. But I'm not going to lie, I miss that body, that mouth and —"

"Let go of my door, you son of a bitch." Nina snatched the door, causing Lamar to let it go. She started the car and peeled out of the parking lot, narrowly missing running over his toes.

"I must say," Alex said, peering over the file that Clinton had handed her, "this is much better than I expected. It was a great idea for you to suggest that people who have family members coming in to town for the holidays let them stay here. The Christmas brunch idea is genius."

Is she actually smiling at me? Clinton thought as he listened to Alex sing his praises for once.

"However," she continued as she scanned the rest of the document. "I don't think we should try to have a New Year's Eve gala. With all that's going on in Charleston during that time, our event might not be successful. Parties aren't really our *thing* anyway."

Clinton nodded. "What if we offer a New Year's Day brunch, much like what we're doing for Christmas? That way we can show our guests that we still want them to be a part of our family in the New Year. Or we could include the New Year's Day brunch in the Christmas package, that way —" Clinton's cell phone interrupted his idea. He looked down at the number and recognized it as Birmingham's. After pressing the ignore call button, he turned to Alex. "Sorry about that."

She nodded as she closed the file on her desk. "Make the changes, get this back to me, and then we can send them to the businesses on our list and play up the part about having their out-of-town family members stay here. Do you think we have time to find a Santa?"

Clinton rose to his feet. "Why not let your

father play Santa? The guests will love that and it gives everything a more familial feel."

She shook her head and smirked. "You know how to work all the angles, don't you? I'm surprised Randall Birmingham let you go."

Clinton almost felt as if her statement was an accusation.

"What do you mean by that?" Clinton couldn't help but wonder if Alex and Birmingham were testing him. "And I quit, remember."

"That's right. Still, as crafty as Randall is, I'm just surprised that he let you walk out the door, especially to us," she said. "Relax, Clinton, it was a compliment."

"Wow, Alex, we must be making some headway. Last week, you still hated me."

She leaned back in her seat. "I'll admit, I haven't given you a fair shake. But my father likes you and you and my sister have this thing going on, so I can't keep being the bitch of the family. Besides, you seem to be a nice guy, Clinton."

"Thank —" His cell phone rang, interrupting their conversation again. Clinton looked down at the display and saw that it was Birmingham calling back. Pressing the silent button, he turned to Alexandria. "Thank you for saying that."

"Don't make me regret it," she said, then returned to the papers on her desk.

He dashed into his office and began to make the changes he and Alex had discussed, but when he turned his computer on, he saw he had a new e-mail message:

You can't run from me forever. All I want is some information that would give me a chance to buy this place out. You have access and you owe me.

Clinton quickly deleted the message. Picking up his phone, he called the very last person he wanted to talk to, his father.

"Hello," Clinton Sr. growled into the phone.

"Dad, have you heard from Randall Birmingham?"

"Hello to you too, son," the elder Clinton spat. "Why do you care if I heard from him or not? You deserted that man to work for his rival. After all that he's done for this family. You have no loyalty, do you?"

"I took another job, I didn't do anything wrong. Listen, if he calls you, don't talk to him."

"Just because you don't work for him, doesn't mean he's not my friend. And I don't bite the hand that feeds me. You think that Sheldon Richardson is going to do things for you that Birmingham has done?"

"For me or you, Dad?" Clinton could feel his anger rising as he spoke to his father. "It seems as if the only time you consider me your son is when I'm taking care of you."

"Why shouldn't you? You're a disappointment and if it weren't for Randall I would've lost my house. Have you forgotten how much it cost to watch your mother die? How much I'm still paying back. Without Randall, I wouldn't have anything."

"Whatever," Clinton said, tired of hearing this same argument from his father. It was as if he blamed Clinton for his mother's death and the debt that followed. "Didn't I take care of your bills? Give me credit for that at least."

"My mortgage is due," Clinton Sr. said flatly.

"How much do you need?"

"Five hundred dollars."

"I'll go to the bank today." Clinton sighed. He couldn't turn his back on his father, but sometimes he felt used.

"That's all right, Randall's going to take care of it."

Clinton slammed the phone down and tore out of his office. He was going to tell Randall Birmingham exactly what he could do with his money.

When he pulled up to the office building where he used to work, he looked behind him expecting to see Alex jump out of the shadows accusing him of working against her family as she'd figured all along. Quickly he dashed inside and headed for the elevators, ignoring the receptionist's greeting. Pressing the button for the fifteenth floor, he seethed with anger as the car rose. Who did Randall Birmingham think he was using his father's finances as a means to get what he wanted? Clinton wasn't going to stand for this bullshit.

The elevator doors opened and Clinton stormed into Birmingham's office, sidestepping his secretary. Birmingham sat at his desk with his back to the door, chatting on the phone and sipping a latte.

Clinton disconnected the call and forced Birmingham to turn around and face him.

"Clinton, what the hell is your problem? That was an important call! What are you doing in my office, anyway?"

"Stay away from my father and don't think that by helping him I owe you a damned thing."

Birmingham rose to his feet as he saw his secretary standing in the doorway with fear etched across her face. "Eunice, everything

209

is okay. Clinton and I are old friends, we're good here."

Clinton's nostrils flared. "Stay away from my family and the Richardson B&B. I'll fight you on this."

"With what army? Son, you have a lot to learn about life. Everything has a price and no favor comes without strings. I gave a lot to you and your family without batting an eye. I hired you, with no experience, because you had good ideas. My plan was to groom you to run this empire. But you walked away without me getting a return on my investment. You owe me. Either get me what I want or I will destroy everything you hold dear, including Nina Richardson."

"Leave Nina out of this." Hot anger sent his body into overdrive and if Birmingham breathed Nina's name again, he was going to deck him.

Crossing over to Clinton, Randall sneered at him. "If you want her out of this, then do what I told you. She's not going to like the fact that you were using her daddy. And Alexandria — well, you already know how she feels about you."

"I know a lot of things, Randall, and if you force me, I will start talking. What do you think people will think of your family image when they find out you're sleeping with nearly every woman in this office and your kids hate you? Do you think you're going to get that contract to build those hotels for the AME Zion Church? You have so much, why is that property so important to you?"

Randall stepped back and leaned against his desk. "Because we always want what we can't have. I'm not worried about your little threats. It's not as if anyone will believe you. But what do you think the Richardsons will do if I tell them that you double-crossed them? You can kiss your job and that sweet piece of ass good-bye. You have forty-eight hours to play ball. If you don't help me, then I will destroy you." Randall waved his hand as if he was shooing a fly away. "Get out of my office."

Clinton slammed out of the office, his body heated from anger. How would he stop Birmingham's smear campaign? Nina asked him not to prove Alex's distrust in him right and that's exactly what he was going to do.

Instead of heading back to the office, he drove home. Sitting in his driveway for a few moments, Clinton tried to wrap his mind around what was happening. Why did Birmingham think he would get involved in a scheme like this and would allow himself to be used because he'd helped his father pay a few bills? He was a grown man with his own mind and he wasn't going to be used like some pawn.

He walked inside and went to the computer. *What if I just resign?* He opened his Word application. When the last document he'd been working on came up, detailing the holiday plans for the bed-and-breakfast, Clinton knew he couldn't run away. He wasn't built like that and he wasn't going to let Birmingham win.

Nina walked out of the Charlotte Hornets' locker room, ready to write her story and take the next three days off. Thankfully, she had gotten out of the locker room without another viral incident.

Her bag was packed for her surprise visit to Clinton's. She prayed that when she pulled up at his place she wouldn't be in for an unpleasant surprise. Suppose he had another woman there?

No, I'm not doing this. Why would I think that he's doing something with someone else?

When Nina arrived at her car, she was surprised to see Lamar there.

"Not you again."

"You can stop the hardcore act," he said, arrogantly leaning against her car. "I was getting ready to leave and I saw your car. We need to talk."

"No, we don't, there is nothing to say that hasn't already been said," she replied.

"Then join me for coffee, for old times' sake."

"Lamar, our old times weren't made over coffee."

"I miss you and you deserve an explanation about what you saw at the diner."

Nina folded her arms across her chest and looked at him incredulously. "Why don't you go fuck yourself? I don't give a damn about you and who you're sleeping with. Just remember, I'm not in your stable anymore."

"Because you're with that clown from the game? Can he make you scream like I do?"

"Clinton's far from a clown," Nina snapped. "He's —"

"Not me and I know I'm what you want." Lamar ran his index finger across Nina's cheek. "We had some good times. The sex was amazing and didn't I always take care of you and give you satisfaction?"

She recoiled at his touch. "So you gave me a few orgasms. You couldn't love me. You couldn't give me what I really needed."

"I can now. I was a fool, Nina. Women like you are rare and I didn't realize that until you walked out of my life."

"Walked out of your life? Please, you decided you wanted to be a saltshaker and spread yourself around town. Don't come crawling around now." Nina raised her left eyebrow. "It's too late to miss what you had, what I gave you so easily. Please move so that I can go home. I have a deadline."

"One night, Nina. Let me change your mind about us," Lamar said as he stepped aside.

"Don't need it, my mind's already made up about you." She opened her door and slid in the car. As she backed out of the parking lot, she watched Lamar staring at her.

Nina drove home, half expecting to see Lamar following her. But he didn't and she was glad. There was nothing left in her heart for him and he needed to get that into his thick head.

Chapter 15

Since he'd left work early, Clinton was burning the midnight oil at home to get Alex the reports for the holiday events. Their relationship had thawed and he wanted it to stay that way.

Adding the last bit of information to his report, Clinton yawned and decided it was time to call it a night. Just as he was about to head to his bedroom, the doorbell rang.

His first thought was to ignore it. He wasn't expecting anyone and it was too late for someone to show up without calling. But what if someone needed help with a broken-down car, or worse, hit a deer or something? Sighing, he crossed over to the door and snatched the curtain back. When he saw Nina standing there, he smiled.

"Nina? You know, I started not to open the door."

"And had I called and told you I was on my way, the surprise would've been ruined."

Her smile seemed to light up the night. Clinton smiled at her and drank in her image in that leather dress she'd had on at the bed-and-breakfast a few months back. He was a smidge disappointed that she didn't have the whip he'd dreamt about.

"Are you going to stand there staring or invite me in?"

"All right," Clinton said, now fully awake. "Let's see what you're working with."

"Well," Nina said. "I'm off for three days and I couldn't think of a better place to spend my time."

"And I couldn't be happier. I always thought that dress looked good on you. But I know where I'd like to see it now."

She licked her bottom lip. "Where is that?"

He closed the door and took her in his arms. "On the floor."

Clinton made quick work of the zipper on the back of the dress and peeled it from her body. Underneath, she was naked.

"Damn!"

"Was this a good surprise, then?"

Clinton's answer was to capture her lips and kiss her until her knees quaked.

In a quick motion, Clinton scooped Nina into his arms. The heat from her body was nearly unbearable as he rushed to the bedroom. When he laid her on the bed, he looked down at her with a smile on his face. "You're so beautiful," he said.

She reached up and stroked his cheek. "Clinton, I need you. Now."

Her eyes shone like diamonds in the dimness of the room as she licked her lips. "I've been thinking about being here all day."

"Is that right? Because this was how my dream started last night." Clinton kissed Nina's shoulders and her skin felt like freshly spun silk underneath his lips.

She reached for his zipper and stroked him until his erection sprang to life. Clinton moaned as she slipped the zipper down and continued to stroke him.

"Slow down, baby," he whispered as he grabbed her hand. "I want to take my time with you."

"Okay," she replied, smiling seductively at him. Clinton brought his lips down on hers, kissing her slowly, deeply, and passionately. Nina moaned in delight as his tongue glided across hers. Then he broke off the kiss and traveled down the length of her neck with deliberate slowness, then down to her perky breasts, licking and sucking each one until her nipples hardened like pebbles. She pressed her body against his, silently urging him to end the sensuous torture that he'd been inflicting on her. But Clinton wasn't ready to stop. Sliding down her flat stomach, he parted her legs, gently massaging her thighs before placing them on his shoulders. He dove into her pleasure pool, lapping up the sweet wetness that spilled from her. She cried out his name as he wrapped his tongue around her throbbing bud. Gently, yet intensely, he sucked until Nina climaxed. Her body went limp against his but Clinton wasn't done. Pressing her against the bed, he looked down at her. "Are you all right?"

"I've never felt like this before," she said through her labored breathing.

"That's because you've never had a man who put your pleasures before his own," Clinton said. "But tonight, that's going to change." He pressed his lips against her neck, making her moan even more. "Because tonight is all about you."

Nina licked her lips in anticipation of Clinton's next move. On so many levels he was right, no other man had taken the time to find out what her needs and desires were. It was all about what she could do to please him.

With Nina on her back, Clinton rose from the bed and stared at her body as the moonlight danced across her. He stepped out of his pants and boxers, showing her just how aroused he was. She inhaled sharply as he eased onto the bed, slipping in between her legs.

"What do you want me to do first?" His lips were so close to her ear that she could feel the heat of his breath.

Closing her eyes as she listened to him open a condom wrapper, she said honestly, "I just want to be loved." When she opened her eyes, she half expected Clinton to have retreated or to be showing some sort of disgusted look on his face, but he smiled at her.

"That's what we all want," he said. "I can give you that, if I'm the person you want. I'm not just talking about sex, no matter how amazing it is."

Nina felt his thickness against her thighs. "I want you in every way," she moaned as she wrapped her arms around his neck. "Every way. Give me what I need."

Silently Clinton vowed to be that one man to show Nina that everyone wasn't like Lamar and anyone else who'd ever hurt her. He was going to give her the love, protection, and passion she needed. Diving into her valley, he sealed his promise with each thrust. Nina matched his intensity as if she were asking him did he really mean what he said.

Spent from their lovemaking, Nina and

Clinton lay in each other's arms. She rested her head against his chest and stared up at him. "I have to tell you something," she whispered.

"What?"

"I've never experienced anything like this."

"Neither have I. You're an incredible woman, you do know that, don't you?"

She shrugged. Clinton propped up on his elbow and looked at her. "You're telling me that no one has told you that before?" he asked.

"I've had a few editors say that but . . . Clinton, you know my history with the opposite sex. So when you say things and do things to me, I don't know how to respond."

"Like this, you lean in and give me a soft kiss on the cheek," he said as he leaned in and placed his cheek against her lips.

Nina kissed him sweetly. "Thank you."

Clinton hugged her against his chest and kissed her on the forehead. "Let's get some sleep. You wore me out, woman."

The next morning as the sun rose, Nina watched Clinton sleep. His chest moved against the sheet and he snored lightly. She wanted to stroke his face and kiss him until he woke up. Instead she just watched him. Was he really the one? Was he really going

to give her the love that she had been longing for? Still, when was the other shoe going to drop?

Stop being so negative, she thought as she
gently ran her fingers across his cheek. *Clinton has no reason to lie to you and you have
no reason to believe that he's going to disappoint you. For once you and a man are on the
same page.*

Quietly she tipped out of the bed and
grabbed Clinton's robe from the back of his
closet. Once she wrapped it around her
body, she headed downstairs and grabbed
her cell phone to check her messages.

"Nina, it's Lamar. I know what you said,
but I know that look, too. You want me just
as much as I want you. That guy can't
compare to me and what we shared."

She deleted the message and pressed her
phone against her forehead.

"There you are," Clinton said, coming up
behind her and wrapping his arms around
her waist. "I was beginning to think that
last night was just a great dream."

"It wasn't," she said as she whirled around
and pecked him on the lips. "Did I wake
you?"

"No, the coldness where your warm body
used to be did." Clinton noticed her cell
phone in her hand. "Is everything all right?"

"Oh, yeah." She tossed the phone on an armchair. "I was just checking my messages. It's a habit of mine."

"Coffee and voice mail messages to start your day, huh? What do you say I cook us some breakfast and get you that coffee I know you're dying to have," he said before kissing her on the cheek.

Nina's eyes followed Clinton into the kitchen and she knew she'd made the right decision. She knew he would give her the respect she deserved, the love she wanted and needed.

"Hey," Clinton called out, "you're going to come taste this coffee or what?"

"I'm coming."

Through breakfast, Nina promised Clinton that she would eventually learn how to cook. "Yeah, right," he said as he loaded more cheese eggs on her plate. "I've come to the realization that you don't want to learn."

"You may be right. But keep in mind that as long as I need to learn, you will have to teach me." She winked at him and Clinton took her hand in his and brought it to his lips. "You're so cute."

"So, what are we going to do on this beautiful Saturday morning? And you better not say Alex expects you in the office."

"I have the day off. Are you telling me that your family doesn't know you're here? You scandalous little lady."

Nina shrugged. "They will find out eventually. Right now, I'm all yours."

Clinton smiled. "That sounds so good. How are we going to take advantage of this good fortune?"

"We could head into town and pretend we're tourists." Nina took a bite of her eggs.

"That sounds good."

"And promise that this won't turn into a business trip. I don't want to hear a word about the bed-and-breakfast."

He gave her a salute. "Yes, ma'am."

"But I probably should let my family know I'm in town sooner rather than later. Think we should have lunch at the bed-and-breakfast or no?"

"You know your sister has been a lot nicer to me lately. Should I be afraid?"

"We all should be. Alex being nice is sign of the apocalypse," Nina quipped as she rose to refill her coffee mug. She could feel Clinton's eyes on her as she poured. Turning around, they locked eyes and smiled at each other.

"That robe has never looked better," he said. "You know what would make it look even better?"

Nina leaned against the counter and grinned at him over the rim of her coffee mug. "What's that?"

"You taking it off." Clinton stood and crossed over to her. Then he untied the sash, slipped his hands underneath the robe, and gripped her hips. Nina placed her mug on the edge of the counter.

"What happened to playing tourists this morning?"

Sliding his hands up and down her sides, he said, "This is what I want to tour right here. These hips, those thighs, and those lips." Leaning in, he kissed her deep and hard, then lifted her up on the counter. "Can we start the tour now?"

Nina pushed her mug aside so there would be no roadblocks for Clinton. "Let's go."

Starting at her navel, he began traveling the contours of her body, treating her as if it were the first time he'd touched her. Nina was putty in his hands as he kissed her neck and massaged her breasts just the way she liked it.

Then, he headed below her navel, re-kissing every spot that he'd kissed on his first trip. When he reached her thighs, Nina quivered in anticipation of feeling his tongue against her throbbing femininity.

Clinton made her feel so sexual, so alive, and so wanted. Her excitement spilled onto her thighs and Clinton lapped it up. Then he buried his face in her wetness, wrapping his tongue around her sweet bud until she screamed for mercy.

He wasn't ready to stop yet. Lifting her from the counter, Clinton headed for the sofa in the living room. Gently he laid Nina against the cushions and spread her thighs apart. She was so hot and ready to feel him inside her. Neither of them thought of protection as he slipped inside her valley. She tightened herself around him, and they were both on the verge of climax as they tumbled off the sofa. Clinton laughed and held Nina against his chest.

"Didn't mean to end up here." He brushed his lips across her cheek.

"Guess we got a little carried away."

"You do that to me," he said. "When we're together it's like nothing else matters."

"I feel the same way. Maybe that's why I keep coming to Charleston every time I have a free moment," she said as they linked fingers.

"You sure that you're not running from something?"

"Like what?"

"Lamar?"

225

Nina dropped his hand. "What makes you say something like that?"

"It's a fair question," he said. "When I met you, you were hung up on this guy and you're both in the same city."

Sitting up, Nina stared at him incredulously. "What are you saying, Clinton?"

"Nothing, I'm just thinking out loud," he said, rising from the floor and holding his hand out to help Nina up.

She ignored his hand and stood on her own. "Why not put all of our cards on the table? I'm not the only one with secrets."

"Meaning what?" he asked.

"Your father and your family."

"My father and I aren't close, so why would I talk about him? He's made it clear that I'm a disappointment to him and he wants nothing to do with me."

"But he's your father and family is important." She turned her back to him.

"Are you trying to change the subject? How did we go from talking about you and Lamar to me and my father?"

"Because I have questions just like you do. If you want to ask me something about Lamar, then just do it."

"Are you over him? Or am I just a diversion to get your mind off him?"

Nina focused her gaze on him. "You really

think that's what's going on? I don't play those kinds of games," she said. "Maybe I need to get dressed and head to my father's."

"So, you're over him?"

"Clinton, I would never play with you the way he played with me. I want one man and that's you. If you're questioning that, then what is all of this?"

"What if he comes back and says what you want to hear, where would that leave us?"

She ran her hand across her face. "I don't want him back. I know you care about me, but I feel like you're holding a part of your life back from me."

"Because of my father? I don't have a relationship with him, so why would I introduce the two of you?" Clinton said. "Nina, be sure that I'm who you want because I love you and —"

"What? You love me?"

"Yes and I'm not ashamed to say it. I love you and I don't have a problem saying it. I love you." He closed the space between them and pulled her into his arms. "Don't break my heart."

"I won't," she said. "But you can't break mine, either."

"Why don't we shower and get out of here?" Clinton gently kissed Nina on the forehead.

As he walked into the bathroom, she watched him with a warm feeling in her chest. He said he loved her and she could tell by the look in his eyes that he was sincere.

About an hour later, Nina and Clinton were entering downtown Charleston. "We're doing the carriage ride?" she asked as Clinton pulled into a parking lot.

"Why not? We can pretend to be tourists and get a romantic tour of the city." He kissed her on the cheek.

"I know there's one thing we don't have to pretend about," she said as she slipped her arms around his waist.

"What's that?"

"That we're happy and going to have the greatest time today."

They walked over to the Palmetto Carriage Works booth and waited for the attendant. Nina leaned in to kiss Clinton on the neck.

"Well, isn't this a pretty picture?" Birmingham said as he approached the couple. "Romancing the boss's daughter is a great way to get a promotion."

Nina and Clinton turned to face him. "What the hell do you want?" Clinton snapped.

"Do I really have to spell it out? Clinton, you know we have unfinished business."

She leaned in to Clinton and asked. "Who is this guy?"

"No one," Clinton said. "Let's go."

Birmingham smirked. "You can't run forever. We'll talk soon."

Nina and Clinton walked for several blocks before she asked him, "Now do you want to tell me who that guy is?"

"Someone who thinks I owe him something because he helped me out a long time ago."

"You're not in any trouble, are you?"

Slowing his pace, Clinton turned to Nina. "Not at all. I used to work for that guy and after my mother's death, my father had some financial issues. He helped me out, but I paid him back every cent that he loaned me."

"What does he want from you?"

"It's not important."

"He doesn't seem like the kind of guy that you can ignore and he'll just go away," she said.

"Don't worry about it, Nina, this is my mess and I'll clean it up," he said a little more forcefully than he meant to.

"That's what I'm talking about, Clinton. You shut me out of so much but expect me to be an open book. I don't want to play tourist anymore. Why don't you take me to your place so that I can get my car and you can take care of your business." Nina stomped away, ignoring his pleas to stop.

CHAPTER 16

Nina sat in the parking lot of the bed-and-breakfast, not really wanting to go inside and not understanding the argument that she and Clinton had gotten into earlier. *What was that all about downtown?* Nina rubbed her hand across her face and sighed. Then she rose from the car and headed inside. She was surprised to see Alex at the front desk.

"Dad finally demoted you, huh?" she said with forced gaiety.

"What are you doing here?" Alex asked as she looked up from the computer.

"Just visiting, I had a few days off and I decided to come here." Nina leaned against the desk.

"And I'm sure Clinton's going to walk through the door at any moment, right?"

Nina shook her head. "I doubt it. We're not speaking right now."

"Aw, trouble in paradise?" Alex rolled her

eyes. "It'll be fine. I'm sure the two of you will be back to being all kissy faced before the sun sets. Don't quote me on this but I think Clinton is good for you."

Nina's mouth dropped open. "Who are you and what have you done to Alexandria Richardson?"

Shaking her head, Alex rolled her eyes. "You have to decide what you want. Do you want me to be happy for y'all or not? I've seen a different side of Clinton and I like the way he treats you." She tossed one of the bed-and-breakfast's signature mints at her sister.

"What time are you getting off from here? Where's Dad?"

"Dad is at a business seminar in Richmond, but I think he's really checking on Robin. Something's going on with her and she's not talking about it."

"You know how Robin is," Nina said. "She thinks she can be Superwoman and never wants us to help her or know that her life isn't perfect."

"That's because we're all too busy cleaning up your messes," Alex said.

"Whatever, Alex."

"I'm just kidding with you. So, you and Clinton must've had a big blowup? What did you do?"

"So, it's automatically my fault?" Nina slapped her hand on her hip.

Alex tilted her head to the side. "I'm going to mind my business as you and Yolanda like to tell me all the time."

"Alex, I don't want to get into this. I'll clean up my own mess this time." She offered her sister a plastic smile. "What's the dinner special tonight?"

"Turkey meat loaf and mashed potatoes."

"Oh my God! I'm going to eat my feelings for real."

"Then let's get it started. Elaine will be here in a few minutes and everyone has been checked in." Alex placed a BACK IN FIVE MINUTES sign up on the front desk and headed to the restaurant with Nina. Just like when they were little kids, they ate in the kitchen with the cook.

"So," Alex said after she and Nina had fixed their plates. "What happened?"

"I thought you were going to mind your business?" Nina dropped her fork against her plate.

"And you should've known that I was going to ask. If this guy did something to hurt you, then I'm going to kick his ass."

"It's nothing like that. Clinton just seems a little secretive."

Alex pounded the wooden table. "He's

married, isn't he?"

"No. It just seems like he's trying to hold back parts of his life and then there was this guy who said they have some unfinished business. It sounded kind of sinister," Nina said.

"Who was the guy?"

She shrugged her shoulders. "He didn't make any introductions. Just that he used to work for him."

Alex nodded thoughtfully. "Interesting. You know, before you and Clinton got so close, I had my suspicions about him and why he wanted to work here and why he's trying to make Dad his new best friend. That guy may have been Randall Birmingham. He's been trying to get this property for years. Clinton used to work for him."

"There's no way he'd do something like that," Nina said defensively.

Alex picked up a roll and broke it in half. "How do you know? What if he was only using you?"

Nina snatched half of the bread from her sister's hand. "You would think that."

"Who said he was hiding something? Your words, not mine. He very well could be hiding his association with Randall. You were probably just gravy. A plaything while he and Randall schemed to steal this property from Dad."

"And you have proof of this?"

Alex shook her head. "Not yet. And he better hope that I never find proof of it. I'm just starting to like him and I don't want that to change."

"Let it go, Alex. He wouldn't have said he loved me if I was just gravy." Nina refused to believe that Clinton was that under-handed and would try to rob the Richard-sons of the business that the family had built from nothing.

"Sometimes, I forget just how young you are," Alex said. "You told him about Lamar, didn't you? He knew what your weaknesses were and what he needed to say to get in your head and heart."

"You don't trust anyone, do you?"

Alex bit into her roll. "Obviously, you don't trust him either. Otherwise, you'd be having dinner with him and not me."

Nina silently chewed her food and looked away from her sister. Was she right? Did Clinton have some other reason for claim-ing to love her?

Clinton wasn't a violent man, but all eve-ning he wanted to put his fist through a wall or, more appropriately, Randall Birming-ham's face. Somehow he had to get it through Birmingham's head that he wasn't going to assist him in his scheme to take over the bed-and-breakfast. It didn't matter to him how many times Birmingham had helped him in the past, he wasn't going to allow him to ruin his future.

Even though Alex had been a lot nicer to him, Clinton knew she didn't trust him completely, and if she got wind of Birmingham sniffing around him, she would blow a gasket.

And Nina.

What would she think? She would doubt everything that he'd ever said to her and question his love for her.

Feeling like a caged tiger, Clinton paced the living room floor until he couldn't stand being in his house anymore. He grabbed his jacket and his keys, then headed to Birmingham's place. He hopped in his car and sped to North Charleston. Tonight, things were going to end with Birmingham, one way or another.

When he arrived at Birmingham's, he sat in the driveway, willing himself to calm down before he knocked on the front door. How many times had he come here in the past for dinner parties or to go over business plans? He thought that Birmingham was someone he could respect and admire, but the more he watched how Birmingham did business, the more he realized that he was a ruthless man who used people as pawns. This man never did anything to help someone without expecting something in return. Clinton couldn't believe that he thought he'd be different.

Clinton stalked to the wooden front door and banged on it with the fury of a SWAT team.

The porch light flickered on and Birmingham snatched the door open. "Have you lost your damned mind?"

Clinton grabbed Birmingham by the collar. "This ends now. I'm not going to let you bully me into helping you. I'm not helping you screw Sheldon Richardson over and I'm not going to let you hang what you've done for me in the past over my head any longer." He pushed the older man against the door.

"I should have you arrested for assault." He rubbed his throat and then glared angrily at Clinton. "You will regret this."

"I won't because I'm going to tell Sheldon everything," Clinton snapped. "And then you'll be exposed."

"I tried to tell your father that he was wrong about you, but he had you pegged all along. You're soft. That's why you couldn't make it working for me. I was grooming you to —"

"Be a cold bastard like you? How about you go to hell and take my father with you. You don't give a damn about what that bed-and-breakfast means to the history of this city. Or how Sheldon Richardson paved the way for you. All you want is something shiny and new to call yours."

Birmingham laughed. "This ain't got shit to do with Sheldon. It's all about Nina Richardson, isn't it? How is she going to look at you when she finds out that you were trying to steal her father's business?"

Grabbing Birmingham's throat again, Clinton snarled at him. "Leave Nina out of this. No one is going to believe your lies. Let it go! This is over." Clinton released Birmingham and stormed off the porch.

"It's not over and you're going to pay for this!" Birmingham called out as Clinton started his car and peeled out of the drive-way. Instead of heading home, Clinton went to the bed-and-breakfast to find Nina.

Clinton knew that he had to tell her everything before Birmingham put his spin on what was going on. He stalked through the lobby, ignoring the desk clerk's greeting, and headed for the family end of the B&B.

As he approached the house, he tried to think of what he'd say to her and how he would make her understand that he wasn't working with Birmingham and he had no intention of trying to steal Sheldon's life-work. He knocked on the door and waited, hoping that Nina was inside.

When she opened the door, dressed in a tank top and a pair of boy shorts, he almost forgot why he'd rushed over.

"Clinton, I wasn't expecting you," she said, quickly wiping a spot of cream from her cheek. "What are you doing here?"

"We need to talk," he said, tearing his eyes away from her tantalizing body. "This afternoon, I shouldn't have pushed you away."

Nina stepped aside to allow him to enter her room. "You shouldn't have, but you did."

"I know. There's something you should know about me: I don't like to depend on other people. I can thank my father for that. He showed me when I was a little kid that people disappointed you. Every time I needed him to show me something about being a man, he ignored me. He showed me what not to do by cheating on my mother, staying out late, and sometimes slapping my mother around. I was a disappointment to

239

my father because I didn't play sports and I wanted to use my brain. But after my mother died, he needed me. Being a good son, I didn't want to let him down."

"So," Nina said, "you got involved with that guy to help out your father?"

"I used to work for him. His name is Randall Birmingham and when I started working for him, I thought that he was going to be that father figure that I was looking for. At first, it seemed that way. I thought Birmingham was a straight-up type of guy. He gave me a lot of business advice and when he learned of my father's plight, he offered to help. I just didn't know his help had strings."

Nina sat on the edge of the sofa and looked up at Clinton. "What did he want you to do?"

"Be his puppet," he said. "Even my father wanted me to just fall in line with what Birmingham wanted. I paid my debt to the man and he still thinks that he can yank my chain."

"I'm glad you felt comfortable enough to tell me this." Nina slid over to give Clinton room to sit beside her. "Since we're coming clean, I have something to confess too."

He closed his eyes and readied himself to hear something about her deciding to give

Lamar another chance. "All right."

"Before I left Charlotte, Lamar said all of the things that I wanted to hear from him. For a spilt second, I nearly fell for it. But then, I thought about you and what we have. I thought about how honest you've been with me and how open you've been about your feelings. Then today, you said you loved me and I know you're the man I want to love and grow with." Nina stroked his cheek. "So, all of these outside people who want to play with our lives can kiss our asses."

Clinton leaned in and kissed her. "Thank you for understanding and being honest."

"Stay with me tonight? I just want you to hold me."

Clinton smiled. "Do you think Alex will approve?"

Nina wrapped her arms around his neck. "Who cares what Alex thinks? We'll just ask her to join us for breakfast."

Sitting in her room, Alex was getting ready to turn in for the night when her phone rang. Thinking that it was Nina, she started to ignore it. The last thing she wanted was to hear anything more about Clinton Jefferson. That man had rooted himself in the Richardson family. Still, she didn't trust him completely. Especially after what Nina said had happened earlier in the day. Alex was willing to bet her beloved car that the man Clinton fought with was Randall Birmingham.

"Yes?" she said when she finally picked up the phone.

"Miss Richardson, this is Randall Birmingham."

Alex looked at the clock on her nightstand. "Why are you calling me so late and what the hell do you want?"

"To set up a meeting with you. I have some information that you may find very interesting."

"Randall, you're a liar and a thief, why would I want to meet with you?"

He laughed, reminding Alex of a diabolical villain from a corny superhero movie. "At least you know who I am, but you have a faker in your midst."

"Is this about Clinton Jefferson?"

"My protégé. You can think what you want to about me, but I believe in winning the right way, not by seduction and underhanded tricks. I think Clinton is taking things too far."

Alex gave Randall her full attention. "Do you have proof of this?"

"I'll give it to you when we meet. Let's

say at the café on the waterfront in the morning?"

Son of a bitch, Alex thought as she agreed to meet with Randall. *I knew you were up to something and now you've involved my sister in this. There will be hell to pay once I have the proof.*

CHAPTER 17

Nina woke up in Clinton's arms and wondered if she could spend every morning like this. She ran her finger down his jawbone and smiled. He loved her and she was growing to love him more and more with every passing moment. What they shared was more than sexual and more than the shell of a relationship she thought she'd had with Lamar. Nina knew Clinton respected her as much as he loved her. His desire for her was born from something more than lust and she craved every moment they shared together.

Nina had left Charleston to make a name for herself out of her family's shadow but now, she'd be willing to move back and make a life with Clinton. It wasn't as if she'd be giving up her career. She traveled a lot anyway. Nina could just as easily make Charleston her home base as she had Charlotte.

"Good morning," she said when he opened his eyes.

"It certainly is," he replied, then kissed her on the cheek. "But any morning with you in my arms is good."

"I like the sound of that. Maybe we should do this more often."

"How about forever?"

"Umm, that sounds good to me," she said. Clinton rolled over and covered her with his body.

"I'm going to hold you to that. Now that we have all of the unpleasantness out of the way we can move on with our lives, even if you do live a few hours away."

"That could change. After the Super Bowl I usually take a few months off. Now I can spend that time with you." She kissed him on the chin. "How many times can I go to the Pro Bowl anyway?"

"I don't want you to think you have to come back here for me. Your life doesn't have to change because we're together," he said.

"It won't. But I can get used to being with you like this and more than just on the weekends."

"And if we were to get married, where would we live?"

Nina shrugged. "I love your house in

245

Summerville. It's quiet and away from my sister and father."

"What about your place in Charlotte? It's so urban chic. I can't see you giving it up for life in the country."

"I'm from the country," she ribbed. "We can split our time here and there. But we have plenty of time to figure this all out. It's not like you're proposing."

"Not yet, anyway," Clinton said. "Ready for breakfast?"

"Yeah, but not from downstairs. I want you on a platter," she seductively whispered.

Alex crossed her legs as she sat at a table in the corner of the café. Randall was late and she was two seconds from leaving. Proof or no proof, that scumbag had some nerve keeping her waiting.

"More coffee?" the waiter asked as he appeared at the table.

"Y—"

"Coffee and cinnamon buns," Randall said. "Sorry for keeping you waiting, Miss Richardson." He dropped a file folder on the table. "Here is the proof that you need."

Alex picked up the folder and flipped through its contents. There were e-mails to Randall from Clinton detailing his job at the bed-and-breakfast, his relationship with

Nina, and requests for payment.

She rose to her feet and left without saying good-bye to Randall. Filled with anger and steam, she got into her car and dialed her father's cell phone number.

"This is Sheldon."

"Daddy, it's Alex. Remember how I told you Clinton Jefferson wasn't all that he was cracked up to be? Now I have evidence to back that up."

"Alex, I thought you'd gotten past this anger and distrust you had of him," he said with a sigh.

"Daddy, I just met with Randall Birmingham. Clinton has been feeding him information about our company and being with Nina to get in good with the family."

"What? I'll be there in a few hours. Don't say a word to Clinton until I get there. I told him not to hurt my baby. I could give a damn about him trying to steal my company, but no one hurts my daughters," Sheldon spat.

"I'll wait for you at the bed-and-breakfast," Alex said, then hung up with her father.

Nina and Clinton crept into his office where he kept a second set of clothes. He had on a plush robe and Nina wasn't dressed much better in a short cotton skirt and a white tank top.

"If Alex saw you now, she'd freak," Nina laughed once they were inside the office.

"No, if Alex saw what I did to her baby sister she would freak." Clinton pinched her ample bottom and grinned.

"She hasn't moved you out of this closet yet?" Nina asked as she perched on the edge of the desk. "I'm sure she just put you here so that she could keep an eye on you."

"Well, I guess she still doesn't trust me."

Nina rolled her eyes. "I do. Alex can be a bit anal. But she'll see as soon as you tell her about Birmingham and what he was trying to do."

Clinton slipped his jeans on and turned to Nina and cupped her face in his hands. "Thank you for believing in me. You know that I would never do anything to hurt you or your family. When your father and Alex know that Birmingham is coming after them, they will know how to stop him and I'm going to do all I can to help."

"Who knew that the world of hospitality was so cutthroat? So, why does this guy want this place? Doesn't he own a lot of properties?"

"He wants what he can't have," Clinton said as he slipped a T-shirt over his head.

"The Richardson Bed and Breakfast is iconic. He was nice to me even though he turned me down and I knew I had to work for him. He's an amazing man and has an amazing daughter." Clinton leaned in and kissed her lips gently. "Guess we missed breakfast, huh?"

Nina glanced at the clock on the wall. "Looks that way. But if we eat now, we can call it brunch."

"Then we can have an even later dinner?" he said as he pulled her off the desk and into his arms. Just as he was about to kiss her, they heard Alex's office door open.

"God, does she ever take a day off?" Nina said.

Through the door, she heard her father curse loudly.

"Wow, your father sounds mad for a Sunday."

"I know and this is unlike him. Maybe we ought to see what's going on." She flung the door open. "Daddy?"

"Nina," Sheldon said. "What are you doing here?" His brow was furrowed and his jaw clenched tightly as he looked at Clinton. "I need to see you."

"Yes, sir," Clinton said as he followed Sheldon into Alex's office. Nina slipped in unseen.

She stood by the half-open door and listened.

"So, you were working for Birmingham this entire time?" Sheldon said in a calm voice that belied his rage.

"No, not at all. He approached me to do some underhanded stuff but I didn't."

"That's bullshit," Alex railed as she opened a folder. "Here are your e-mails and canceled checks that Randall wrote to you."

"Alex, this isn't what it seems."

"Shut up!" Sheldon yelled. "I don't care about you feeding secrets to him because I run this business just like any other property, but for you to use my daughter —"

"Use your daughter? Mr. Richardson, I have not —"

"What are you talking about, Daddy?" Nina asked.

Everyone turned and looked at her. "I didn't want you to find out like this. But he's been using you, Nina. It's all been a lie," Alex said.

"No," Nina said, shaking her head. "You're wrong. Clinton wasn't working for that man. He told me everything about what —"

Alex crossed over to Nina with the canceled checks. "It's true, Sis. I really wanted him to be everything that he said he was."

250

Tears welled up in Nina's eyes as she looked at the checks and the dates on them. Turning to Clinton she shook her head. "You liar!"

"Nina, no, you know that —"

She slapped him as hard as she could. "Go to hell!" She ran out of the office with tears streaming down her face. Once again, she'd been fooled by a man who was supposed to love her. How could Clinton do this to her and her family? She'd believed his story about not wanting to hurt or deceive her family and she believed him when he said that he loved her.

"How could I have been so stupid?" she exclaimed as she slammed into her room. But she knew that she was going to get the hell out of Charleston. There was no way she could stand for her father's pity or Alex's silent I'm-sorry-but-I-told-you-so looks every time she turned around. But most of all, she didn't want to hear any more of Clinton's lies. She didn't want to be reminded of how sweet his kisses were or how he made her feel when he touched her and made love to her. It was all a lie, a joke, and a part of a plan to steal the bed-and-breakfast.

Nina quickly changed into a pair of jeans and a sweatshirt and crept out of the bed-

and-breakfast, not bothering to say good-bye to anyone.

When she got into the car, she sobbed until her shoulders shook and her eyes were red and raw. Why was it that every time she opened herself to a man, she ended up heartbroken? Taking a deep breath, Nina decided not to cry anymore. She wasn't going to give Clinton the satisfaction. She started up the car and peeled out of the parking lot.

She'd been driving for about an hour before her cell phone rang. "What?"

"Eww, somebody has an attitude," Yolanda said. "Hello, Sis."

"I really don't want to talk right now."

"What's wrong? I was calling to tell you that I'm coming to Charlotte tomorrow. Are you going to have time for your sister?"

"I have a deadline," Nina lied. "So, no."

"Look, I'm not going to continue with this charade. I talked to Alex and she told me what happened with Clinton. Then she said you took off, so deadline or not, you're making time for me. Are you still driving?"

"Yes, and I don't want to talk about this today or tomorrow." Nina glanced down at her speedometer. She was going nearly one hundred miles per hour. Sighing, she slowed the car down. "Why does this always happen to me?"

"It's not your fault. I could kick Clinton right where it hurts. Not only did he hurt you, but he was trying to steal Dad's property. It would've been one thing if he had just done that underhanded crap but to involve you —"

"What part of 'I don't want to talk about this' don't you understand?" Nina snapped.

"Nina, I know you don't want to talk about Clinton, but I don't want you to get down on yourself like you were with Lamar and for God's sake don't let this push you back into his arms."

"I'm hanging up now." Nina ended the call and tossed it on the passenger seat.

Seconds later the phone rang again. "What?" she snapped.

"Nina," Sheldon said. "Are you all right?"

"What do you think, Daddy?"

"I hope you're not speeding."

"No, I'm not," she said.

"I fired Clinton. I hope you know that I don't give a damn about him coming in here and being Birmingham's spy, but he hurt you and I will never forgive him."

"It doesn't matter. We know the truth now and we can move on."

"It does matter, because I know you're hurting right now. If I wasn't a good Christian man he would've been leaving this place on a stretcher."

Nina smiled for the first time since she'd started driving. "I know, Daddy. I love you and I'll be fine."

"I know you will and you're going to meet Mr. Right one day," he said.

"Thanks, Daddy."

"I love you and call me to let me know you made it home safely," Sheldon said.

Nina promised that she would, then ended the call. She turned the cell phone off because she didn't want to hear from anyone else.

"This is Nina, please leave a message and I'll call you back." Clinton had heard her voice mail greeting ten times in the last half hour.

"Damn it," he growled. Clinton couldn't let things stand the way they were. She had to know that he wasn't using her. Birmingham had really done it this time and Clinton was going to make him pay. Sheldon and Alexandria thought that he was a spy and Nina hated him, thinking that he had been pretending to love her. But that was the biggest lie of all. He loved her more than anything and she had to know that. He'd find another job, but he'd never find another

Nina. Those checks weren't his, but the checks that Birmingham had been giving to his father.

How long had this bastard been planning this? he thought. *That's why he was helping my father.*

In order to clear his name, Clinton was going to have to confront his father and make him admit that Birmingham gave him that money. Though he dreaded talking to his father, Clinton rushed out to his car and headed to his childhood home.

The drive to the Deas Hill area of town seemed to take three hours: Every light was red, people were driving at least ten miles under the speed limit, and every big rig that was on the road seemed to be in front of him.

When Clinton finally arrived at his father's house, he sat in the driveway for a few moments. Did his father have such a low opinion of him that he would turn to a man like Birmingham for help? Was he that greedy and proud?

Slamming out of the car, Clinton pounded on the door and waited for Clinton Sr. to open it.

"Boy, what the hell is wrong with you?" the elder Clinton asked when he snatched the front door open.

"What's wrong with me? Why have you been taking money from Birmingham? Thanks to you, I've been fired." Clinton pushed past his father and walked into the living room.

"The man said if I needed help that he would take care of it." Clinton Sr. folded his arms across his chest. "What does that have to do with your failure? That's all you've ever been is a big failure. You can't do anything right for long."

Clinton closed his eyes, feeling as if he were an eight-year-old again, cowering in a corner as his father spat out how disappointed he was in him. "You know what," Clinton said. "You've never been much of a father, husband, or a role model. It's no wonder that I followed Randall Birmingham for all of those years like a little lapdog."

"Too bad you didn't learn to be a man like him, someone who goes after what he wants. You are content to be a lapdog," Clinton Sr. snapped.

"Well, not anymore and you're going to clear my name with the Richardsons. That money went to you and not me. You're going to tell Sheldon Richardson that."

Clinton Sr. waved his hand as if he were swatting flies. "Unlike you, Randall has been loyal to me, more like a son than you have ever been."

Balling up his fists, Clinton pounded them into his thighs. "A stranger on the street could've been more of a father to me than you. This is useless." He turned toward the door, then looked back at his father. "You don't even care that you cost me something perfect, someone that I really love. I can find another job, but Nina was precious and she was the kind of woman that I could see myself spending my life with. You're such a bitter old fool that you don't give a damn or understand what I'm going through right now." Clinton slammed out of the front door and stood on the porch. Tears stung his eyes. Just as he was about to turn and head to his car, the door swung open.

"Son," Clinton Sr. said. "You're right about me. I'm bitter and I'm old, but the last thing I want to do is ruin things for you. Randall has been helping me out for years, but I never knew it was going to hurt you. Hell, he acted as if he were my friend and doing me a favor."

"I sent you money and you never said a word about him. You never said anything about *your friend.* Didn't you think that when I quit working for him that he should've stopped helping you? You were

just being greedy and damn the consequences, right, Dad?"

"Look, if you want my help, this is no way
to go about getting it," Clinton Sr. snapped.

"Just go to hell, old man." He bounded
off the porch and got into his car. Clinton
knew his father wasn't going to do the right
thing. The only thing he could do was head
to Charlotte and convince Nina that he
really did love her.

CHAPTER 18

Nina arrived at her place and she wasn't surprised to see her sister Yolanda was already there.

As she stepped out of the car, she rolled her eyes. "Don't start."

"No hello?"

"Yolanda, I know why you're here and I'm fine. I don't need you to babysit me and send reports to Dad and Alex," Nina said as she popped her trunk to remove her bag.

"That's not why I'm here, solely. I have some meetings with some people tomorrow and I'm not going to waste money by staying in a hotel."

Nina pushed her bag into Yolanda's hands. "Make yourself useful."

Yolanda took the bag and followed Nina inside. "Listen," she said. "I'm not going to take much more of your attitude."

Nina turned around and looked at her sister. "You can always go home, Yolanda."

"Not going to happen," she said. "Besides, I'm here on business, remember? Some of these NFL and NBA players and their wives need fashion tips. Working with Daddy when *USA Today* did that article on him gave me a whole new outlook on how I could expand my business. Fashion consulting. Aren't you tight with some of those people you write about?"

Nina ignored her sister as she stormed into her bedroom. She didn't care about her sister's business plans when she was in the middle of another heartbreak. "Lord, whatever I've done in a past life or in this one, haven't you punished me enough?" She flung herself across her bed.

"Nina, you didn't bring this on yourself," Yolanda said from the doorway.

With tears streaming down her cheeks, Nina sat up and turned to her sister. "No, this is all Clinton. That lying dog! But what's wrong with me? Losers must see something in me that screams, 'Come, get some.'" She wiped her eyes with the back of her hand. "I'm not going to do this, I'm not going to cry over another man again."

Yolanda took a seat on the bed beside Nina and hugged her tightly. "We could always roll down to Charleston and kick his ass."

Nina cast her eyes upward at Yolanda. "He lives in Summerville and gas is too expensive for that."

"Go wash your face and take me out to dinner. I'm not about to let you sit in here and feel sorry for yourself," Yolanda said as she let her go. "By the way, have you heard from Robin lately?"

Before Nina could answer, her phone rang. Yolanda looked at the caller ID. "It says 'Charleston, SC,' but it isn't Daddy's or Alex's number."

"It's probably Clinton. Don't answer it."

Being that Yolanda never listened to anyone, she answered the call. "Hello?"

Clinton thought Nina had finally answered the phone, but there was something different about her voice. "Nina?"

"No, this isn't Nina and you have some nerve to call my little sister after you used her to try and steal my father's business. And to think I defended you and encouraged Nina to open —"

"I don't mean any disrespect, but I didn't call to speak to you, Yolanda. Put Nina on the phone."

"She doesn't want to talk to you and you'd be smart not to call her again." Yolanda ended the call.

Clinton pressed redial and prayed that Nina would pick up.

"What part of 'she doesn't want to speak to you' don't you understand?"

"Let her tell me that," Clinton said, struggling to keep his voice even. In the background he heard Nina tell Yolanda to hang up the phone.

"Don't call back, you've done enough damage."

"But it's not —" The phone clicked in his ear. Clinton turned off on the exit that took him into Uptown Charlotte. It didn't matter if he had to sit outside of her place all night, he was going to talk to Nina.

When his phone rang, he prayed that it was Nina. "Nina?"

"I guess her father showed her the package I gave Alexandria," Birmingham said with a laugh.

"You slimy son of a bitch. Do you care what you've done?"

"Don't really give a damn. I asked you to do one thing. You owe me for everything that you know and the fact that your father still has a roof over his head. I own you, Junior."

"No one owns me and I'm going to bring you down, Birmingham. For as much as you know about me, I know the same about you.

Underhanded business deals, lying to your stockholders, and let's not forget all the women you run around town with. How do you think your wife will feel about that?"

Birmingham laughed and it incensed Clinton. "This is a big damn joke to you," Clinton snapped.

"No, Clinton, you're the joke. Do you really think that your father is going to be able to make the Richardsons believe that I wrote those checks to him? They're going to look at him as a father who's trying to protect his son. You're screwed, buddy."

Clinton ended the call and tightened his grip on the steering wheel. What if Birmingham was right? What if Nina never believed him?

He pulled into the parking lot where Nina lived, cut the engine, and looked up at her place. What was he supposed to do now? If he knocked on the door, her sister would probably slam it in his face if Nina didn't do it herself. But he'd come too far to sit in his car looking like a stalker. He hopped out of the car and slowly walked up to Nina's front door. His heart pounded faster and faster with each step he took. Losing Nina would be the worst thing that could happen to him because he loved her so much and having her think of him as a liar hurt to the bone. Clinton had never loved a woman the way that he loved Nina. She touched his heart with just a smile, though he knew convincing her of that wasn't going to be easy.

He urgently pressed the doorbell and waited. The curtain moved back and he saw Yolanda glaring at him. She opened the door and stood in the crack. "What are you doing here?"

"I came to see Nina and I don't want to argue with you."

Yolanda folded her arms across her chest. "You're not walking through this door. You didn't just pick a fight with my baby sister, but my whole damned family. I have half a mind to —"

Nina appeared behind her sister and grabbed her shoulder. "Yolanda, I'll handle this."

The cold look that Nina gave him was like a laser slicing his heart in half. She looked as if she hated him when it was only hours ago that those ebony eyes sparkled when she looked at him.

"Why are you here?" Nina demanded as she stepped on the stoop, refusing to allow him to enter.

"Because I have to explain, Nina. Things aren't what they seem to be. I was never trying to take anything from your family. Birmingham set me up."

"Those checks, those e-mails, he just made it all up? Do I look like a fool? I mean, I know I made a fool of myself by letting you into my bed and my heart. You're worse than any man who's ever hurt me because you used me. Not just for sex but for money and to get closer to my father!"

Nina stepped closer to him with fire flickering in her eyes and the threat of violence in her body language. Without warning she pounded her fists against his chest. "I hate you, Clinton. How dare you make me love you when it was all a lie!"

He grabbed her wrists before she could hit him again. "It's not a lie because I do love you and I didn't use you. The only lie is the one Birmingham made up —"

"Bullshit! The only lie is me believing you loved me. Let go of me and get out of here."

"Not until we talk about this," Clinton said. "Please, Nina, why would I come all of this way if there was any truth to what Alex said?" He dropped her hands. "I can't force you to believe me, but look at what we shared and tell me it was a lie. If you honestly believe that I could fake my feelings for you, then I'll leave and you'll never see me again."

She stepped back from him and the look in her eyes told him that she didn't believe what they shared was a lie. "If you don't get off my property, I'm going to call the police and have you removed." Nina dashed inside and slammed the door in Clinton's face.

He placed his hand on the door and started to knock again, but he knew that Nina wouldn't listen to him until he had proof that he hadn't used her. Clinton got back into his car and headed for a hotel because he didn't have the strength to drive back to Charleston.

Nina watched from her window as Clinton walked away from the door and got into his car. Part of her wanted to run outside and tell him that she believed him, but how could she ignore what was in black and white? Those checks had his name on them, those e-mails, cruel and revealing, said that he was only dating her so that he could endear himself to her father.

"Nina," Yolanda said. "You didn't fall for his lies, did you?"

She turned away from the window and toward her sister. "No, I didn't." Nina sighed and wiped her teary eyes.

"I know that look and I know you're considering calling that fool and giving him another chance. You've done it before and I'm not going to let you do it again. He didn't just hurt you, he tried to hurt Daddy." Yolanda sat down on the sofa beside Nina. "For once, Alex and her suspicious mind was right."

"I just wish that she wasn't and he wasn't a lying creep. I fell for him hard and it's not going away. He seemed so different."

"Good acting."

Nina pinched Yolanda on the arm. "Why am I such a loser when it comes to men?"

"Because you have a good heart and you will give anyone a chance, even those who don't deserve it. Clinton's lucky I have a business meeting tomorrow and I need to keep my manicure intact or I would've went all upside his head when I saw him at the door."

"But it doesn't make sense," Nina said as she rose to her feet. "Why would he drive here if he'd only been using me? Now that the plot has been exposed, what's his purpose?"

Yolanda blew on her nails as if her polish were wet. "The sex must be good to him. That man is no better than Lamar or any other loser from your past. Little Sis, trust me. Let this one go. I'm hungry, let's go get something to eat."

"Fine, we can walk to a restaurant or something," Nina replied. She didn't want to go out, but she didn't want to hear Yolanda and her theories about Clinton and his appearance on her doorstep.

"Let's go dancing after we eat dinner," Yolanda said. "You need to do something to take your mind off things."

"How are you going to be ready for your meeting in the morning if you stay out all night running the streets?" Nina asked, believing that her sister's visit was less about business and more about babysitting.

"Who said my meeting was in the morning? I just said that it was tomorrow. I'm going to go change, you do something with your face. Tear stains aren't attractive on you."

Nina touched her wet cheek, not realizing that she had been crying. She didn't want to go out, but she couldn't sit around and cry all night.

I'm going to get through this, Clinton was just another sorry-ass man. I will never fall in love again. It's time for me to be the heartbreaker.

Nina rushed to the bathroom, feeling emboldened by her revelation. She was going to go out with her sister and pretend that she didn't have a care in the world and she was sure that if she stayed out long enough that she would actually come to believe it.

She couldn't have been more wrong.

Nina and Yolanda headed to a dance club after they'd grabbed a quick bite to eat at Mert's Heart & Soul restaurant.

"Charlotte is turning into a happening city," Yolanda commented as they waited for an Uber. "Maybe I should move my business here."

"Oh no," Nina said. "I don't need you here watching my every move and reporting it to Daddy."

"The world doesn't revolve around you, Nina. I want a change. A change would do you good too," Yolanda said. "You can write anywhere. Staying here is going to bring up a lot of memories that are going to cut you in the heart every time you see Lamar or Clinton shows up on your doorstep."

"To hell with Lamar and Clinton. I'm going to start over and fall in love with the one person I know won't hurt me."

"Who is that?" Yolanda asked as the black car pulled up on the curb.

Nina opened the door and smiled at her sister. "Me."

They slid into the back seat. "That's the spirit," Yolanda said.

After a short ride to the club, the women were greeted with a long line of would-be partiers. Nina shook her head. "This is a bad idea. I don't want to stand in that line."

"What else do you have to do? Cry over Clinton?"

Nina glared at her sister as the exited the Uber. "No, I'm through with tears."

"You'd better be, Richardsons don't cry, we survive."

Nina smiled, but she clearly wanted to go home, dive under the covers, and cry.

Despite the number of people in the line, everyone got in the club fairly quickly. Nina and Yolanda were prepared to take their problems to the dance floor when Nina heard a familiar voice call her name. She whirled around and saw Lamar standing there with a smile on his face.

"I didn't think the club was your thing. You're looking sexy as hell tonight."

"What do you want?" Nina rolled her eyes.

"A lot of things, but right now, I'd settle for a dance."

"Who is this guy?" Yolanda asked, giving him a hateful glance.

"This is Lamar."

Yolanda held on to Nina's arm. "Oh. Sorry, Lamar, it's a sisters' night and you're not invited."

He smiled. "So, she told you about me?"

"Every slimy detail."

"Nina, where's your new man?" he asked.

"Lamar, go away, please."

He leaned in close to her ear. "You don't have to put on a show for your sister, I know what you really want."

"Is that so? If you know what I want then why are you still here?"

"I'm done. I tried to make things right with you, but you want to keep your ass on your shoulder. You don't have to worry about me anymore."

"Good," Nina snapped. "Because you were never good enough for me to begin with. Why did I waste my time with you when all you wanted was a good lay and your face in the newspaper? Lamar, go to hell and I mean that with everything in me. It's men like you that make women just snap. Go out and find you another victim because I resign from that position." She pushed him aside and Yolanda flipped her middle finger up at him as they headed for the middle of the dance floor.

"Good job, Sis," Yolanda yelled over the music. "It seems as if you are on your way back."

CHAPTER 19

When Clinton woke up, he didn't get on the road for Charleston. What did he have to rush back for? He didn't have a job to get to and he was sure his father hadn't lifted a finger to help clear his name. Birmingham was right. He'd been beaten. Nina's reaction to him last night had been enough proof to show him that until the truth came out, he'd have a snowball's chance in hell to win her back. He knew he couldn't wallow in self-pity all day, so he pulled himself out of bed, showered, and checked out of the hotel. Then, against everything that his common sense told him, he headed back to Nina's to see if she would talk to him.

On the drive over, his cell phone rang.

"Hello?"

"Clinton, this is Sheldon Richardson."

"Mr. Richardson, sir, I'm surprised to hear from you."

"I figured you would be. You know, I don't

like to be thought of as a fool and that's what Randall did. I discovered those e-mails you allegedly sent to Randall were falsified."

I told you so! "Mr. Richardson, I hope that you believe me when I tell you that everything Birmingham told you and your daughter was a lie."

"It looks that way but those checks," he said.

"Were written to my father, Clinton Jefferson Senior."

"That's the same thing he said when he came to my office and that prompted me to looking into this thing further. I'm not willing to offer you your job back at this moment, but I will say this — if there is an ounce of truth to what Randall is saying, a job is the last thing that you're going to have to worry about. I told you not to hurt Nina and from what I understand, that's precisely what you did."

"Birmingham's lies hurt her. I love Nina, Mr. Richardson, and excuse me for being frank, but I could give a damn if I never work for you again."

"Is that so?" Sheldon said.

"The only thing that matters to me right now is getting Nina back."

Clinton could almost hear Sheldon's smile through the phone. "You must really love my daughter if you're turning down gainful employment. Right now, Alex and a computer technician are going through your hard drive to see if you and Randall were communicating."

"Mr. Richardson, I knew when I took this job that Birmingham wanted your property, I just had no idea he'd be so dirty and cause all of this division."

"Son, the only ones who lost anything were you and my daughter. This bed-and-breakfast means a lot to me, but not half as much as my four daughters. In a couple of years, I'm going to pass this place on to them and for all I know, they may sell it. Still, I'm not going to let Randall get away with this — especially since he made my daughter feel as if her heart had been ripped out of her chest."

Clinton felt a little better as he pulled into Nina's parking lot. "Have you talked to her today?" he asked.

"I called her and left a message. She's avoiding me."

"Me too."

Nina was glad to see Yolanda walking out the door, but when her phone rang and she saw her father's face on the screen she didn't answer. Nina had been up until about

274

four a.m. with her sister at the club. What was surprising to her was that Yolanda woke up at eight thirty to make her meeting. She planned to do nothing but sleep the morning away. But every time Nina closed her eyes, she saw Clinton's face. Then she reached out for him, only to wind up holding her pillow tightly. Her phone rang again and she ignored it, thinking that it was her father again. Or even worse, Alex.

Just as she was about wrap up in her favorite blanket, the doorbell rang. "No one wants me to sleep today," she groaned as she kicked out of the covers and headed to the front door. Nina, figuring it was her sister, opened the door without looking out the window first. "What is it, Yo— Clinton, what the hell are you doing here?"

"If you don't want to let me in, that's fine, but please check your voice mail."

She rolled her eyes and sighed. "Why don't you just say what you said on the message and leave?"

"Your father called you this morning," Clinton said.

"How do you know that?"

"We just talked. He and Alex have taken a look at the stuff Birmingham gave them and the lie is unraveling. I never sent him those e-mails and those checks went to my father.

Nina, I love you, and if you need to verify that I wasn't using you, go ahead. But don't question my love for you. I made a promise to never hurt you and I plan to keep it."

Nina wanted to fall into his arms and cover his face with kisses. She wanted to tell him that it had been a struggle for her to believe that he would use her in such a way. But she steeled herself and looked at him. She'd promised herself that no one would ever hurt her again and even if this was a lie, what about the next time? But what about what she felt and the fluttering in her chest as she looked at him? Nina wanted to ignore what her heart was saying to her because she'd been burned by love too many times.

"Will you just leave?" Nina said.

"No, I won't." He took a step closer to her. "I know why it seemed as if Birmingham was telling the truth. I can understand why you're gun-shy. You have to know that I love you."

Nina shook her head. "I can't do this," she said. "I promised myself that I wouldn't allow anyone else to hurt me and that includes you."

"I don't want to hurt you, Nina. Tell me you know that I'm not like those men who hurt you in the past."

She turned her back to him, feeling as if she didn't know anything. If her father had forgiven him, why couldn't she? Nina knew that Clinton wasn't the problem, it was her, and if it wasn't this time, then he'd hurt her someway. She had to stop it right now.

"I need some time alone," she said. "There are a lot of things I need to sort out and with you here, that's going to be impossible."

"So what happens when I leave?"

Nina faced him, her eyes shining with unshed tears, and shrugged her shoulders. "There's no crystal ball with the answers. I need some time to myself to process what's happened to me over these last few months. This isn't just about what happened between us, Clinton. Maybe I never got over all of my feelings about Lamar before I jumped into this with you. I'm glad you weren't trying to steal my father's hotel, but this has nothing to do with that."

Clinton folded his arms across his chest and stared at her. "Lamar's the lesser of two evils in your mind?"

"This isn't about him, this is about me and what I want." Nina took a step back from Clinton, she felt as if she couldn't breathe with him standing so close. *I'm either making the best decision of my life or the biggest mistake.* "It's over."

"You mean that? This is what you really want?"

Though her soul screamed out no, Nina nodded. "It has to be. There will always be questions as to why we're together. Are you trying to endear yourself to my father or do you really love me? You're going to be wondering if I'm still harboring feelings for Lamar. It's a recipe for disaster."

"How can you seriously think that?" he asked, his voice peppered with anger. "I haven't even asked for my job back at the Richardson B&B. I don't want it, I want you."

She shook her head. "What do you mean, I thought my father would've given you your job back since —"

"Damn that job. I can find another one, but I can't find another you." Clinton pulled her into his arms and forced her to meet his gaze. "That night at dinner, I knew I wanted you more than anything I've ever worked for. Your father could've fired me on the spot and I wouldn't have cared. Tasting your lips and feeling your skin against mine was like heaven. We can't end like this."

"Clinton, please," she said, trying to pull out of his grasp.

"So, you're scared? That's what this is

about? You've been looking for something to get you off the hook because you're afraid to love me? There's no loophole, it's all or nothing, babe. You have to stop thinking love hurts because we both know that it can be beautiful."

Tears flowed freely down her cheeks as their eyes locked. "Clinton, I do love you and I'm scared because I don't want to find out that you're going to hurt me too."

"Nina, do you realize how much I love you?"

"How much do you love me?" she asked.

Clinton wanted to say something corny like more than the moon and the stars, but he brought his lips against her ear. "Let me show you." He scooped Nina into his arms and headed for her bedroom. He didn't have sex on his mind as he laid her on the bed. Clinton just held Nina as she cried silently against his chest.

"I love you," he whispered. "And I'm going to say it until you believe it."

She cast her eyes upward and met his gaze. "I love you, too."

"This time love isn't going to hurt you. What we have is real and nothing or no one is going to change that."

"What about my crazy sisters?"

"Just wait until you meet my crazy father,"

Clinton said.

Nina kissed him gently and nestled against him. "Are we really going to do this? I mean, Alex is going to freak out and Yolanda doesn't like you right now either."

"I'll win them over," he said, holding her tighter. "As long as we have each other, nothing else matters."

Nina closed her eyes and drifted off to sleep, silently praying that this was no dream, he said he loved her.

Clinton watched Nina as she slept, noting the angelic smile on her face and the subtle movements of her chest as she inhaled and exhaled through her mouth. His love for her made him ache. He couldn't lose her, but he knew that Birmingham wasn't going to stop messing with his life. He felt as if he and Nina had built a solid foundation — still, he wasn't going to let Birmingham get away with his little ploy.

Gently he stroked her cheek, trying not to wake her, but her eyes fluttered open.

"Hello, beautiful," he said.

"How long have I been sleeping?"

"I don't know, about as long as I've been looking at you."

Nina blushed and turned her head away from Clinton's heated gaze. "Oh, God, I hope I wasn't drooling."

He pinched her cheek. "Just a little."

"Shut up."

Clinton took her face into his hands. "Nina," he said huskily. "I want you so badly."

She rolled over on her stomach and looked up at him with a glimmer of desire in her eyes. "Then take me," she said as she inched up his body and planted a deep kiss on his lips.

Clinton wrapped his arms around her waist, pressing her against his arousal. "Oh, I plan to," he said when their kiss broke off. Slipping his hand between her thighs, Clinton stroked her most sensitive area, feeling her heat through her shorts. "Those have to come off." He unbuttoned them and snatched them off.

"Anything else you want to remove?"

He reached for her tank top and pulled it off in a swift motion. "This has to go too."

"What about you? You're still fully dressed. Let's change that," she said as she pulled his shirt over his head. Then Nina rained kisses down the center of his bare chest and stopped at the waistband of his pants. With nimble fingers, she unbuttoned his pants and slipped her hand inside his boxers, and his erection sprang forward. Clinton closed his eyes and tossed his head back when he felt the warmth of her breath against his cock. The moment that she took him into her mouth, he nearly lost it. He held the back of her neck as she bobbed up and down, taking him deeper into her mouth. Seconds before he climaxed, Nina pulled back.

"You taste as good as you feel," she said seductively.

He couldn't respond as he looked into her eyes, his mind blown by the experience that she had just given him. Clinton flipped Nina on her back and returned the oral pleasure that she'd given him. He pulled her hips closer to his lips so that he could taste every drop of her feminine juices. She moaned and groaned as Clinton's tongue danced across her throbbing bud. Nina wiggled underneath him as if she was trying to get away, but he wasn't having it. He continued his kiss until Nina exploded.

"You definitely taste as good as you feel," he said as he released her. "I love every part of you, everything about you just drives me crazy with desire. I don't ever want to lose you."

Reaching up, she stroked his cheek. "You won't."

Smiling, he covered her mouth with his,

kissing her until they were both dizzy and wanting more. With a free hand, he reached for his pants and pulled a condom from his pocket because he needed to be inside her.

Nina took the package from his hand. "Let me," she said as she ripped open the wrapper and slid the sheath over his erection. In a quick motion, Nina was on top of him, grinding against him slowly, taking him deep into the heat of her passion. Clinton reached up, palming her breasts and feeling her nipples growing hard against his fingers.

"Nina, Nina, Nina," he moaned as she bounced up and down in a sensual rhythm. Clinton easily caught her beat, rotating his hips and touching her every sensitive spot. She was wetter and hotter than he'd remembered. But every time he made love to Nina, it was as if they were making love for the first time all over again. She never ceased to amaze him or find some new way to make his toes curl or make him scream her name.

Nina was his sensual goddess, a sexual muse who turned him inside out every time she looked at him. She leaned against him and kissed him, taking his tongue into her mouth, sucking and nibbling it. Clinton allowed her to control his body, their kiss, and her pleasure. But he couldn't hold back his climax as Nina tightened herself around his shaft and leaned back, grabbing his ankles.

"Oh baby," he cried as he exploded. Nina collapsed against his chest, their bodies drenched in sweat.

"Wow," Clinton whispered against her ear. "That was simply amazing."

Nina fingered his nipple and kissed his cheek. "I love you."

"I love you, too. We're never leaving this bed," he said breathlessly.

"That would be great, but Yolanda's going to be bursting through that door sooner or later."

"Umm, then we'd better make the most of the time we have alone together," Clinton said, his arousal rising as he flipped Nina on her back. "Because I have some moves I want to show you."

CHAPTER 20

A week passed since Nina and Clinton had reconciled. He was back in Charleston, but he hadn't returned to the bed-and-breakfast because he didn't know if he wanted his job back.

Besides, he had a score to settle. He'd spent most of his downtime gathering the records he'd kept during his employment with Birmingham. He had evidence of his former boss cooking the books and lying to his stockholders as well as evidence of a mistress whom Clinton used to make monthly payments to.

Part of him wanted to bury Randall Birmingham with this information, but that wasn't his style. The only thing he wanted from the man was for him to leave the Richardsons alone and to give up his quest to possess the bed-and-breakfast. Since he had all of the information and evidence he needed, Clinton was ready to head to

Birmingham's office to confront him. But he was stopped by a knock at his front door.

When Clinton pulled the curtain back to see who his visitor was, he was shocked to see Alexandria standing on his porch.

"Alex?"

"Clinton, I'm probably the last person you expected to see, but I need to talk to you."

He stepped aside. "Come in." Clinton dropped his file folder on the sofa. "What's going on?"

"Why haven't you come back?"

"Sorry?"

"Your job is waiting for you. I feel like such a fool. I know what kind of man Randall Birmingham is, but I fell for his lies." Alex pushed her hair behind her ears. "It was never my intention to hurt you and Nina. But I did and I'm sorry."

Clinton folded his arms and peered curiously at Alex. "This is really big of you, Alex."

Alex dropped her head, then looked up at him quickly. "You're a good guy, Clinton. More than that, you make my sister happy. Clinton, I was wrong and I don't admit that often."

"Thank you, Alex. But I told Nina that I'd find another job because I don't want her to think that I'm with her because I work for her father," he said.

"We need you. Your work is stellar. We're getting a lot of press and a lot more clients because of your marketing. Nina knows that those things Randall said were lies."

"Made a promise to Nina. She means more to me than a job. I don't want there to be any questions as to why we're together."

Alex nodded. "I can respect that. But I know my sister and I know she doesn't think you two are together because you work for Daddy. Think about it before you make a decision. Unlike Randall, I don't want to let you go. But I can't make you stay if you really want to go. Just promise me you won't ever work for Randall's trifling ass ever again. You're better than that."

Clinton smiled. "You don't ever have to worry about me doing anything with Randall but bringing him down. I hate what he tried to do to your family and what he did to my reputation."

"Then come back where you belong. I know I didn't make things easy for you, but after talking to Nina and my dad, I know that I was wrong. Just think about it." Alex headed for the door, then turned to Clinton. "My father likes you as an employee and a boyfriend for his daughter. You're practically family."

Family, he thought once he was alone. *I would love to start a family with Nina.* That thought excited him and thrilled him at the same time. He'd never thought about marrying any other woman he'd ever been involved with and the thought of starting a family had never crossed his mind. Until Nina.

Before he made his decision, Clinton was going to make sure Birmingham would no longer be a problem for the Richardsons.

Nina sat at her computer, staring at the screen. While she should've been working on her story about the upcoming playoffs in North Carolina high school basketball, she couldn't get Clinton off her mind, the way he kissed her and how her body responded when he touched her. She crossed and uncrossed her legs as she throbbed.

"Okay, I have work to do," she said aloud, and began to type. Just as she was about to get into the flow of writing, her front door burst open and Yolanda walked in.

"Give me my key back," Nina said when she looked at her sister. "What are you doing here?"

"I had an epiphany," Yolanda said. "I'm moving my flagship store to Charlotte."

"What?"

Yolanda kissed her sister on the cheek and twirled around the room. "When I was here last week, I saw what a happening place this is. So, I figured with all of the professional people in Uptown, Risqué will be a hit here."

"Why do I feel as if there is more to this story?" Nina asked as she put the final touches on her article.

"There isn't. So don't go looking for something that isn't there. Besides, Richmond is dead for me. Business is on the decline. So many people are trying to swagger jack my style and I'm tired of looking at my books being in the red all the time. I'll be closer to my family and we can be roommates for about a month."

"I've been thinking," Nina said, turning around in her chair and facing her sister. "Maybe I should relocate."

"What?"

"I'm a freelance writer, I can write anywhere — why not Charleston?"

Yolanda smiled knowingly. "This is about Clinton, isn't it? You are so in love with him that it's sickening. He's good for you, though."

Nina nodded. "I know. Maybe I'm moving too fast, what if I go back to Charleston and things go south?"

Yolanda rolled her eyes. "Why do you always expect the worst? Never mind, don't answer that, let me rephrase the question — why do you keep expecting the worst from Clinton? Aside from that thing with the hotel when we all thought he was a liar and a thief, he's a stand-up guy."

Nina couldn't disagree with her sister, Clinton was a man of his word. He proved that he loved her and she didn't have anything to fear, except for the tiny voices that warned her that there was no happily ever after.

"After I file this story, I think I'm going to head to Charleston and talk to Clinton about our future," Nina said.

Yolanda waved her hands. "That's not what you want to do. You rush down there talking about the future, you might scare the man away. Find out what Clinton wants before you browbeat him with what you want."

"So you're saying don't open up to him? Clinton and I aren't like that. I can tell him anything and he doesn't shrink away like some others did."

"At least call him first," Yolanda said. "I guess you need a house sitter, huh?"

"Not really, but you can stay." Nina picked

up the phone to dial Clinton's number. Before she could dial, she got an incoming call from Alex.

"Alex, everything okay?"

"Maybe. Have you spoken to Clinton today?"

"I was just about to call him. What's going on?"

"I need you to talk some sense into him."

"What do you mean?" Nina furrowed her brows.

"Well," Alex said with a sigh. "He thinks that you don't want him to come back and work for us."

"I never said anything like that."

"We need him and you need to let him know that his employment has no bearing on your relationship."

Nina thought back to what Clinton had said when he showed up on her doorstep that day.

Damn that job. I can find another one, but I can't find another you.

"Alex, maybe you should talk to him," Nina said.

"I did and he said he didn't want you thinking that he was with you only to have job security. As much as I didn't like him when he first started working here, I can admit that we need him and he's a decent guy."

"Wow, talk about a one-eighty."

Alex gritted her teeth. "Call your boyfriend and tell him to get his butt back to work."

"I'll do one better, but I'm going to need your help," Nina said.

Clinton walked into Birmingham's office, not surprised to find his administrative assistant sitting in his lap. He cleared his throat, announcing his entrance. "Should've snapped a picture for the missus."

"Clinton, get the hell out of here," Birmingham said as he pushed the young blonde to the floor.

Folding his arms across his chest, he leaned against the wall. "Miss, you might want to head back to your desk so that you can grab the phones or whatever it is you get paid — on the books — to do."

The young woman straightened her skirt and blouse before dashing past Clinton.

"What do you want?" Birmingham asked angrily.

"To let you know that your plan didn't work. And, you're going to leave the Richardsons alone."

Birmingham flipped his hand at Clinton.

"I don't need you to get that bed-and-breakfast."

Clinton crossed over to Birmingham's desk and dropped the file of incriminating evidence on it. "But you need me to stay out of jail and divorce court. See, these documents are authentic and proof that you're a piece of shit."

Birmingham flipped through the file. "You son of a bitch. How-how did you get all of this?"

"It looks like I did learn something from you after all," Clinton said.

"As soon as you walk out the door, I'm shredding all of this," he said.

"I have copies and if anything happens to me or anyone I love, packages will be mailed to your stockholders, the Securities and Exchange Commission, and your wife. Do you really want to test me?"

Birmingham dropped his head. "What do you want from me?" he said in a tight whisper.

"Leave the Richardsons alone, stay away from me and my father, and drop dead!" Clinton stormed out of the office, feeling as if he could look happily toward a future with Nina.

When he got into his car, his cell phone rang. "Yeah?"

"Clinton, it's me," Nina said.

"Hey, darling, how are you?"

"Lonely. I want to see you. Do you realize that summer is almost over and then the holidays are right around the corner? I haven't looked forward to the holidays in years. It usually meant football games and being away from my family."

"Really?" he said.

"But this year is going to be different," she said. "Do you think you can meet me somewhere?"

"That's going to be pretty difficult with you being in Charlotte."

"Who said I was in Charlotte?"

A slow smile spread across Clinton's face. "Where are you?"

"In a secret spot at the B&B."

"I'll be there in fifteen minutes."

"Follow the notes in the lobby," she said before the line went dead.

Clinton sped to the bed-and-breakfast, making it there in ten minutes, because he was excited to see what Nina had in store for him.

"Hi, Clinton," the desk clerk said when he walked in. She had a huge grin on her face.

"Hello, Elaine."

"I have something for you." She handed him a rose-scented envelope. Immediately he recognized Nina's handwriting.

"Thanks," he said, then ripped the letter open.

Come through the kitchen, pick up the wine, and follow the instructions.

Clinton headed for the kitchen, wondering if the staff would let him through. When he arrived, he found the entire staff was all smiles and the cook handed him a bottle of 1997 Pinot Gris with a note taped to the front.

"Here you go, Clinton," the stout man said with a huge grin on his face.

"Thanks," he replied. Clinton ripped the note open.

Walk out of the kitchen and follow the trail of lights past the pool. When you come to the door with the wreath it will be open. There's an ice bucket for the wine, drop it in there and walk into the sitting room. I'll be waiting.

The kitchen staff smiled at Clinton as he folded the note and tore out of the kitchen. Once he reached his destination, he could barely place the wine in the bucket because he was filled with such anticipation.

"Nina," he called out before he reached the sitting room.

She walked out into the front room in a form-fitting red dress. "I thought I said follow the instructions and this isn't the sitting room."

Clinton looked down at the stilettos she had on and couldn't wait to peel the dress off her and watch her walk around in nothing but those shoes. He closed the space between them and wrapped his arms around her. "I'm not good at doing what I'm told," he breathed against her ear.

Nina pushed against his chest. "Not so fast. I lured you here under false pretenses."

"What? And here I thought I was going to be seduced."

"You are as soon as you answer a question for me. Why haven't you come back to work?"

"What? Did your sister tell you —"

Nina placed her finger to his lips. "You loved your job, I know that. My father loved you and Alex grew to respect you. What we have has nothing to do with the fact that you work here. You got this job before you met me. You shouldn't give it up because of what we have."

"I don't want you to think that I'm using you to stay employed."

She shook her head. "That never crossed my mind. You told me what it meant for you to work here and how much you admired my father and this property."

"True, but . . ."

Nina folded her arms across her chest. "No buts. Clinton, you're being really silly if you allow that man's scheme to keep you unemployed. You're practically family."

"Am I?"

She pulled him closer to her. "Go back to work so Alex will stop blaming me. Or at least go back to work so that we can make love on top of your desk."

A slow grin spread across Clinton's face. "That's a hell of a reason to go back to work."

"Then it's settled?"

"Yes. I'll come back to work. But you're going to have to make it worth my while."

Nina released him and picked up the remote to the radio from the settee. Marvin Gaye's smooth voice filled the air, singing about needing sexual healing. She moved her hips like a professional dancer and put Clinton in a trance. Reaching out, she pulled at his waistband, urging him to dance with her. He fell into her sexy rhythm, then captured her mouth with his, placing a heated kiss on her. Her mouth was sweet and he devoured her tongue as she slipped it between his lips. A soft moan escaped her throat and Clinton felt as if he would burst through his fly as she fingered his zipper.

He lifted her from the floor and wrapped her legs around his waist.

"I want you so bad that it hurts," he moaned as they broke off their kiss.

"Then let me ease your pain. The bedroom is right behind you."

Clinton slowly walked forward, balancing Nina in his arms as he headed for the bed. The room was aglow with the light of several flickering candles. Rose-scented incense burned on a small table that held chocolate-covered strawberries and whipped cream.

As he gently laid her on the bed, he stared down at her — his eyes filled with love and a mixture of lust. "You're beautiful," he said. "Perfect."

She wiggled her forefinger at him. Clinton followed her silent command and joined her in the bed. He slipped his arms around her and unzipped her dress, then peeled it from her body, kissing every inch of skin he exposed.

Once she was completely naked, Clinton took the whipped cream and traced her hard nipples with the cream. "Now this is a dessert I can't wait to taste," he whispered before taking one of her nipples into his mouth and licking the sweetness away. Nina moaned as he continued sucking and kissing her breasts. She grabbed the back of his neck, encouraging him to kiss deeper, harder, and faster.

"Oh, Clinton."

He pulled back and looked into her eyes. "Do you know how much I love you?"

Nina nodded, unable to speak as she felt his erection pressing against her thighs. She wrapped her legs around his waist and pulled him against her. "Do you know how much I need you?" Nina moaned.

"Then aren't we the perfect pair," he said before kissing her lips.

As their bodies joined, Clinton was taken away by ecstasy. Nina felt so good, so right. Her body was his wonderland and every thrust, every motion she made drove him wild. He liked it when she took control, he loved it when she allowed him to control her.

Today, she was all about being in control as she shifted her body so that she was on top of him. Like a wild mustang, she rode him hard and fast. He gripped her hips and dove deeper into her lithe body, feeling as if he were floating on the warmest cloud. When she tightened herself around him, Clinton cried her name out so loudly that he was sure anyone within several miles heard him.

Nina gripped his shoulders as they climaxed. He wrapped his arms around her and held her against his chest. Neither of them spoke as they basked in the afterglow of their lovemaking. She kissed his neck gently as he stroked her back.

Moments later, the couple was up and eating the dinner that Nina had the kitchen prepare for them.

"How did you get everyone to assist you with this?" he asked as he took a bite of his steak.

"You're well liked and when I told everyone that we're a couple, they were happy to help."

Clinton smirked. "And this place?"

"Used to be storage area. But Daddy turned it into a honeymoon hideaway a few years back," she said. "He said he did it because newlyweds often forget that other people are around. This gave them a little privacy when they rented the honeymoon suite."

"Honeymoon hideaway?"

"And I think he made that decision after we were all grown because he never wanted any of us to get the idea to sneak a boy in here. And when I say any of us, I mean Yolanda."

Clinton smiled, thinking that he'd marry
Nina in the summer, winter, spring, or fall.

CHAPTER 21

The next morning, after Clinton and Nina had said good-bye and he'd returned home to change his clothes, he was back at the bed-and-breakfast, but this time in Sheldon Richardson's office.

"Good morning, Clinton," the older man said, then motioned for Clinton to sit. "I was just about to have my morning jolt, would you like a cup?"

"Yes, sir, that would be great."

Sheldon poured two cups of coffee, then walked over to his desk. "What can I do for you this morning?"

"It's like déjà vu. I'm here looking for a job," Clinton said with a smile as Sheldon offered him cream and sugar for his coffee.

"You don't have to ask for something that's already yours," Sheldon said. "That business with Randall was beyond low. Alex was easily fooled because she hardly trusts anyone whose last name isn't Richardson, and those checks made you look guilty. Then Clinton Senior came into my office and we talked man to man and father to father, and I knew that we'd come to our decision too hastily."

"You have to know that I would never do anything to hurt this company —"

"That's secondary since I know you and Nina are an item. It's my daughter who I don't want you to hurt. What my daughters don't realize is that I know everything. Nina has met some pretty rotten apples. I sense that you're different."

"I love Nina very much. She's like no other woman I've ever met," Clinton said, his lips curving into a smile.

Sheldon leaned back in his chair. "She's most like her mother, even though she didn't know her. Nina's very giving and caring. The way some men are these days, that's her blessing and her curse."

Clinton nodded, remembering how heartbroken Nina was when they'd initially met. "Nina is a breath of fresh air. She makes me want to be a better person."

Sheldon took a sip of his coffee. "All right. Well, welcome back. And Alexandria has taken the liberty of moving your things to your new office."

"New office?"

"One with windows and a little more space," he said with a laugh. "I love my daughter, but she was wrong for stuffing you in that glorified closet."

Clinton nodded. "Like you said, she didn't like me when I first arrived here."

"She didn't trust you. But you're practically family now." Sheldon rose to his feet. "Come on, let me show you to your office."

Clinton followed the older man down the hall, thinking about family. He needed to see his father and thank him for what he did for him. Maybe it was time for the two of them to finally become real father and son. Clinton Sr. stuck his neck out for him and that meant something.

"Here's your new office," Sheldon said.

Clinton glanced around the spacious office, which looked like Grand Central Station compared to his old one. He had a real oak desk, a burgundy leather chair, and a view of the Charleston Harbor. "This is nice," he said.

"I thought you'd like it," Alex said from the doorway.

"This is nice, but how did you know I was going take the job?"

"Nina assured me," Alex said with a sly smile. "Besides, I was ready to beg you if I had to. I'd like to think that I can do everything here, but you have a brain for marketing." She extended her hand to him. "I was really rude to you when you first got here and you didn't deserve that."

Clinton shook her hand, then enveloped her in a tight hug. "That means a lot coming from you, Alex," he said.

Nina arrived in Charlotte expecting to have her house to herself, but she was surprised to see Yolanda still there.

"You're not going home, are you?" she teasingly asked her sister.

Yolanda looked up from the files in her lap. "While you were out romancing Clinton, I was busy putting things in place to open my shop. I found a lovely space in what you all call Uptown Charlotte. I'm really excited about this."

Nina couldn't help but wonder why her sister wanted to come to Charlotte all of a sudden. But Nina knew not to press her too hard. When she was ready, she'd tell her all about it. Right now, all she could think about was Clinton. A slow smile spread across her face as she plopped down on the sofa.

"Lamar came by here," Yolanda said with a snort.

"What?" Nina's smile quickly turned to a

frown. "He was supposed to be through with me."

Yolanda closed her file. "I told him to take a flying leap. He said that he knows you want him and he will see you again."

"Whatever," Nina quipped. "Maybe if he paid this much attention to me when I thought we were dating things would have turned out different."

Yolanda gave her sister a piercing look. "Are you sure you're over him? This thing with you and Clinton happened real quick, so do you really think you've given yourself enough time to heal?"

"Yes, I'm over him. He tossed me aside like I was garbage. Had other women he was seeing when I thought I was the only one and I'm supposed to give a shit?"

"Good to hear because you have a good thing with Clinton and I don't want to see you ruin that."

Nina rolled her eyes. "See me ruin it?"

"Don't get mad, because I say this with love, but you do make some bad decisions when it comes to the heart. You make up scenarios in your head, come up with crazy schemes, and end up alone."

Nina rose to her feet and glared at her sister. "I know what I'm doing and I know I love Clinton."

"And several months ago, you knew you loved Lamar," Yolanda said matter-of-factly. "Nina, be sure you know what you're doing and who you want. When you first met Clinton you just wanted to use him to make Lamar jealous."

"And you said it was a bad idea," Nina exclaimed. "Clinton showed me how I should be loved. I seriously don't want anything to do with Lamar."

"Just make sure you've truly closed yourself off to him. Because if he's bold enough to just pop up, he's not going to go away if you don't make it clear that he's not welcome." Yolanda threw up two fingers and walked out of the room.

Nina watched Yolanda as she walked away and thought about what she'd said about Lamar. She did need to make it clear that he didn't have a chance in hell to be in her life or her heart again. Reaching for her cell phone, she dialed Lamar's number. As the phone rang, Nina wondered if she was making a mistake reaching out to him. But she needed to tell him to stay away from her and stop thinking he had a chance. Clinton had her heart and there was nothing he could do to change it.

"Yeah," Lamar said when he answered the phone.

"What do you want?"

"Nina?"

"My sister said you came by my place and I need you to stop doing that. Besides, last I heard, you were through with me."

"Such hostility. Does it have to be this way?" he asked. "I'd like to think we can be friends."

"We can't and you can't keep thinking you have a chance. I love Clinton and that's the man I'm going to be with. A man without a harem."

"Had I told you I was seeing other women, would you have given me a chance?"

"You robbed me of that choice. I'm not going to argue with you, I'm not going to try and understand why you treated me the way you did. We're over. If I see you at a press conference, I'll be professional."

"That's how we're doing this? I mean, you were seeing that guy and —"

"Done explaining myself to you. Stay the fuck out of my life." Nina ended the call and she wasn't feeling as if she'd lost something. She felt at peace.

Yolanda seemed to appear out of nowhere and eyed her sister suspiciously. "Who taught you how to talk like that?"

Nina tossed a pillow at her sister. "Look in the mirror."

Yolanda rolled her eyes. "Well, let me take you to dinner, Mini Me."

Nina nodded. "As long as you're paying."

Sitting in his new office, Clinton couldn't keep from smiling. Everything was going right in his life — dream job and the woman of his dreams. He couldn't wait to see Nina and feel her arms wrapped around him. But he couldn't take off when he'd just gotten his job back.

"Knock, knock," Alex said at his doorway. "Busy?"

"I was about to call it a day. What's going on?"

Alex placed a notice on his desk. "It's a quick turnaround, but there's a marketing conference in Charlotte in a couple of days and I figured you'd like to go."

"I'd love to go," Clinton said, realizing he could work and play.

Alex smiled as if she knew why he was so excited to attend. "Oh, your holiday promotion is a hit. This is the first time we're booked for Thanksgiving and Christmas."

Clinton nodded. "That's great. With some more promotions like this, the bed-and-breakfast is going to have its best year ever. Do you think we can get your father to play Santa?"

Alex sat on the arm of the leather chair across from Clinton's desk. "I'm sure he will. He used to do it when Nina was a little girl. The kids are sure to get a kick out of it."

"And you can be an elf," Clinton joked.

"That's not happening. Are you going to let Nina know you're coming to town?"

Leaning back in his chair, he replied, "I think I'll surprise her. Alex, let me ask you a question."

"Shoot."

"Do you think Nina's ready to settle down and get married?"

Alex's jaw dropped. "You're considering proposing?"

"I love her more than I thought I could ever love anyone." His eyes glistened with joy.

"Don't take this the wrong way. But do you think this might be a bit of a rush? I want you and Nina to be certain."

Clinton shrugged. "It feels right."

"Then go for it," Alex said as she rose to her feet. "Just make sure you do right by her or you're going to have to deal with me."

Clinton saluted Alex and grinned. She said go for it and that's just what he was going to do. But before he could ask Nina to be his wife, he was going to have to talk to his father. The Jefferson men needed to make peace with each other.

After shutting down his computer and packing his briefcase, Clinton headed for his father's North Charleston home. The last time they'd talked, Clinton had no idea that his father would be the one to make his dreams come true. The least he could do was try and make an effort to build on what was going on between them.

Besides, if he and Nina were going to start a family together, then he was going to have to repair the fractured one he belonged to.

Clinton arrived at his childhood home and fought all of the bad memories that were a part of the place. As he placed his car in park, he decided that it was time to make new ones. Slowly he walked to the front door and knocked softly. Seconds ticked by before Clinton Sr. opened the door.

"Son," he said.

"Dad."

"Well, don't just stand out there. Come in."

Clinton followed his father inside. The house was in mild disarray with newspapers strewn across the floor and coffee table. "What's all this?"

"Been looking for a job," he said before settling into his leather recliner.

"Why?" Clinton took a seat on the sofa next to the recliner.

"Money's tight now that Birmingham isn't helping me out anymore," Clinton Sr. said. "Not that I want his tainted support."

"What do you need, I'll take care of it for you."

Clinton Sr. looked at his son, his eyes glassy with tears. "Why would you do that? I've never been much of a father to you and I see that. Long time ago, I had dreams and then reality set in. I wasn't going to be a football star and when I had a son, I was going to make sure he was going to be one. You have my name, but you got your smarts from your mama. I resented the fact that you wanted to keep your nose in a book.

"You didn't let me pin my dreams on you. It made me so mad when I realized that things weren't going to work out the way that I figured they always would. How can I expect you to help me now?"

"Because you're my father and no matter what happened in the past, we have to move on," Clinton said. "When you stood up to the Richardsons for me, I knew that things were changing. Birmingham tried to do a number on me and you could've ignored it."

"May not seem like it, but I know what's

right and what's wrong. Birmingham was trying to make you look like a liar and a cheat. That's never been our style. Sheldon Richardson is a good man and I couldn't have him thinking that you were trying to cheat him."

Clinton rose to his feet and closed the space between him and his father. "I want to ask you something. How did you know you wanted to spend the rest of your life with Mom?"

The older man smiled as if a pleasant thought crossed his mind. "The first time I kissed your mother, I knew I'd never be happy with anyone else."

Clinton couldn't help but think about the affairs his father had over the years and the arguments that he'd heard his parents have.

"But," Clinton Sr. said as if he'd read his son's mind. "I ruined the love of my life when my dreams fell through. In the beginning, though, your mother and I had the greatest relationship. She made my soul sing like no other woman ever has. I regret how I treated her in the last years of our marriage. I wanted my dreams to come true and when they didn't, I blamed her. But your mother never walked away. That's why I know she's an angel I never deserved. If you find a woman like that, you hold on to her, but don't make the same mistakes that I did."

Clinton nodded. "That's just how she makes me feel."

"The Richardson girl?"

He nodded. "I love her."

"Then hold on to her and don't let her go for nothing," Clinton Sr. said.

CHAPTER 22

Nina and Yolanda ate sushi and drank a lot of sake to celebrate. After the third carafe of the potent drink, Nina looked at her sister. "What are we celebrating?"

"You being an adult and making a boss chick move." Yolanda downed her sake. "Wait, that's me. I guess we're celebrating you not sabotaging yourself."

Nina downed her own sake. "And telling Lamar where to go and how to get there."

Yolanda pointed her finger at her sister. "That part." The women giggled and Nina ordered another platter of California rolls and thanked God that she and Yolanda had decided to use a ride share service tonight.

"So," Yolanda said as she sipped some water. "Do you see yourself with Clinton for now or forever?"

Nina furrowed her eyebrows. "What kind of question is that?"

"One that you need to answer. I believe

Clinton is a good man and the right one for you, but I want to make sure you're ready and not just —"

"Pause. This is not a conversation to have while we're drunk. But I do love Clinton and I . . . Let me have some coffee before we go there."

Yolanda sighed. "Don't listen to me. Honestly, I've never seen you happier and I know when you and Clinton do this always and forever thing, I'm going to lose my road dog." She patted Nina on her shoulder. "But it'll be worth it."

"Aww, you're going to miss me and I haven't even gotten married yet. Is that why you're camping out in my house?"

Yolanda turned away from her sister and took the final swig of sake. "Yeah, let's go with that."

Nina raised her right eyebrow. "What's going on, for real, Yo-Yo?"

Yolanda shook her head as she reached for the last California roll and stuffed it in her mouth. Nina propped her chin up on her fist. "Stuffing your face isn't going to stop my questions. I do this for a living."

Yolanda chewed slowly and pointed a chopstick at her sister. "But I'm older than you and if I don't want to share, then I don't have to. And we need more sake."

"You're cut off and if you don't tell me, I guess you can talk to Daddy." Nina pulled out her phone and waved it in Yolanda's face. "Last chance."

"I'm out of here and if you call Daddy, I'm going to give you the ass whooping you missed as a child!" She stormed out of the restaurant.

Now Nina was sure something serious was going on. After paying the bill, Nina headed out to look for her sister. She went to the fashion boutique across the street, hoping that Yolanda was inside scoping out the competition. She wasn't. Nina called her and it went to voice mail.

Then she sent her a text: Stop acting like a baby. Where are you?

I'm on the train. See you soon. We'll talk later. K?

Okay, I guess.

Nina decided to walk home and think about what was really going on with Yolanda. Halfway into her walk, she decided to call Clinton. When his voice mail picked up, she was disappointed because she needed to hear his voice.

When she arrived home, she kicked her

shoes off and headed to the kitchen for a bottle of water. Heading for her bedroom, Nina grabbed the latest copy of *Sports Illustrated* from the coffee table. Then there was a knock at the front door. "Yolanda?" she called out. She was greeted by silence. Nina stalked to the front door, half expecting to see her sister standing there. But to her surprise, it was Clinton. Yanking the door open, Nina leapt into his arms and showered kisses on him.

Once he was able to catch his breath, Clinton said, "I should do this more often."

"What are you doing here?"

"There's a marketing conference that Alex signed me up for. She figured that I'd want to come and surprise you. Everything all right with Yolanda?"

Nina sighed and told him about the scene at the sushi bar. "She said she's riding the train and we'll talk later, but I don't like this." She led Clinton over to the sofa. He took her hands into his as they sat down.

"What's going on?"

"Your guess is as good as mine. She hasn't told me anything." Nina looked into his eyes and felt his concern. She couldn't love him more if she tried. "I'm glad you're here."

He leaned in and kissed her cheek. "So am I."

318

"Are you hungry? I can order takeout for you." She grinned.

He pulled Nina against his body, "Actually, I do want something to eat." Rubbing his lips against her neck, he said, "And what I want isn't on any menu at any restaurant."

Turning her head, Nina brought her lips on top of Clinton's. He slipped his hands underneath her blouse, touching her as if he were doing it for the first time. "You feel so good," he said when their lips parted.

Nina ran her tongue over her lips, capturing Clinton's lingering taste. "You feel even better."

"My conference doesn't start until tomorrow. So, you got me all night and I plan to make the most of it." Slowly he unbuttoned her top and slid it from her shoulders. Each inch of flesh he exposed, he kissed. When he unsnapped her bra and her breasts spilled forward, Clinton took each one in his mouth, circling her nipples with his tongue until her knees began to quiver. With one hand, Clinton unsnapped her pants and pushed them down. With the other, he slipped between her thighs, feeling the wetness that had pooled there.

"Missed me?" he whispered.

"Yes," she moaned breathlessly as his finger entered her heated core.

Pressing against her, Clinton made sure she *felt* how much he'd missed her. "I've been thinking about this all day. And this sofa is too small for me to do everything I want to do to you."

"Well, there is a big bed upstairs waiting for us."

Clinton lifted her from the sofa and they headed up to her room. Laying her on the bed, he leaned in to her and kissed her on the forehead.

"You're beautiful," he said as he stepped out of his pants.

Nina nearly ripped her clothes off, anticipating the pleasure that he was about to deliver. "I love you," she said, unabashedly and without worry that he would cut and run.

"I love you, too," Clinton replied as he joined her on the bed. For a moment, they lay in each other's arms, just touching and exploring the other's body as if it were the first time they were about to make love. He traveled her curves with his finger, making every nerve in her body tingle. Love and desire rippled through her body.

Nina sought out Clinton's lips, reveling in the sweetness of his mouth as he kissed her with deliberate precision. Nina melted against him as he pressed his flesh against hers. It felt as if they were melding their bodies together. She wrapped her legs around his waist and rolled over so that she was on top of him. Clinton palmed her breasts, teasing her nipples with his thumbs as she slid her hands down the center of his chest heading for his throbbing member, stroking him softly and slowly until he moaned with pleasure.

"I need you, inside me." Her wanton need was on full display.

Clinton was happy to oblige her request as she spread her thighs apart and he felt the warmness from her core. He was harder than a stone as she mounted his erection and enveloped him in her wetness. Gripping her hips as she rocked back and forth, Clinton murmured her name with his lips pressed against her ear. "You feel so good."

With her eyes closed and head thrown back, Nina replied, "You feel better."

Sliding his hands up and down the small of her back as she rode him deep and fast, Clinton was brought nearly to climax when she sped up her rhythm and tightened herself around him. He fell in sync with her, matching her passion thrust for thrust. Nina gripped his shoulders and he took her breasts into his mouth, sucking and kissing her hardened nipples until Nina cried out fervently.

Clinton flipped Nina over, pinning her against the bed, and rained kisses across her neck and down her chest and they ground their bodies against each other. Sweat covered their bodies and their animalistic cries filled the air as they reached their sexual peak at the same time. Nina never felt so connected to another person, so wanted, needed, and loved. She clung to Clinton and decided at that moment that she never wanted to let him go.

He kissed her cheek and when he looked at her, Nina could see the love in his eyes and nearly burst into tears. Was she really getting her happy ending?

Clinton wiped a stray tear from her eye with the pad of his thumb. "What's with the waterworks?"

"I'm just so happy," she said as she took his hand and kissed it. "Can this all be real?"

"If that didn't feel real, then I really must be doing something wrong," Clinton joked.

"Clinton, what I'm talking about is what I feel inside. I didn't think I could love you as much as I do and to know that you love me, too."

He silenced her with a soul-searing kiss that sent a shiver down her spine. When they broke off the kiss, Clinton stared longingly into Nina's eyes. "A wise man told me that when you find a love like this, you don't let it go," he said. "And I don't plan on letting you go, ever. Marry me."

She pressed her hand against Clinton's chest and propped up on her elbow. "What?"

"If I had a hundred more years on this planet, I'd never find a woman who thrills me like you do, who sends chills down my spine just by saying my name." He kissed her again. "Say yes."

"I-I don't know," she whispered, pushing out of his embrace. "This is all happening so fast and —"

"What's stopping us?"

"Me," she said, swinging her legs over the side of the bed. "I just don't know if I'm ready for marriage and I don't want to disappoint you."

"Disappoint me? There's no way you could do that. We love each other and this seems like that next logical step. I'm not going to let you out of my life."

Nina stood up and looked at him. "Are you sure this is what you want?"

Clinton reached into his discarded pants and pulled out his mother's engagement ring. "What do you think?"

Nina wiped the tears from her eyes and

took note of the marquise cut diamond and ruby ring. "This is too much."

He took her hand in his and slipped the ring on her finger. To their surprise, it fit perfectly.

"This is fate. This was mother's ring and she was the most important woman in my life. Now, you are. So, are you going to marry me or what?"

Tears of happiness streamed down her face. "Yes," she cried. "Yes, I'll marry you."

Clinton grabbed Nina around the waist and lifted her into the air. "I love you," he said as he captured her lips and planted a passionate kiss on her. They fell back on the bed and celebrated their engagement all over again.

The next morning, Nina woke up thinking the night before had been a dream. But the sparkling ring on her finger told her otherwise. Clinton was in the shower getting ready for the conference and she dipped into the kitchen, finding her sister standing at the coffee maker.

"All I want to know is what was that man doing to you all night long?" Yolanda asked.

"When did you get in? Where did you go?" Nina asked as she pulled two coffee mugs from the cabinet.

"I just explored the city. But it seems as if you were otherwise occupied anyway. I've never heard such noise. I thought for sure someone would call the police." Yolanda filled the two mugs. "I had no idea you were such a freak."

"Shut up." Nina popped her sister on the arm.

Yolanda grabbed Nina's left hand. "What in the — Is this an engagement ring?" Yolanda shrieked so loudly that Clinton burst into the kitchen shirtless and his face full of shaving cream.

"What happened?" he asked, looking from Nina to Yolanda.

Yolanda rushed over to Clinton and hugged him tightly. "Welcome to the crazy Richardson family. I guess that's what all the noise was for last night," she said.

Clinton blushed as he let her go. "Well, I'm sorry if we kept you up last night." Glancing over at the stove, Clinton furrowed his brows. "Who's cooking?"

"Not Nina," Yolanda said as she returned to the stove. "But she did get the coffee mugs."

Nina poked her tongue out at her sister as Clinton headed back into the bathroom.

"See," Yolanda whispered, "aren't you glad you got that asshole Lamar out of your life?"

Looking down at her ring, Nina couldn't have been happier with that decision. "Yes, I am. But we still need to talk about what's going on with you."

"After we eat, okay?"

Nina nodded as she sipped her coffee.

Moments later, the trio was sitting down to a breakfast of grits, eggs, toast, and turkey bacon. Yolanda, unlike her little sister, was handy in the kitchen.

"So," Yolanda began in between bites. "Are you guys going to live in Charleston? You know Alex isn't going to let you go again. When's the wedding going to be? And you know what, I'm picking the gown."

"Slow down, Yo-Yo," Nina said. "We just made it official last night. We're going to need time to talk about all of that."

Clinton nodded in agreement.

"Well," Yolanda said. "You don't have to worry about selling this place if you decide to move to Charleston."

Nina dropped her fork on the side of her plate. "You're really moving, aren't you?"

She nodded. "Clinton, you can take her to Charleston and everything will be fine."

Nina eyed her sister suspiciously. "What are you running from?"

Clinton took his plate to the sink. "I'll see you all later," he said as he kissed Nina on the cheek and headed for the door.

Once Clinton was gone, Nina grabbed Yolanda's hand. "What's really going on?" she asked.

Yolanda smiled weakly. "I need to get away from Richmond because I'm in over my head."

"With your business?"

She shook her head and walked over to the coffee maker. "A few weeks ago, I witnessed something outside of my store."

"What?" Nina asked.

"A murder. I didn't want to tell anyone about it because I didn't want to put you all in danger. I want a fresh start without all the drama. I came to Charlotte instead of going home because I figured these people who committed this crime could find me." Yolanda's hands shook and sloshed coffee over the counter and floor.

Nina walked over to Yolanda and wrapped her arms around her. "You can't cut and run. You have to go to the police and tell them what you saw."

Yolanda faced her sister and shook her head. "These people are dangerous and I'm not getting involved. The store's been closed and I've given up the space in Richmond. Some movers have boxed my merchandise up and they're shipping it here. The scary thing is, a bullet whizzed right by me and hit the picture I had of all of us on the wall. That bastard who did the shooting said if I talked to anyone, he'd make sure he killed me and everyone that I loved."

"Yo-Yo, why didn't you tell me?"

She shrugged her shoulders. "What could you do? Tell Daddy? Tell Alex? No, I'm not getting you all involved in this. It's all over now."

Nina kissed her sister's cheek. "I hope you're right." Nina thought about her sister being threatened by some thug, which put a cold chill on what should've been a happy day.

CHAPTER 23

Twisting in his seat, Clinton struggled to focus on the speaker at the marketing conference. His mind was back in Nina's town house, right where his future wife was waiting. He'd heard of whirlwind romances, but never did he believe he'd be a part of one. But if this was how it felt, then he was all for it.

Following the morning session, Clinton decided to take a walk around uptown taking advantage of the unseasonably warm fall day. Strolling through the streets of uptown, he decided that there was way too much action going on for his tastes. He couldn't count the number of bankers he'd passed who'd been screaming into cell phones, bicycle messengers who dashed in and out of traffic not caring if they knocked someone over, and the out-of-town visitors who held up traffic as they drove down the congested streets at a snail's pace. All of it made Clinton long to whisk Nina away to his Summerville home and lock the door. Charlotte, he surmised, was a great place to visit, but he hoped that Nina still had a longing for the quiet life of the South Carolina countryside.

"Hey," a voice said, breaking into his thoughts.

Clinton looked up and saw Lamar standing in front of him.

"You're Nina's friend, right? Thought I recognized you."

"I'm her fiancé."

The smug smile on Lamar's face quickly curled into a scowl. "Fiancé? Damn, that girl moves quick. I was just by her place."

Clinton hid his disappointment. "What?"

"Guess that's why she stood me up for dinner. She's settling?"

He's lying, Clinton thought.

"Oh well." Lamar shrugged. "I wish you nothing but happiness with your new *fiancée*. With you being in Charleston and Nina here, that's going to mean a lot of lonely nights, but don't worry, I'll keep your side of the bed nice and warm. 'Cause you know our girl has needs."

Anger bubbled in Clinton like an exploding volcano. Without warning, he coldcocked Lamar, nearly knocking him off his feet.

"You had your chance with Nina and like a fool you gave her up!" Clinton bellowed, not giving a damn about the people stopping to look at them. He wanted to hit him again, but restrained himself. "Stay away from her."

Lamar leapt to his feet and lunged at Clinton, who dodged his punch. "Don't get mad at me because you can't control your bitch," he huffed.

Clinton grabbed Lamar by his collar and pushed him against the side of a building. "You bastard. You're not even worth my time." Clinton pushed him in the chest and turned to walk away.

Lamar smiled sardonically. "You sure Nina feels the same way?"

Lamar's cold laughter sent waves of anger down Clinton's spine. Was Lamar telling the truth and did he need to worry?

Turning around and glaring at him, Clinton resisted the urge to punch Lamar in his smug face again. Beating Lamar down wouldn't get him the answers he needed.

Taking off down the street, Clinton had to find out if anything Lamar said had any truth to it. He headed for his car, which was parked in a garage on College Street.

As he drove to Nina's, all he could think about was why would she accept his marriage proposal if she was still seeing a clown who had no respect for her?

Clinton screeched into the parking lot of Nina's building, catching her as she was walking toward her car. He threw the car in park, hopped out, and ran over to her.

"Clinton, hey," she said with a smile on her lips.

He grabbed her arm. "We need to talk."

She furrowed her brows as she stared incredulously at him. "You're hurting my arm. What the hell is wrong with you?"

Clinton released her arm and shook his head. "Why, Nina?"

"Why what?"

Running his hand over his face, he groaned. "Are you still seeing him? Lamar made sure I knew he was at your house."

Her face blanched. "It's not like that. He came over, but —"

Clinton shook his head and squeezed his eyes shut. "What do you need to do to get over him? Sleep with him? Have some more time with him to make sure I'm the right man for you? Were you going to keep my engagement ring on or take it off before you hopped into bed with him?"

Nina struck his cheek as hard as she

could. "How dare you? If you have such a low opinion of me, then why do you want to marry me?" She twisted the ring off her finger.

"Maybe I made a mistake," he snapped.

Nina pressed the ring in his hand. "Then here's your chance to correct it."

Clinton closed his fingers around the ring and without another word, he got into his car. He didn't even turn around to see the tears falling from Nina's eyes.

Nina wasn't sure how long she'd been sitting in her car until her cell phone rang.

Wiping fat tears from her eyes, she answered it. "Hello?"

"Nina, are you going to Independence? The coach is waiting for you, but he said he won't wait much longer," her editor said.

"I'm sorry, I'm on my way."

Since Independence High School had won another state championship despite losing in the regular season, she was scheduled to have a sit-down interview with the coach about his program, but her mind wasn't on football. She was devastated by Clinton's rejection. All because of something Lamar had said. He wouldn't even listen to her explanation.

If he questions how I feel about him, then

this is for the best, she thought as she started her car and tore out of the parking lot. Nina desperately tried not to cry as she headed for the interstate, but her tears won out and blurred her vision as she turned onto I-277. A blaring horn was the last thing she heard before everything went black.

Red lights and sirens swirled around Nina's mangled car. The eighteen-wheeler she'd pulled out in front of never had a chance to stop as her car swerved in front of him. The Charlotte Fire Department called in the Jaws of Life to cut Nina from the car.

"She's not breathing," a fireman said as he pulled her from the car and placed her on a stabilizing board.

Emergency medical technicians took over the scene trying to stabilize Nina. Her vital signs were low and her heart rate was dropping by the second. A police officer pulled Nina's purse from the car, searching for her identity and next of kin. Everyone on the scene or anyone who saw the crumpled red Mustang felt as if she wasn't going to make it.

"Her name's Nina Richardson," the officer told the EMT.

The young blond nodded and turned to her. "Nina, Nina, can you hear me?"

What happened? Nina said silently. *What's going on? Clinton, I'm so sorry. You have to know I don't love Lamar, I love you. Only you.*

A tear spilled from her eye and rolled down her cheek.

The EMT turned to his partner. "We're losing her, fast."

They loaded Nina into the rescue squad and sped to Atrium Health Center.

Yolanda shook hands with the Realtor as she took the keys to her new retail space.

"Thank you so —" The chiming of her cell phone interrupted their conversation. "Hello? Alex, slow down, I can't understand you . . . Nina? Accident? Yes, yes, I'm still in Charlotte, I'll find my way there. I'll be careful. See you and Daddy soon."

Without saying another word to the Realtor, she dashed out of the building. *Oh God,* she thought, *please don't let this have anything to do with me.*

Yolanda, who had been about three miles from the same interstate where Nina had crashed, found her way to the hospital. Rushing into the emergency room, she banged on the nurses' desk.

"Hello, somebody!"

A haggard-looking nurse appeared at the desk and frowned at Yolanda. "Yes?" she

335

said with a sigh.

"My sister was in a car accident and was brought here. Her name is Nina Richardson."

The woman punched a few buttons on the computer. "She's here and in surgery. I can have a doctor speak with you." She reached underneath her desk and pulled out Nina's belongings. "These were in the car with her."

Yolanda ripped the plastic bag open and searched for her sister's cell phone. She had to call Clinton and let him know what was going on.

Time froze for Clinton as he sat in his car looking at the engagement ring he'd given Nina less than twenty-four hours ago. He couldn't believe the things he'd said to her. Maybe it was the ghost of Ayesha reappearing in his mind and heart. Still, he wasn't going to play second fiddle in her life if she had any question about being with Lamar.

When his cell phone rang, he almost didn't hear it because he was so deep in thought. "Yeah?" he rumbled into the phone.

"Clinton, it's Yolanda."

"Listen, I know you and your family are close, but this is really none of your business, it's between me and Nina," he snapped.

"What are you talking about?" she questioned.

"Why are you calling me?"

"I don't know what's going on with you and Nina, but she was in a serious car accident. She's in surgery at Atrium Health Center. You really need to get here."

Clinton's heart nearly stopped beating. Accident. Surgery. What if she didn't pull through and the last words they exchanged were angry ones? Dropping his phone, Clinton started for the hospital, though he had no idea where he was going.

As he ripped through the uptown traffic, he spotted a blue hospital sign that led him directly to Atrium Health Center. Parking in the emergency room parking lot, he ran into the waiting area and sought out Yolanda. He found her standing next to the nurses' station with her hand on her hip and a scowl on her face.

"I've been here for an hour, what in the hell is going on with my sister!" Yolanda screamed at the nurse. The woman, who looked more tired and agitated than the law should've allowed, threw Yolanda a cold look.

"When the doctors have some informa-

337

tion, they will tell you. Standing here and screaming at me isn't going to do you or your sister any good."

Clinton approached the women, fearing that they would come to blows without intervention. "Ma'am, we just need to know how Nina Richardson is doing, we're not from here and this is very stressful," Clinton said calmly.

The woman gave him a terse smile. "I understand that and everyone in here is worried about a loved one. Give me a second and I'll check to see if she's out of surgery."

Clinton thanked the woman, then drew Yolanda into his arms. "Everything is going to work out fine," he whispered.

"This is all my fault."

"Why?"

Yolanda shook her head and blinked away the hot tears forming behind her eyelids. "They've found me, I know it. Now Nina's fighting for her life."

Guilt jabbed Clinton in the heart. He blamed himself for Nina's accident. She was probably upset after their argument and shouldn't have been driving. Why didn't he hear her out instead of accusing her of sleeping with Lamar?

"Nina and I had an argument before she

left, it was bad and I know how she gets," Clinton revealed. "If anyone is to blame, it's me."

Yolanda looked up at Clinton, her eyes watery. "You don't understand," she began.

"Is the Richardson family in here?" a doctor asked.

"Yes, here," Clinton spoke up.

The doctor walked over to Clinton and Yolanda. "I'm Dr. Max Terry, Nina's surgeon. She suffered some serious injuries in the wreck because the truck struck on the driver's side of the car."

"How is she?" Yolanda asked nervously.

"It looks as though the worst is over, she had several broken ribs and a punctured lung. We feared her internal injuries were more significant, but after her surgery, we discovered they weren't. However, her left arm is broken in three places and there may be some eye injury because of the shattered glass that struck her face. Then there's the possibility of head trauma."

"But she's going to pull through?" Clinton asked.

The doctor sighed. "The first forty-eight hours are critical. Her condition is very grave at this time. I don't want to give you false hope, because at any moment she could slip away."

Yolanda's knees buckled at the doctor's admission and Clinton struggled to keep her upright.

"Where is she now?" Clinton asked.

"In the intensive care unit. Give us a few more hours to see how she reacts to the medication we've given her before you go in to see her."

"I need to see my sister now, even if it's through glass," Yolanda said, her voice forceful and sad at the same time.

The doctor nodded and motioned for her and Clinton to follow him.

With each step, Clinton felt cold dread creep up his back. If Nina died he knew he'd never love again and never forgive himself for the rude things he'd said to her just moments before her accident. How would he ever be able to find another woman who had the wit, the sparkle, and the heart that Nina had.

Has! Clinton corrected. *Nina's going to pull through this and this ring is going back on her finger where it belongs.*

CHAPTER 24

Nina felt as if she was having an out-of-body experience. She could've sworn she was talking and she was telling the doctors and nurses who kept poking and prodding her to find her family. They weren't listening, though. She kept hearing things like her vital signs weren't looking good and her lung had collapsed again. Pain ripped through her body every time she took a breath.

What happened to me? she wondered. *The last thing I remember is Clinton telling me that it was over. Why, why did he do that? Lamar. I don't have time to deal with this. I'm so tired.*

"Doctor, Doctor, she's flatlining," a nurse screamed frantically. "We need a crash cart, stat!"

A team of nurses and doctors rushed to Nina's side at the same time that Clinton and Yolanda appeared at the window outside of the ICU.

341

"Clear," the nurse yelled as the doctor placed the paddles on Nina's chest. Seconds ticked away before the doctor charged the paddles and placed them to Nina's chest again.

"We have a rhythm," the doctor said.

I just want to sleep, Nina thought. *I want to put all of this behind me.*

Then she heard Yolanda's wailing. "No! Nina."

Her eyes fluttered open and she whispered her sister's name.

"Miss Richardson," the doctor said. "Do you know where you are?"

She nodded.

"We're going to place you on a respirator until we know you can breathe on your own. Your sister is here and your fiancé."

She shook her head. *I don't have a fiancé, he dumped me.*

"They're really concerned about you and you're going to have to fight to recover. You're a loved woman and they need you to pull through this," he said.

"Clinton," Nina murmured.

The doctor motioned for Clinton to enter the room. Slowly he walked in and stood by Nina's bedside. She cast her weak eyes up at him.

"Make it brief," the doctor cautioned.

Clinton nodded and took Nina's hand in his. "I'm so sorry," he whispered. "Please come back to me. Nothing that happened before this moment matters. I want to marry you and I want to spend the rest of my life with you. But I need you to fight and come back to me and Yolanda and even Alex. Your dad, Alex, and Robin are on their way here right now. Nina, we can't lose you."

Do you mean it? Do you really want to marry me or are you saying it because I'm lying here in this hospital bed? How could you think I was untrue to you because of something that Lamar said?

When she opened her mouth, nothing came out.

"Shh, don't try to speak," he said. "I was wrong. Just know that, I was wrong and I will never forgive myself if . . ." Tears spilled from his eyes as he looked down at her. Nina mustered as much strength as she could to squeeze his hand.

I love you so much. And it's okay, because I'm going to fight to come back to you and my family. It was my fault. I shouldn't have tried to rush to the interview and I shouldn't have let you walk away from me when you and I had unfinished business.

"Nina, keep fighting, baby," Clinton said.

The doctor tapped Clinton on the shoulder. "You're going to have to leave now."

Leaning in to kiss Nina's scarred face, he muttered he loved her, then left the room.

Next, the doctor allowed Yolanda to visit with her sister. She walked into the room with bloodshot eyes and tear-stained cheeks. "Oh my God," she moaned as she looked at Nina.

Yolanda, please don't fall apart right now.

"Nina, I hope this wasn't because of me. You'd better not die on me."

This wasn't about whatever you're running from. I wish you'd go to the police and stop trying to hide.

Yolanda held Nina's hand and cried silently. "Right now, I wish I had Alex's strength. Maybe when she walks in this room she'll say the right words to snap you back to health or maybe I'll wake up and this will be just a nightmare."

Yolanda walked the length of the bed, eyeing all of the machines and tubes hooked up to Nina.

"I hate hospitals. But this isn't going to be like the last time, God can't be that cruel. You're coming home and everyone is going to take care of you. I can see Alex right now forcing you to go to bed at eight o'clock." She smiled at Nina, then kissed her forehead gently. "Come back, Sis. I can't terrorize Alex alone."

"Ma'am, she needs her rest now," the doctor said to Yolanda.

Wiping her eyes, she nodded. "I'm going to be outside her door all night," Yolanda informed the doctor.

"I know you want to be here for her, but she's going to need you to keep your strength up as well."

"I'm not leaving my sister in this hospital alone."

From the doorway, Clinton said, "She won't be alone because I'm going to be here with her."

No one noticed the smile on Nina's spilt lips.

When Clinton and Yolanda returned to the ICU waiting room, Sheldon, Alex, and Robin were huddled in a corner. Robin was the spitting image of her father only more feminine. She had long brown hair that hung down on her shoulders and a heart-shaped face that was filled with sadness and fear as she clutched her father's arm. Alex pointed to Clinton and Yolanda and everyone turned to them.

Sheldon spoke first. "How is she?"

"Very weak, Daddy," Yolanda said as she

flung herself into Sheldon's arms.

"Oh my God," Robin moaned. "Why is this happening?"

Clinton closed his eyes because the answer to that would have Nina's entire family ready to put him in a hospital bed.

Alex wrapped her arms around her sister. "It was a horrible accident. That damned Mustang. She had to have it and look what happened."

"It wasn't the car," Yolanda said. "And don't come in here with your negativity."

"Girls," Sheldon said in a controlled voice. "Nina doesn't need this. We're here to rally around her and pray." He turned to Clinton. "How are you holding up?"

Unable to speak, he just shook his head. Silently the two men exchanged meaningful looks that spoke what they couldn't verbalize.

Alex, Robin, and Yolanda looked as if they would burst into tears at any moment. Alex grabbed Yolanda's hand. "Are you all right? I know this is hard for you."

"I hate hospitals, nothing good has ever come out of a hospital." She shivered as if an arctic wind had blown over her.

"Do you think the doctor will let us see her?" Robin asked.

"They just kicked me out, she looks so

small and broken in that bed," Yolanda said, then burst into tears. Sheldon held her tightly and rocked back and forth.

"She's going to be fine, Nina has a lot to live for."

Yolanda looked up at her father, her eyes shining with tears. "So did Mom."

"This is different," Alex said. "It has to be."

Clinton wrapped his arms around Alex. The pain she was feeling had been written across her face. When he'd seen her shiver, he knew exactly how she felt. Then he felt her tears on his shoulder as he stroked her back. Alex pushed back from him and offered Clinton a lopsided smile. "Thank you, Clinton."

"Guys, Nina's going to pull through because we're getting married," he revealed.

Everyone looked at Clinton and found a small reason to hold on to a bit of happiness.

"You're good for her and I couldn't be happier," Alex said.

Sheldon nodded. "I know you love my baby as much as any of us do."

Yolanda blinked her tears away. "She knows it too."

"So, you're Clinton," Robin said. "I've been so caught up in my drama that I haven't had a chance to meet you." She extended her hand to him. Clinton shook her hand.

"I hate that we're meeting under these circumstances," he said softly.

Robin nodded and tears ran down her face. "Not the best way to meet my future brother-in-law."

The doctor walked into the waiting room. "Excuse me," he said. "I have some news about Nina Richardson."

"We're her family," Sheldon said, his face shadowed with concern. "What's going on?"

"It's quite remarkable," he said with a smile. "We were going to put her on a breathing machine because of her collapsed lung, but to our surprise, it has reinflated and she's coming out from under the medication. Her vitals are rapidly improving and I can allow one of you to go in and see her for a few brief minutes. She's not out of the woods, but her condition has been upgraded from critical to serious."

"Thank you, Jesus," Robin and Alex moaned.

"I'm going to go and see her," Sheldon said, and everyone agreed. The doctor led him into the ICU area where Nina was.

Clinton watched the three sisters as they huddled in the corner, silently praying that

God didn't take Nina away from them and thanking Him for bringing her this far. He couldn't help but believe this was all his fault. He had been the reason that Nina was lying in the hospital bed. Tears fell down his cheek and hit the tip of his shoes before he realized that he was crying. Alex looked at Clinton and drew him into the sisters' circle.

"I know you love her and you have to believe that she's going to make it through this," she said in a tender voice. "She doesn't need your tears, she needs your prayers."

Just as the group joined hands to pray, Sheldon came running down the hall. "She's awake, my baby just woke up."

Everyone rushed to Nina's room, happy and surprised to see her with her eyes open. The doctor cautioned them to visit her only for a few minutes and one at a time.

One by one, the Richardson sisters entered Nina's room. When it was Clinton's turn to see her, he wasn't sure if he should've gone inside or just allowed her family to see her. But when she smiled weakly at him, he knew coming into her room had been the right thing. Despite the angry words that they'd shared before the accident, the love they shared was still strong.

"I'm sorry."

Nina shook her head. "Not your fault."

"I love you so much and the thought of losing you was more than I can bear."

Nina reached for Clinton's hand. "I'm not going anywhere," she said. Her voice was raspy and low.

He kissed her hand. "Please don't. When you get out of here, this is going back on your finger where it belongs." Clinton pulled his mother's engagement ring from his pocket and held it up for Nina to see.

"Lamar didn't mean any —"

"Shh, I know. Don't worry about him or how foolish I was. Just get better so that we can plan our wedding."

Tears flowed down Clinton's cheeks. Seeing Nina looking like a broken doll in the bed with all of those tubes hooked up to her was almost more than he could handle.

"Don't cry, Clinton," Nina said.

He stroked her hand, then kissed her on the cheek. "I'm going to let you get some rest, but I'm going to be outside your door."

She squeezed his hand. "Stay with me tonight."

Clinton nodded. If she wanted him by her side then he wouldn't leave it. As Nina drifted off to sleep, Clinton rose to his feet and stretched. The door to her room opened and Sheldon walked in. His eyes were bloodshot and his shirt wrinkled.

"How is she?" he asked Clinton.

"Resting."

"Can't believe I almost lost my little girl. I think I've lost enough. She doesn't know it, but she's more like her mother than anyone else. Nora had spunk just like Nina, she wore her heart on her sleeve just like Nina, and she loved hard. I can't lose her all over again."

Clinton stood there feeling helpless and guilty. "Mr. — Sheldon, I feel like this is all my fault. Nina and I had an argument before she got into her accident."

Sheldon rubbed his forehead. "You're not to blame for this," he said. "When Nina told me she was getting the Mustang, I didn't say it, but I didn't want her to get it. Thought it was too fast for her and thought that something like this would happen. She's the kind of person who drives too fast. Add being angry or emotional to the mix and I knew something like this was going to happen. When she gets out of here, I'm buying a her a Buick."

Clinton smiled. "A Buick?"

"I don't think so." Nina's raspy voice startled them for a moment.

Sheldon and Clinton turned to Nina. "Aren't you supposed to be sleeping?" her father admonished.

"I was until I heard you say you were putting me in a Buick," she said.

"Go back to sleep," Clinton said as he stroked the back of Nina's hand. "Or your doctor is going to kick us out of here."

"All right," she said.

Tears welled up in Sheldon's eyes as he watched Nina drift off back to sleep.

"Sheldon, why don't you go and get some rest?" Clinton suggested.

"I think I will. I'll be in the waiting room with her sisters." The two men hugged and Sheldon whispered to Clinton, "Take care of my baby."

Clinton took a seat beside Nina's bed and silently promised that he would take care of her for the rest of his life.

CHAPTER 25

Two weeks later, Nina was released from the hospital, and despite her pleas to go to her home, Clinton and her family whisked her to Charleston where she was waited on hand and foot.

Resting against the pillows in her room at the bed-and-breakfast, she waited for Yolanda and Robin to get out of her room. But that wasn't going to happen anytime soon as they looked at her as if she'd break into a million pieces if she moved one inch.

"You two can leave and I won't die," Nina said.

"Don't even joke like that," Robin remarked dramatically. "We almost lost you and . . ."

"Calm down," Yolanda said. "Nina is just being Nina. But we're not going anywhere."

"I hope you don't plan on getting another Mustang," Robin said. "You're too hot-headed to handle that much horsepower."

Nina folded her arms across her chest. "Channeling Alexandria Richardson now?"

The door to her room opened and Alex walked in. When the conversation stopped, she figured her sisters had been talking about her.

"What did I miss?" she quipped.

"Nothing," Nina said. "Can you get your sisters out of here?"

Alex shook her head and joined Yolanda on the settee near the window. "Little Sis, why don't you accept the fact that you're stuck with us and enjoy it?"

Nina rolled her eyes. "I'm really fine."

Yolanda nodded. "You sure are with your busted leg and broken arm. You're awesome. What the hell were you thinking, driving and crying? I thought I taught you better than that."

Robin furrowed her brows. "And you were crying because?"

Alex crossed her legs. "Let me guess, you and Clinton had an argument."

Nina closed her eyes. "I don't remember. Instead of talking about me, why don't the three of you catch me up on what's been going on in your lives? Y'all have been real quiet about that."

Robin rose to her feet and stood next to the window. "You all are going to find out

354

anyway, so I might as well tell you. I'm getting a divorce."

"What?" the three sisters exclaimed in unison.

"Not you," Yolanda said. "I thought you had the perfect marriage."

"Nothing in life is perfect," Robin said in a near whisper. "Logan and I have just grown apart, and I don't know if we can work things out. Especially after what I've learned about my husband."

"Which was?" Alex asked.

Robin hugged herself tightly. "I don't want to talk about it."

Nina shook her head. "You don't get out of it that easily. What did you find out?"

"Logan is a father."

No one knew what to say after Robin dropped that bombshell. Nina wanted to hug her sister tightly, she couldn't move from her bed.

"But-but . . ." Yolanda sputtered, looking for the right words to say. "Not Logan."

"He claims that he never slept with this woman, but the DNA test didn't lie. That slimy bastard," Robin spat.

"I'm floored," Alex said. "Logan always seemed like a stand-up guy and this just doesn't seem like him."

"You know what, Alex, you go to him and

try to work things out then," Robin snapped. "I'm sorry, I didn't mean to lash out at you."

Alex shrugged her shoulders. "Whatever. I get that you're upset, but you should be logical. What if the DNA test was tampered with?"

"Stop watching so many soap operas. He cheated on me and made a baby with some other . . . I wanted to have Logan's child. But . . ."

Yolanda turned to Robin. "Does Daddy know?"

"Yes," Robin replied. "He helped me move when he was in Virginia at that conference. Logan was irate when he came home and I was gone. He went on and on about how this woman had been stalking him and wanted him to break his vows but he didn't. He swore that the DNA test would clear him and I believed it like a fool. You guys used to laugh at me and called me Miss Optimistic. But that Robin is gone."

"I'm sorry you're hurting, but don't let him steal your joy. I could beat his ass for hurting you."

Yolanda pinched Alex on her arm. "Whoa! This is a side of you I haven't seen in a while."

Alex pinched Yolanda back. "Shut up."

Before Yolanda could retort, there was a knock at the door.

Robin crossed the room and opened it. Clinton walked in and smiled.

"Am I interrupting something?" he asked as he looked around the room.

Robin shook her head. "Have a seat, Clinton, we were just leaving."

"No, we weren't," Alex said.

"That's right," Yolanda said. "Because we all need to talk to you."

Nina groaned. "All right, all of you get the hell out of my room so I can spend some time with my fiancé!"

"So rude," Yolanda said as she and Alex rose to their feet.

"That's your sister. And she learned that behavior from you," Alex said as she followed Robin and Yolanda out the door.

Clinton smiled as the Richardson sisters walked out of the room. "They're giving you a hard time?"

"Smothering me is more like it." Nina held her arm out to Clinton and he hugged her gently.

"They're doing it because they care," he replied. "How are you feeling?"

"A lot better now that you're here."

"You really scared us. I thought I was going to lose you," he said. "That car has got to go. Besides, we can't put our babies in the back seat of a Mustang. And we certainly aren't going to put a baby seat in mine."

Nina groaned. "Not you, too, Clinton. That car is totaled, but as soon as I get a check from the insurance company, I'm getting another one. No arguments. Maybe I'll get an EcoBoost instead of a GT this time."

He kissed her on the forehead. "I know. But seriously, where will Clinton the third, Clinton the fourth, and little Clintina sit?"

Nina laughed, then touched her side. Laughing hurt her ribs. "You're crazy if you think I'm going to name my daughter Clintina. But I do want a big family. And you can drive the minivan. And I don't hear you talking about getting rid of your Mustang."

"And I'm not getting rid of mine. It's an investment, a classic car. I tell you what, instead of a minivan, how about a stylish SUV?"

"Whatever, but I don't do big cars." Nina nestled closer to Clinton and closed her eyes. "This isn't how I imagined we'd spend time in bed together."

"You need to recover, but trust me when you're one hundred percent we'll make our time in bed together more exciting," he said.

"Umm, I like the sound of that." She reached up and stroked his cheek.

"Knock, knock," Sheldon said as he walked into the room. "Oh, I didn't realize that you two were . . ."

"It's all right, Daddy," Nina said. "Clinton was just holding me because your daughters spent the morning terrorizing me."

Sheldon smiled and took a seat near the window. "They just love you, honey. You gave us all quite a scare. That's why we're all here, *terrorizing* you. So, you two are back together and everything is right with the world, huh?"

Clinton nodded. "I never should've let her go in the first place."

"So, the wedding? Is it going to be in Charleston, Charlotte? Where are you two going to live?" Sheldon asked.

Clinton dropped his arms from around Nina. "We haven't worked that out," he said. "I know we're going to have to make some big decisions soon." He brushed his fingers across Nina's cast. "The most important thing right now is for Nina to heal."

Sheldon nodded. "I understand. You know, I would be happy to have you two live here."

"Daddy," Nina said. "Do you really think we should live where Clinton works? Alex would never give us a moment of peace. I can see it now, three in the morning, she's knocking on our door wanting to go over a business proposal."

Clinton and Sheldon broke out laughing. "She would do that," Clinton said as he eased off the bed. "But I appreciate the offer."

Sheldon rose to his feet. "All right, but the offer stands."

"Thank you, Daddy," Nina said as Sheldon headed out the door. When the couple were alone, Clinton turned to Nina.

"Do you want to move to back to Charleston?"

"I want to be wherever you are. That's the thing about freelancing. I'm free. It was a risky career move, but I like flexibility."

Clinton perched on the edge of the bed and was about to kiss his fiancée when the door opened and her sisters returned.

"Eww," Yolanda said. "I know you two were not about to . . ."

Nina sucked her teeth in disgust. "Well, if we were, you busted that groove up. Why are y'all back?"

Robin folded her arms and turned to Alex. "Because someone said we needed to talk to Clinton."

Alex smiled. "If you're going to marry Nina, then we need to ask you some questions."

"Can this wait?" Nina asked. "I'm tired."

"That's fine because we don't want to talk to you anyway," Yolanda said as she walked over to Clinton and linked arms with him. "Let's go have lunch. Nina, you go to sleep, all right?"

Clinton looked helpless as Nina's sisters dragged him out of the room.

The moment Clinton and the Richardson sisters entered the bed-and-breakfast's restaurant, he knew this wasn't going to be a friendly chat. Robin smiled sweetly at him and offered him a seat at the head of the table. Yolanda and Alex sat on either side of him and Robin called for the waitstaff to bring in their lunch.

"So," Yolanda said. "What in the hell happened between you and Nina before the accident?"

Clinton cleared his throat. "We had a disagreement."

"We know that," Alex said. "But what was it about and why did you allow her to get in that car when she was so upset?" She folded her arms across her chest.

"I wasn't there, I'd already left because she'd given me my engagement ring back and it was over."

"Why?" Yolanda and Robin asked at the

same time.

"Because I thought that she and Lamar had slept together," he said in a low voice, embarrassed that he had actually listened to that man.

"Lamar? He's still sniffing around her?" Yolanda asked. "I remember the night that she saw him and told him to kiss off. Who told you that those two had something going on?"

Heat radiated from Clinton's collar. How was he going to explain to these women that he'd been a fool and nearly killed their sister? "It was a misunderstanding and we've worked past it."

"Not really, because we have to be sure that you aren't going to be a problem for Nina," Robin said, quickly dropping the nice sister façade. "Because if you are, we'd prefer it if you didn't marry her."

"Wait a minute, I love Nina. How could I predict what was going to happen?"

"How could you believe that Nina was unfaithful to you? She loves you!" Yolanda exclaimed. "She's never been so happy. Maybe you're the cheater."

Clinton rose to his feet, trying to keep his anger in check. "I know you all love your sister and this family is really close. But Nina doesn't need protection from me. I'd appreciate it if you three would mind your own damned business."

The sisters looked at Clinton with their mouths wide open. "Oh, he's going to fit in this family just fine," Yolanda said with a laugh.

Alex and Robin nodded in agreement.

"Clinton, sit down and have lunch, please," Alex said. "Nina told us what happened and trust me, we're not always like this. But it's nice to know you're honest."

Yolanda shook her head. "Because if we were, there's a man in Virginia who would be in a world of hurt right now."

Robin's smile faded. "Excuse me, I'm going to check on the food." She bolted from the room, leaving Clinton wondering what was going on.

After lunch, Clinton headed back to Nina's room happy to be marrying into the Richardson family, though he was a little concerned about Robin. Something was going on with her. Since he wasn't really family yet, he didn't feel comfortable enough to ask her what was happening in her life. Besides, he was certain that she and her sisters would handle whatever was going on. That's just how they seemed to work.

"Knock, knock," he said as he entered the room.

Nina had been trying to climb out of the bed when Clinton quickly crossed over to her. "What are you doing?"

"I'm going crazy in this bed! And I'm itching in places I can't reach lying down."

He lifted Nina into his arms. "You need to rest and recuperate. You were hit by a truck, babe."

She rolled her eyes. "Really, I'd forgotten all about that. I just want to get into a warm bath. Can you help me do that?"

"You know I can't. Those casts can't get wet."

She pouted. "Then you can give me a sponge bath."

Clinton nodded. "I'll do that. First, let me get you in this chair." He sat her in a rocking chair, then he eased her nightgown off her body. It was hard for him to look at the scars on her body and not blame himself for them being there.

Nina noted his silence. "What?"

"I'm so sorry that I . . ."

She shook her head as his finger trailed down one of her scars. "We're not going to do this. We're not passing blame around."

"I'm going to get a towel and some warm water. Don't move."

"If I could, I'd be out that door so fast." Her laughter warmed his heart as he walked into the bathroom to fill a small basin with warm water.

When he returned to Nina's chair, he smiled at her and started the sponge bath. He washed her feet, moving up the calf on her free leg and then between her thighs.

"Are you okay?" He stroked her with the warm cloth and Nina moaned.

She nodded as he moved the cloth across her stomach. "They didn't give me baths like this in the hospital."

"Tried to ask the nurses to let me, but they said no." Clinton winked at her as he dipped the cloth in the water and lathered it up again. He rubbed it across her breasts and up and down her neck and shoulders. "Still good?"

"Never felt better."

He rinsed the cloth again and wiped the suds away. Clinton dried her with a soft towel, then reached for a bottle of lotion from her dresser. Of course, it smelled like roses. Smoothing it across her body, Clinton said a prayer of thankfulness. He was blessed that Nina didn't die and they'd have a future together.

"I'm so sorry," he murmured as he propped up her broken leg on some pillows.

"Clinton, you don't have to keep apologizing to me."

"I don't know what I'd do without you." He grabbed a clean gown and helped her into it.

"Hopefully, you'll never have to find out."

"You scared the hell out of me, babe." Clinton let go of her hand and pulled another chair up beside hers. "And I feel like this is my fault."

Nina sighed. "We both could've handled things better."

He stroked the back of her hand. "I could've listened instead of accusing you. Nina, I just felt so jealous when —"

She brought her finger to his lips. "You never have to worry about another man coming between us. If I wasn't ready to spend forever with you, I wouldn't have taken your ring."

"I know that and I can't believe I let Lamar's lie get to me like that."

"Well, I should've sat in the parking lot until . . . there is enough blame to go around." A tear slid down her cheek. "Things could've been a lot worse."

"Yes. I'm with your family though. No more Mustangs."

"Really?" She blinked in rapid succession.

"Yes."

"How about I promise to slow down and you don't make me cry anymore?"

"I can do that." He kissed the back of her hand. Nina wished she could make love to her man. As if he could read her desire, Clinton leaned in and kissed her on the forehead.

"We're going to have the rest of our lives to make love every day."

"Promise?"

"Absolutely." He kissed her again, with fire and passion. Nina's moan hung in the air as the door to her room opened.

"Oh my God!" Yolanda exclaimed. "I know y'all aren't doing what I think you are."

Alex turned her back and Robin smiled.

"We're trying to have a moment here." Nina shook her head at her sisters.

"Don't you think you should be in bed resting?" Alex said as she started toward Nina.

"I think I need to lock my door."

"Come on, guys. Let's leave them alone, for now." Robin ushered her sisters out of the room.

"Guess we'll see you two at dinner, since Nina can get out of the bed." Yolanda waved her hand as she left.

Nina turned to Clinton and whispered, "Are you sure you want to be a part of this madness."

He winked at her. "Of course."

CHAPTER 26

Several weeks passed before Nina could return to her normal activities, but as soon as her doctor released her from his care, she couldn't wait to head to the Ford dealership and pick out a new car.

Sheldon had loaned Nina his Lincoln Continental, and it felt as if she were steering a spaceship. Before she headed to pick out a car, Nina knew she wanted to kiss Clinton. He'd been so good to her during her recovery, spending his days and nights at the bed-and-breakfast working and taking care of her. When she'd been in severe pain, he'd sleep on the settee in her room so that he could give her pain medicine every four hours. He worked with the physical therapist so that he could help Nina with her exercises.

I couldn't have a better fiancé, she thought as she parked the car, nearly dinging Alex's car as she exited.

Nina bounded into the lobby, smiling as she waved at the front desk clerk.

"Nina," Alex called out. "What did the doctor say?"

"Clean bill of health."

Alex enveloped her sister in a tight hug. "I'm so glad. You had us worried for a while. I guess all those exercises you and Clinton were doing behind closed doors worked wonders."

"You sound like Yolanda."

Alex dropped her arms. "Please, I was actually talking about the therapy he's been helping you with. I keep my mind out of the gutter, unlike your sister."

Nina nodded. "I'm glad to see you and Clinton working so well together."

"It's a relief to have him here. So much so that I'm going on vacation. The Bahamas are calling me and I'm going to answer."

Nina raised her right eyebrow and smiled. "Who are you? And here we thought you weren't listening to us at all."

Alex thumped Nina on the forearm. "Shut up. Besides, Clinton and Daddy can run this place without me for a week or two."

"I hope when you go, you'll leave your cell phone and your laptop here," Nina said. "And I'd love to continue this conversation, but I have to find Clinton."

"He's in his office," Alex said. "Have fun, but remind him that we have a meeting in an hour."

Nina dashed off, waving to her sister. She wasn't sure if she could get used to all of these changes in her family. First Yolanda and her move to Charlotte, then Robin's divorce, and now Alex was going to get a life.

As Nina walked into Clinton's office, he hung up the phone and turned to her with a huge smile on his face. "I was just about to call you," he said. "How did it go at the doctor's office?"

"Great, he said that I'm healed." Nina hopped up on his desk and took his face into her hands.

"So, how are we going to celebrate?" She offered him a seductive smile.

"Well," he said, rubbing his nose against hers. "I could think of a thousand ways, but they'll have to wait."

"Yeah, Alex said that you all have a meeting in an hour?"

"Thanksgiving is in a week and we have to make sure we have everything together for the families that are coming in."

"Oh, yes, Thanksgiving." She kissed Clinton gently. "You know Alex is talking about taking a vacation?"

"What? You're kidding, right?"

"No. I think all of my sisters have lost their minds. But hey, if this means they will leave me alone and let me live my life, then I love it."

Clinton shook his head. "Your sisters aren't going to leave you alone any more than you're going to leave them alone. That's the kind of family you have and you all love it. How is Robin, by the way? She had me a little worried when she was here a couple of weeks ago."

"She hasn't called lately. I'm hoping she hasn't killed Logan. Yolanda and I were so looking forward to doing that."

Clinton squeezed his future wife's cheek. "See what I mean."

"What?" Nina asked.

"You all meddle in each other's lives and that's not going to change. If it did, something would be wrong."

Nina shrugged. "I guess you're right. And you'd better get to your meeting or Alex will blame me for making you late." She hopped off the desk and blew him a kiss. "I'll see you tonight in Summerville and in your bed."

Clinton stood up and drew her into his arms. "I'll be waiting."

After leaving Clinton's office, Nina sought

out Yolanda. She knew that her sister would go with her to pick out her new car. As she was about to walk into Yolanda's room, she heard yelling.

"Who is this? Why are you doing this to me?" Yolanda yelled. "I have no idea who you are and I don't care to."

Nina heard a thump, then she burst into the room. "Yolanda, what's going on?" Glancing around the room, she saw her sister's phone in pieces.

"I've got to get out of here," she said, then dashed out of the room. Nina ran after her and grabbed her arm.

"Yolanda. What is going on?"

"They found me."

"Who? Are you talking about what happened in Virginia?"

Yolanda nodded solemnly. "I've got to get away from here before they show up and someone gets hurt."

"Where are you going to go? If they found you here, they'll find you in Charlotte and you'll be alone there."

"I'd rather them do that than come here and hurt you or someone else in the family."

"Will you please go to the police?"

"Shh," Yolanda said, grabbing her sister's arm. "I don't want Dad or Alex to hear this, all right. I have to deal with this on my own and the best thing for me to do is to leave, okay?"

"And live looking over your shoulder for the rest of your life? That's crazy, Yolanda."

"Putting you all in danger is crazy and you better not tell Dad or Alex about this," she hissed at Nina.

"So, I'm supposed to let you walk out that door and into the line of fire of those thugs?" Nina glared at her sister. "It's not going to happen and if you don't march your ass into Daddy's office and tell him what's going on, then I am!"

Nina turned on her heels and headed for the stairs with Yolanda behind her protesting all the way.

"This is insane. Daddy is going to over-react and —"

Nina turned around and looked at her sister. "Overreact? Someone is trying to kill you."

Yolanda burst into tears. "I'm so scared." Nina hugged her.

The sisters walked into Sheldon's office and waited for him to hang up the phone. He smiled initially when he saw his daughters, but when he noted Yolanda's red-rimmed eyes, he knew that something was amiss.

"What's wrong?" he asked.

"Daddy," Yolanda said. "I'm in trouble."

Sheldon pressed the do not disturb button on his phone. "Trouble? Tell me everything that's going on."

Nina nudged Yolanda.

Sighing, Yolanda began telling her father her story. "I decided to move to Charlotte for more than one reason. Before I left Richmond, I witnessed a murder."

"Did you go to the police?" he asked. Yolanda shook her head. "Why not?" Sheldon asked. "I mean, they could've protected you from those thugs."

"Yeah, right," Yolanda snorted. "There are so many people who have died waiting for the police to help them."

"I didn't raise you girls to fear the police or to run from you problems," he said.

"They're stalking her, Daddy," Nina exclaimed. Yolanda shot her an angry glare. "And," Nina continued, "she wants to go back to Charlotte without me."

"Without you?" Sheldon and Yolanda said in unison.

She nodded. "Clinton and I aren't going to have a weekend marriage and I'm not going live in Charlotte while he's here working here. I have the luxury of being able to work anywhere."

"That settles it," Sheldon said as he picked up the phone. "You need protection and I know just who to call. Are you going to be living in Nina's place?"

Yolanda folded her arms and nodded.

"Good," he said as he punched in some numbers.

Yolanda turned to Nina. "I told you that I didn't want to tell him this," she said.

"And I don't want to see my sister in a body bag," Nina replied as she rose to her feet. "I have to go, all right?"

"Thanks a lot, Nina."

Clinton sat in his meeting not paying attention to a word that anyone was saying. He wanted to be wrapped in Nina's arms, with her lips pressed against his and his hands roaming her body.

"Clinton," Alex said. "Are you ready to make your presentation?"

"Oh, yes, sure," he said, rising to his feet and grabbing his notes. Just as he stepped behind the podium, the door opened and Randall Birmingham walked in with two Charleston police officers.

"That's him," Birmingham said. "That's the man who stole the money from my business account."

Alex leapt to her feet. "What are you doing here and what is the meaning of this?"

"Ma'am," the taller officer said. "Please sit down."

The second officer grabbed Clinton and whipped out his handcuffs. "Clinton Jefferson, you have the right to remain silent, anything you say can and —"

"What is this all about?" Clinton demanded as the officer tightened the cuffs. "What are the charges?"

"Financial fraud, embezzlement, and assault," the officer said. "It is all in the arrest warrant."

Birmingham smiled as Clinton was led out of the conference room in front of several of the bed-and-breakfast's clients and potential clients. Alex dashed after them.

"Clinton," she said. "I'll have our lawyers meet you downtown." She turned to the people who hadn't left the room. "This is all a big misunderstanding. If anyone has any questions about our holiday promotions, please call or e-mail me. Good afternoon."

Alex ran outside and grabbed Birmingham's arm. "You son of a bitch! What are you trying to pull?"

He grinned and shook his head. "Pull? I'm trying to get the man who tried to rob my company and make him pay."

Alex shook her head. "This is about Clinton telling you to kiss his ass and not giving you what you wanted."

"So, you're his cheerleader now? I thought you didn't trust him."

"It's you I don't trust!" Alex slapped him as hard as she could. "You piece of shit."

Birmingham stroked his jaw. "I guess you want to join Clinton in a jail cell, huh?"

"That would be a lot better than spending another second in your presence. Get off our property or you're going to be arrested for trespassing." Alex turned on her heels and stormed away.

When Clinton arrived at the police station, he was beyond angry. Birmingham was at it again, but he wasn't going to stand for this. His reputation was at stake and he was embarrassed as hell. Being led out in hand-cuffs with potential clients watching was too much and Birmingham was going to pay.

This son of a bitch isn't going to get away with this. He knows that I didn't steal a damned thing from him, Clinton thought as the officers processed him. About an hour later, he was sitting in a holding cell with a drunk man who kept calling him Ollie.

Sitting in the corner of the cell, Clinton found himself in a place where he'd never thought he would be. He'd never been in any type of trouble and had never seen the inside of a jail cell. Until now. It wasn't as if he was some young kid, he was a successful businessman and he had a lot more to lose now.

"Clinton Jefferson," the jailer called out. "Your lawyer's here."

Clinton bolted to the door of the cell and waited for the wide man to open it. Just the few hours he'd been in jail had been too long. He looked up at the man who'd represent him, David Harrington, the bed-and-breakfast's attorney. The two men shook hands as the jailer led them to a private room.

"Please tell me that you've gotten my bail set and I can get out of here," Clinton said.

David shook his head. "Unfortunately, the court is backed up and I can't get an arraignment hearing until the morning. These are some serious charges and with all the identity theft going around, judges are taking these cases seriously."

Clinton banged angrily on the table. "I didn't steal a damned thing. This is Birmingham's vendetta against me because I wouldn't help him get the bed-and-breakfast. I thought it was over when the truth came out the first time."

"The first time?" David asked, folding his hands underneath his chin.

Clinton told David about the plot that Birmingham had hatched when he started working at the Richardson Bed and Breakfast.

"Now, that's a horse of a different color," David said when Clinton finished. "Let me call the judge and let him know what's really going on. You might be going home tonight."

Clinton nodded as his attorney pulled out his cell phone and made the call. The first thing he was going to do when he got out of jail was find Birmingham and one way or another, this thing between them was going to end tonight.

CHAPTER 27

Nina was about to head to Clinton's office when Alex nearly bowled her over. Nina grabbed her sister's arm. "Where's the fire?" she asked Alex.

"Clinton's been arrested."

Nina shook her head in disbelief. "Arrested, for what?"

"This is Randall Birmingham causing problems again, I have to tell Daddy before someone else does," Alex said as she pushed by Nina.

Without saying a word, she headed outside, got into her father's car, and headed for the Charleston County Detention Center. She was going to bail her man out and this Birmingham person was going to deal with her.

Nina had never seen the inside of the detention center. She expected a scene from a low-budget prison movie, but she found a man sitting behind a desk. It was as if she'd walked into a hotel, a one-star hotel with bad service, but a hotel nonetheless.

"Excuse me," she said to the desk sergeant. "I need some help."

The man sucked his teeth as he looked up at her. "Visiting hours are over and if you're not on the inmate's list twenty-four hours in advance, you're not getting in."

Nina folded her arms across her chest. "First of all, I'm not here to visit anyone, I need to bail my fiancé out of this place. His name is Clinton Jefferson."

"What do you want me to do about it? Are you a bail bondsman?"

"No, but can you check and see what his bond is?"

The man sighed as he began typing something into the computer. "Clinton Jefferson, you say?"

"Yes." She sighed in frustration.

"He's been released. About two hours ago."

Nina dashed out of the center and sped to Clinton's house. Her trip was impaired by late-evening traffic and the fact that Nina wasn't too sure of herself on the highway. Her accident still haunted her. When her cell phone rang, she didn't reach for it, since her phone wasn't connected to the Bluetooth in her dad's car.

If it's important, they will leave a message, she thought.

Anger flowed through Clinton's veins like blood as he took an Uber back to the Richardson Bed and Breakfast. As soon as the driver pulled into the parking lot, Clinton opened the door and hopped out of the car.

His bond hearing kept replaying in his mind. Though he was released on his own recognizance, Clinton was still angry. He should've never been in front of a judge in the first place. *I didn't do anything,* he bitterly thought as he got into his car.

If he was going to be treated as a criminal, then maybe he needed to find Birmingham and do something to him that would warrant jail time. But he knew he couldn't make a bad situation worse.

Nina.

What was he going to say to her? This was the last thing that Nina needed right now. They should've been focused on their wedding and building their future together. Birmingham was standing in the way of his happiness and he wasn't going to have that. Not after everything he and Nina had made it through.

Just as he was about to peel out of the

parking lot, Sheldon appeared in his rear-view mirror. Clinton slammed on his brakes, placed the car in park, and exited the vehicle.

"Sheldon, I . . ."

The older man shook his head. "Alex told me everything and I know that Randall is up to his dirty tricks again. Fool me once, shame on you, but Sheldon Richardson is nobody's fool twice. Don't let this man make a fool of you."

"What do you mean?" Clinton asked.

Sheldon clasped his arm around his future son-in-law's shoulder. "You're leaving here with a head full of steam and I'm guessing you were going to find old Randall. Rough him up a bit and make him confess to setting you up?"

Clinton nodded. "I was arrested in front of many of our clients and it makes you look bad."

"What would make me look bad is having my daughter marry a man in prison. I know what Birmingham is trying to do, so if you're going to confront him, I'm going with you."

"Sheldon, I can't let you —"

"This is and has always been about my bed-and-breakfast. This man has been trying to get his mitts on my property for years.

This has to stop, because I'm not selling and he can't keep coming after you. You're family now and I'm going to show you how we protect family."

Clinton and Sheldon jumped into the car and headed for Birmingham's office. Clinton told Sheldon that he was sure the man was still there plotting and planning as he usually did.

"It's a damned shame that the man won't leave you alone," Sheldon gritted. "He knew that I wasn't going to sell, and after that stunt he pulled trying to make it seem as if you were a spy . . . unbelievable."

Clinton slowed his car as they pulled up to a traffic light. "So, what are we going to do?"

Sheldon smiled. "He isn't the only one who knows how to play dirty." Reaching into his pocket, he produced a USB drive. "When he watches the eleven o'clock news tonight, he's going to wish he had never messed with my family."

As the hours ticked by and Nina still didn't see Clinton, she began to worry. Did something happen? A car accident? Or maybe that fat pig at the detention center had lied to her. Clinton could still be sitting behind bars waiting for someone to bail him out.

She picked up her cell phone and called Alex.

"Yes, Nina?"

"Have you seen Clinton?" Nina's voice was frantic with worry.

"His car was in the parking lot, but it's not anymore. But I haven't seen him," she said.

"Well, he's not at home and I'm worried that he might do something crazy," Nina said as she nervously nibbled on her lip.

"Like what?"

"Go after Randall Birmingham."

Alex snorted. "If he did, I wouldn't blame him. Do you know how it looked to have Clinton dragged out of that meeting in handcuffs? And you know the good old boys in the Charleston County Detention Center didn't care about who Clinton was or the fact that he'd never been in trouble before."

"Please don't say that," Nina said. "I'd hate to think that something happened to Clinton while he was sitting in jail over some bullshit that he didn't do. What if someone roughed him up?"

"Nina, stop borrowing trouble and just wait. Where are you?"

"In Summerville."

"Just come here and wait for him, then we

can find out what's really going on," Alex said.

Nina exhaled loudly. "All right, but I don't know how long I can sit on my hands and wonder where he is."

"You can always busy yourself with some work," Alex said. "I have some filing that needs to be done."

"Whatever. I'll be there shortly." Nina ended the call. Silently she prayed that Clinton was all right and would be at the hotel when she arrived.

Her prayers were in vain because when she arrived at the bed-and-breakfast an hour later, neither Clinton nor her father was anywhere to be found.

"Where are they?" Nina asked Alex as they settled in Alex's office with a batch of cookies.

Alex chewed on one of the crispy chocolate chip cookies and glanced at her sister. "Just calm down," she said. "They'll be here soon."

"And if they aren't? What if something terrible happened?" Nina hopped out of her chair and nearly knocked the platter of cookies over.

"If Daddy is with Clinton, they may have gone to the lawyer's office or something. I doubt Daddy and Clinton are out doing something illegal or dangerous." Alex pushed the platter up on the desk and glared at her sister. "Now, calm the hell down."

"Sorry," she said as she sat down. "But Alex, this is strange. If Clinton was released from jail hours ago, then where is he?"

Birmingham laughed when he saw Clinton and Sheldon standing in his doorway. "Well, this is a sight," he said. "What did you two come here for?"

"You know what this is about," Clinton snarled. "You have some nerve to march into my place of business with the police. You know damned well I didn't steal anything from you."

Leaning back in his chair, Birmingham clapped his hands as if he'd been watching a Broadway play. "Sheldon, you'd better watch this one. He's an excellent liar. You know, when you left the company, I had no inkling that I'd need to change my account numbers and passwords. He cleaned me out. Thank God the bank offers fraud protection."

"Cut the bullshit, Randall. I know what you wanted this young man to do and since he hasn't done it, you're trying to ruin his life. I'm not having it. He's family and this ends now," Sheldon hissed. Then with a quickness that belied his age, Sheldon leapt across Birmingham's desk and grabbed him by the throat. "If you don't recant these ridiculous charges and leave my family alone, I'm going to hurt you. Then I'm going to take your properties the way you've tried to take mine."

Birmingham glared at him. "Just how do you plan to do that?"

Clinton dropped a file on his desk. "I'm going to sue you for defamation of character and we're taking this fight public. I'm tired of talking and trying to reason with you. When I'm awarded millions of dollars, you won't be able to buy a cheeseburger."

Sheldon let Birmingham go. "This is what you're going to do if you want to remain in charge here. First, you're going to drop these charges against Clinton. Second, you're going to stay far away from my bed-and-breakfast. I want you to move your headquarters out of Charleston, out of this state, actually. If you don't, bits and pieces of this information will be leaked to the media while the lawsuit, which we will be filing in the morning, drags on. Your stockholders will jump from this sinking ship like rats on the *Titanic.* The choice is yours."

Clinton smirked as he watched Sheldon

work over Birmingham. He had no idea that his future father-in-law had it in him. *Guess it just goes to show you that you can't judge a book by its cover.*

"Do we have a deal?" Sheldon asked as calmly as if he were inviting the man to a dinner party.

"You think I'm going to let you blackmail me?" Birmingham hissed.

Sheldon shook his head. "This isn't blackmail, this is just what you deserve. You have less than twelve hours to make everything right and decide what you're going to do. If not," he said as he picked up the file, "the authorities and your stockholders will be getting this information." Then Sheldon held up his USB drive. "And I know a bunch of reporters who are dying to get their hands on this."

Birmingham glared at Sheldon and shook his head.

Clinton and Sheldon turned to walk out of the office as Birmingham picked up the phone to call the district attorney.

Once they were outside, Clinton turned to Sheldon and smiled widely. "I had no idea that you were that tough."

"I didn't manage to stay in business this long by having a soft touch. I've always ignored Randall because I knew there was no way he could've gotten to my business. He's duplicitous and I've known that from the first day he came into my office asking to buy into my company. There was something about him that I didn't trust and I always trust my gut feelings about people. Well, almost always. I don't think I've ever given you the apology that you deserved for me thinking that you were working with that snake and using my daughter. I know that you love Nina and she loves you. I guess hiring you was one of the best decisions I could've made."

Clinton smiled. "It certainly changed my life. Nina's the best thing that's ever happened to me."

"You weren't so bad for her, either. But remember, while I don't meddle, I will settle things if I have to. Especially when it comes to my baby." Sheldon winked at Clinton, then laughed.

He clasped his hand on Clinton's shoulder and the two men headed for the car.

When Clinton and Sheldon arrived at the bed-and-breakfast, Nina was standing out front pacing back and forth.

"Where the hell have you two been?" she demanded when they got out of the car.

The two men looked at each other and shook their heads. "You'd better watch your tone, young lady," Sheldon said with a smile tugging at his lips. "We had some business to handle."

Clinton took Nina into his arms, despite the fact that she stood there with a scowl on her face and her hands on her shapely hips. It only took one gentle kiss on her neck to melt her anger.

"They didn't hurt you in jail, did they?" Nina asked when she finally gave him a tight hug.

"No, but that doesn't mean I want to go back there," he said. "I don't think that's going to be a problem, though. Your father is one man who I don't want to piss off."

"My daddy?"

"Yes, you should've seen him in Birmingham's office. He was a man on a mission and a great actor."

Nina furrowed her eyebrows. "Okay, I'm lost."

Clinton pulled the file folder from his jacket that he and Sheldon had threatened Birmingham with, then opened it. Inside were blank sheets of paper. "He thought we had documentation on all of his shady business dealings and a multimillion-dollar lawsuit. Your dad played it to the hilt." He ushered Nina inside and they headed for her room.

"So, this is over now, charges dropped, and this Randall Birmingham is going to leave us the hell alone?" Nina asked as she unlocked the door.

"If he's smart he will. Playtime is over with this guy."

Nina sat down on the bed and smiled. "But I have to say, I like it when my man takes charge."

Easing onto the bed beside her, Clinton took her into his arms. "Do you now? Because, I'm a take-charge type of guy."

Nina licked her lips and smiled. "Prove it."

Taking her into his arms, Clinton brought his lips down on top of hers, kissing her deeply and passionately. With one hand, he unsnapped the buttons on her blouse, even popping a few of them off. Her skin felt like silk underneath his fingertips as he un-hooked her bra. He pulled Nina onto his lap and gazed deep into her eyes as they broke off their kiss.

"I love you so much," he moaned before kissing her again. Their tongues danced as Clinton continued to peel Nina's clothes off. She reached down and tugged at his belt buckle, but he grabbed her wrist.

"Remember, I'm in control." He flipped Nina on her back and held her wrists. With a deliberate pace, he explored the curves of her body, using his tongue as his guide. Starting with her breasts, he kissed and sucked until her nipples hardened underneath his kiss. Nina moaned as he inched down her stomach, tasting her as if she were made from the nectar of the gods. Clutching his shoulders, she nearly exploded as his lips made their way to the folds of skin between her thighs. Her legs shook as his tongue found her throbbing bud and sent ripples of pleasure through her nervous system. She tossed her head back and called out Clinton's name over and over again like a mantra. Reversing his direction, Clinton found his way to Nina's lips and she could taste her essence on his tongue as he kissed her deeply, making her heady with passion.

"Clinton, I need you," Nina moaned as he covered her body with his. He slipped his hands between her thighs and felt the heat radiating from her core, and when he felt how wet and ready she was for him, Clinton got even harder. Wrapping her legs around his waist, he fell into her hot wetness and felt as if he'd died and gone to heaven. No other woman had moved him the way Nina did. It was more than sex, they had a connection that he reveled in. She was a part of his soul and as they ebbed back and forth on the edge of ecstasy, Clinton knew he'd never love another woman again as much as he loved Nina.

CHAPTER 28

As the sunlight peeked through the blinds in Nina's room, she opened her eyes and stared down at Clinton, who slept soundly. *God, I love this man,* she thought. Nina didn't think she'd be able to open herself up to another man after the way Lamar had trampled her heart. But Clinton was different, he was gentle, he was patient, and he loved her as much as she loved him. Gently she stroked his cheek trying not to wake him, but his eyes fluttered open.

"Good morning," he said.

"Morning," she replied with a smile on her face. "Do you want some breakfast? We could go downstairs and —"

"I just want to lie here with you in my arms." Clinton kissed Nina on her forehead. "When I was sitting in that jail cell, the one thought that kept me sane was knowing that I'd be back in your arms soon enough."

"No more jail cells for you, mister. I was

beyond scared when I heard you were arrested."

"That's all behind us. Your father took care of Birmingham and he won't cause us any more problems. We just have a wedding to plan now."

She leaned against his chest and kissed his collarbone.

"I say let's get married tomorrow," Clinton quipped.

Nina smacked him playfully on the shoulder. "That's not going to happen. Imagine trying to elope around this bunch. Besides, I want Daddy to walk me down the aisle into your arms."

Clinton brushed his lips against hers. "We're going to do whatever you want, babe."

"It's your wedding too and we're never doing this again."

"Oh, no doubt. We're in this forever."

Clinton cupped her face in his hands and kissed her slow and deep. When they broke the kiss, Nina smiled like a Cheshire cat. "Let's get married Christmas Day."

"Are you sure you want to share our anniversary with Santa Claus?" Clinton laughed.

"Every day I'm with you is like Christmas, so let's just make it official," Nina said, then kissed Clinton on the tip of his nose. "Anyway, Santa Claus has nothing on you."

"Then Christmas Day it is. So that gives us about a month to get this wedding planned?"

Nina nodded. "At least I won't be flying around the country missing homemade turkey and stuffing this year."

"Sounds like fun. And speaking of fun . . ." Clinton placed her hand on his growing erection. "Let's replay last night."

Nina stroked him to the point of a near climax. "I'm down for —" A knock at the door stopped their flow. Nina groaned.

"Nina, Clinton, open the door," Alex said.

"Could her timing have been any worse?" Clinton whispered.

"Maybe if we ignore her she'll go away."

"I know you two are in there," Alex said. "Open this door."

Clinton shook his head. "She's not going away."

Wrapping her body in a sheet, Nina walked over to the door, and once Clinton had put on his boxers and a T-shirt, she opened it. "What do you want?" Nina asked.

Alex walked in the room and shook her head. "Sorry to interrupt, but not really." She ignored Clinton's and Nina's annoyed looks. "Is anyone going to tell me what happened with Randall? Dad's in meetings all morning and —"

"Why don't we talk about it over breakfast? It'll give me and Clinton a chance to get dressed."

"All right," Alex said, smiling slyly at her sister. "Fifteen minutes?"

"How about thirty?" Clinton suggested.

Alex waved good-bye to the couple and headed out the door.

About thirty minutes later, Clinton and Nina joined Alex in the dining room. She had arranged for an array of breakfast foods to be served as well as gourmet coffee, which Nina knew was a peace offering.

Nina smiled. "This is really nice, Sis."

"I felt kind of bad for busting up your groove this morning," Alex whispered as Clinton poured coffee for the ladies. "So, what happened?"

Clinton and Nina sat down and looked at Alex. He said, "Nina and I had a wonderful night and —"

Alex nodded and held her hand up. "That's nice, but what happened with that snake Randall?"

Clinton told her the events of the previous night as Nina munched on honeydew melon.

"So he's finished terrorizing us?" Alex asked.

Clinton nodded. "I don't think he wants to deal with your father."

Alex smiled smugly as she buttered a piece of wheat toast. "Daddy didn't make it this far by being a pushover, Randall should've known that." She bit into the bread and turned to Nina. "Are you going to join us for Thanksgiving this year or are you covering the Cowboys again?"

Nina cut into her turkey bacon and shook her head. "Not this year. I'm looking forward to the holidays this year." She and Clinton exchanged a meaningful glance.

Alex looked at them and eased back in her chair. "What am I missing?"

Nina drummed her fingers against the table. "Oh, nothing." The smile on her face was as bright as the sun. "We're getting married."

"I know that," Alex said.

"On Christmas Day," Clinton said.

Alex clasped her hands together. "What? That is so romantic. And Clinton, you will never be able to forget your anniversary. Are y'all going to have the wedding here?"

Nina was thrilled with Alex's excitement about the wedding. Squeezing her sister's hand, she smiled. "Getting married here would be apropos since this is where we met."

"And she nixed my idea of flying to Vegas tonight."

Alex rolled her eyes. "I'd hurt you both."

Nina nudged Clinton. "I told him that."

"Glad you did." Alex pursed her lips, then relaxed. "But I'm thinking a winter wonderland theme with —"

"There you go," Nina said. "Can we take it one step at a time?"

"Sorry, but we need this happiness right now. I'm still trying to process everything going on with Logan and Robin."

"And then there's Yolanda."

Alex raised her right eyebrow. "What about Yolanda?"

Nina bit her bottom lip, surprised that their father hadn't shared Yolanda's situation with Alex. Now she wished she'd kept her mouth shut. "Nothing."

"You can't open up that can of worms and say nothing. What's really behind her move to Charlotte?"

"Ask your sister. I'm not getting into this. Besides, we were talking about a winter wonderland."

Clinton smiled at the two women. If someone would've told him when he started his job at the bed-and-breakfast that he'd be sitting at a table with Alexandria Richardson planning his wedding, he would've told that person that he or she needed to seek mental health help.

"All right," Clinton said as he walked over to Nina and Alex. "We'd better tell the rest of the family about our wedding day. I don't want Yolanda to come down on me because we didn't tell her about this."

Nina turned to her fiancé. "You know she will. Believe it or not, she's actually tougher than this one."

Alex rolled her eyes. "Whatever. Are you going to tell me what's going on with Yo-Yo or not?"

Nina shook her head.

Alex rose to her feet. "Keep your little secrets," she said, her tone telling everyone how offended she was to be left out of the loop. "I'm going to book my cruise."

Once Alex was gone, Clinton turned to Nina. "She's going to find out what's going on, why didn't you just tell her?"

"Because Yolanda doesn't want any of us involved in her drama. Besides, Alex would just try to fix everything and it would just cause more conflict."

Clinton drew Nina into his arms. "Let's just focus on us right now and we can worry about everything else later."

A slow smile spread across Nina's face. "Remember what we were about to do before Alex knocked on the door?"

He nodded enthusiastically. "Oh yeah."

"Then, let's go pick up where we left off," she whispered naughtily.

Hours later, Nina and Clinton emerged from the room ready for lunch and to start planning their wedding. They were surprised to see Sheldon, Alex, and Yolanda in the dining room.

"It's about time you two came up for air," Yolanda said with a wicked grin.

Alex shook her head at her sister. "You're so crass. Dad is sitting right here."

Yolanda folded her arms across her chest. "And he has four daughters."

Sheldon cleared his throat. "Before you all say something that causes me to go get my belt, let's move on."

Nina and Clinton sat side by side, not feeling a bit embarrassed about how they spent the morning. He poured Nina a glass of tea and winked at her as she accepted it.

"Alex said you all have set a wedding date," Sheldon said as the waitstaff served them lunch.

"Yes," Nina said, a tad bit annoyed that her sister blabbed without giving her a chance to tell her father herself. "We're going to get married on Christmas Day."

Yolanda clapped her hands together. "This is going to be so exciting. Burgundy and cream with poinsettias all around and winter roses."

"Whose wedding is it, mine or yours?" Nina teased, though she knew Yolanda was going to do the majority of the designing for the wedding.

"I was thinking a winter wonderland theme," Alex said.

Nina threw her hands up. "Do Clinton and I get a say in this at all?" She nudged him and he shook his head.

Yolanda glared at her sister. "If I let you have a say, there'd be footballs hanging everywhere. And I'm going to be the maid of honor, right?"

"No, I'm the oldest and that's my job," Alex said. "Right, Nina? Clinton?"

Clinton sipped his tea and laughed. "You're on your own with this one," he said to Nina.

"Maybe Robin should be the matron of honor, since she's the only one of us who's ever been married," Nina said.

Yolanda picked up her glass of iced tea and took a long sip. "We see how that worked out for her," she said. "Has that fool explained himself yet?"

"We're not going to talk about Logan and Robin while we're planning my wedding," Nina said. "We'll deal with him later."

Sheldon shook his head. "No one is dealing with anyone. Logan and Robin have to hammer out what's going on between them without interference from you three."

The sisters pouted and nodded. "Okay, Daddy," they said in unison.

"I mean it," Sheldon said. "Marriage is between a man and a woman and Robin doesn't need the three of you making things worse for her. Besides, each one of you have your own problems."

Yolanda looked uncomfortable as she took another sip of tea. Nina wanted to ask her sister about things in Charlotte and those invisible thugs stalking her, but she held her tongue.

All throughout lunch, the family bounced wedding ideas off Clinton and Nina. Sheldon was thrilled that the couple had decided to have their wedding at the bed-and-breakfast. He and Nora had been married there as well.

Alex, ever the businesswoman, wanted the wedding to be elegant and use some of the photos for their holiday promotions. Nina was not having that at all.

Yolanda wanted to pick all of the fashions,

and have her boutique provide the wedding gown and bridesmaid dresses. Clinton just wanted to enjoy his shrimp and grits because for all he cared, he and Nina could get married in the middle of the Charleston Harbor wearing wet suits and it would still be the happiest day of his life.

"So," Sheldon said, interrupting the wedding talk. "Where are you two going to live after the wedding?"

Nina and Clinton exchanged glances. "Summerville."

"But what about your writing career?" Alex asked. "Have you talked to any editors here about freelancing and there aren't any professional teams here —"

"I know and I haven't talked to any editors yet, but I was thinking about doing some teaching as well. The College of Charleston has some guest teaching positions and I might apply for one," Nina said.

"Are you sure that's what you want to do?" Yolanda asked.

Nina nodded. "I never do anything that I don't want to do."

"I'm glad you're coming home," Sheldon said. "I know I shouldn't feel this way, but I want to keep my eye on you for a little while after that accident. Having you closer is going to make that a lot easier."

"Daddy," Nina murmured.

He reached across the table and squeezed her hand. "Nina, I know you like to think that you don't need anybody and you're the most independent woman on the earth. But at the end of the day, you will always be my baby."

Tears welled up in her eyes as she smiled at her father. "I love you, Daddy."

Clinton's heart swelled as he watched Nina and Sheldon.

Nina looked around the table. "Since the accident, I've had time to think about what's really important to me. I don't have to prove to anyone that I'm good at my job and I can write sports just as well as any of my male colleagues. I don't have to prove anything to anyone anymore. I can write and I can teach other people to write. This is what I want. Besides, this is a great place to raise a family and if it was good enough for Mom and Dad, then it will be good enough for me and Clinton."

Sheldon clasped his hands together. "This is a celebration, then. My baby's coming home."

CHAPTER 29

Nina walked out of the dressing room of Yolanda's Charlotte boutique and her sisters collectively gasped. The formfitting Simone Carvalli wedding gown hugged her curves and gave her caramel skin an ethereal glow.

"This is the one," Nina said as she spun around.

Alex brought her hands to her mouth. "You look like Mommy." She pulled her phone out and showed Nina a picture of their parents on their wedding day.

Tears welled up in Nina's eyes as she looked at her smiling mother. Yolanda rushed over to her. "Nope. No teardrops on the dress. But you do look like Mommy."

Robin nodded as she downed her champagne. "Beautiful. Just beautiful."

Nina looked down at the length of the dress. "Yolanda, can you shorten it?"

"Yes. How short?"

Alex shook her head. "Why would you do

that, it's perfect the way it is."

Robin thumped Alex's shoulder. "Let her have her dress as short as she wants it. We just have to make sure she doesn't wear high-top sneakers."

"It was just a suggestion," Alex said.

"Knee length, does that meet your approval?" Nina kicked her leg out.

"Yes," Alex and Yolanda said in concert.

"And," Nina began. "It's a winter wedding, I can wear boots."

"No, you won't!" Yolanda dashed to the back of the boutique and returned with a shoebox. "These are the shoes for this dress." She opened the box and handed Nina the silver heels.

"They are gorgeous." Robin nodded, then got a little misty-eyed. "I'm going to take a walk."

"Robin," Alex called out to her sister. Robin threw up her hand.

"I'm fine, just give me a minute."

When she walked out the door Alex locked eyes with Yolanda. "I swear I want to hurt Logan."

"So do I, but Daddy said mind our business."

"I feel bad that I'm getting ready to get married and she's hurting so much." Nina sighed and reached to unbutton her dress.

Yolanda and Alex crossed over to her and helped her take the dress off. "She won't talk to us about what happened when she went home after Thanksgiving."

"I wish we could find out Logan's story," Alex said.

"You just want to punch the man in the face." Yolanda laughed. Nina walked into the dressing room and put her clothes on.

"We all want to punch him in the face." Nina crossed over to the counter and reached for a glass of champagne.

"No." Yolanda moved the champagne out of Nina's reach. "You have to drive back to your town house."

Nina rolled her eyes. "And you think one glass of champagne is going to hurt me?"

"Were you drinking the last time you got in an accident?" Alex asked.

"Whatever." She grabbed a bottle of water. "Happy?"

"Thrilled." Alex and Yolanda burst out laughing.

"What are we going to do about Robin?" Nina asked just as her sister walked in the boutique.

"I hope y'all haven't been talking about me all this time?" Robin rolled her eyes.

"Things with you and Logan aren't any better?" Nina asked.

Robin shook her head. "But don't let me put a damper on your wedding plans. This isn't about me."

Yolanda took Robin's hand in hers. "We really wish that you would let us help you through this."

Robin raised her eyebrow. "The only thing that's going to help me through this is for Logan to sign these damned divorce papers. He just won't let our marriage go."

"Maybe you two should try to work things out," Nina said. "I know you still love him."

"If Clinton ever cheats on you and produces a child, let me know how apt you'll be to forgive him. He keeps denying that this child is his, but the DNA test didn't lie. He's the father." Robin rose to her feet and stalked over to the window. Silently tears fell from her cheeks. "I wish I didn't still love him."

Nina crossed over to her sister. "But you do and I know that love is too important to let go."

Robin turned around and smiled at her sister. "You're so happy and so in love. Life isn't a fairy tale and Logan and I aren't going to work anything out because I don't trust him anymore."

"We'll see. You've always been my role model. I wanted to be like you, with a happy marriage and . . ."

Robin patted Nina on her shoulder. "You can't believe everything that you see. Obviously, Logan and I weren't that happy if he could turn to another woman the way he did. I'm heading back to your town house. I think the movers are coming and I feel like I'm bringing the mood down here." She walked out of the boutique.

"Don't you think we need to go after her?" Nina asked.

"No," Yolanda said. "Just give her some time to be alone. You can't fix our problems by running to Daddy or giving a lovesick speech, Nina."

Nina turned to Yolanda. "Forgive me for caring about you and Robin."

"Thanks to you, I have a man shadowing my every move and he is getting on my nerves. I can't run my business without him hovering over my shoulder. I swear, he watches me when I go to the bathroom."

"Would you rather be dead?" Nina snapped.

Yolanda rolled her eyes. "Tell me something," Nina continued. "If the shoe was on the other foot, wouldn't you have done the same thing?"

Sighing, Yolanda admitted that she

would've told her father as well. "All right, I get it."

"What in the hell is going on with you two?" Alex asked. "I know Yolanda is hiding something about why she just moved here from Richmond."

Yolanda rolled her eyes. "We'll talk about it after the wedding. We have enough drama as it is."

Nina folded her arms across her chest. "Alex, will you be my maid of honor?"

Alex smiled. "Yes." She crossed over to Nina and gave her a tight hug. "I'd be honored. I'm going to check on Robin, she's had enough time to cry alone and y'all can fix whatever this is between you two."

Once Yolanda and Nina were alone, Yolanda tossed a cookie at her. "See there. That's why I didn't want to get Daddy involved. I have to admit, though, if Charles would take that stick out of his ass, he might be an all-right type of guy. He has the looks and the body, all he needs is a personality."

"That's the Yolanda I know and love. You want to bed the bodyguard."

"Shh, don't let Alex hear you say that," Yolanda replied with a wicked glint in her eyes. "But our relationship is strictly professional."

■ ■ ■ ■

Clinton closed his office door and rubbed his temples. The bed-and-breakfast was jumping because of holiday promotions and his upcoming wedding. But Clinton seemed to have a migraine every day. He couldn't wait to have Nina as his wife, but all of this planning was getting on his last nerve.

Just as he was about to pick up his phone and call Nina, there was a knock at his door.

"Come in." Clinton was shocked to see his father walk into his office. "Dad, what's going on?"

"I just came to check on you." He took a seat across from Clinton's desk. "Your wedding's coming up soon."

The younger man nodded. "Nina's very excited. Her sisters have turned this into the event of the year."

"How do you feel?"

"Never been so looking forward to the day after Christmas," Clinton said with a smile.

"Yeah, I remember those days before your mother and I got married."

Clinton folded his arms across his chest. Though he and his father had made some headway with their relationship, he still wasn't sure he could take hearing stories about his mother from him. Part of him didn't want to make things easy for his father, because it wasn't as if it was easy for him growing up with Clinton Sr. constantly putting him down. But holding on to old bitterness wouldn't be fair to Nina and their union. He had to make more of an effort to make things right for their future.

"You know," Clinton Sr. said. "There's something I need to tell you that I should've told you a long time ago."

"What's that?"

"I'm proud of the man that you are. Your mother made you a good man because I was too stupid to do it."

"Thanks."

The elder man rose to his feet. "I mean it. For so many years, I let my failures dictate how I treated you. That's not right and I can clearly see how wrong I was."

"Why now? Are you dying?" Clinton asked, though he didn't mean for his words to come out so coldly.

"Guess I deserve that. I want to be a part of your life, Son. I want to have a chance to know my grandchildren."

"Grandchildren? You're looking into the future now? Or do you know something I don't?"

Clinton Sr. chuckled. "You mean to tell

415

me that you and that pretty little girl don't plan to have a bushel of children?"

Clinton shrugged. "We haven't discussed that, but I'm sure we will have at least one child in the future."

"And I know you will be a better father than I ever was. I hate what I did to us. I can't blame anyone but myself for the strain on our relationship. It's understandable why you don't want anything to do with me."

"It's going to take a long time to undo the years of damage between us," Clinton said.

"I'm willing to work at it."

"So am I. I'm looking forward to seeing you at the wedding."

"Of course. She's a lucky woman because you're a good man."

Clinton didn't know if he should've hugged his father or shaken his hand. The two men stood in the middle of the office, looking at each other awkwardly. "Thanks, Dad."

The older man nodded and walked out the door. They'd start healing and have a better relationship one day. But today, Clinton was just happy his father didn't feel like his enemy.

CHRISTMAS DAY

The grand ballroom of the bed-and-breakfast had been transformed into a winter wonderland. Crystals hung from the ceiling, glistening like frozen raindrops. Red roses decorated the altar where Clinton stood waiting impatiently for Nina to walk into his arms.

He wasn't surprised that this wedding wasn't the most traditional. There weren't a hundred guests in the room. Just close friends of the Richardsons and Clinton's father and fraternity brothers. Sheldon's barbershop crew had taken Clinton to the side to share scotch and a warning. "Nina is all of our baby," Leroy Foxx said as he poured Clinton a glass of scotch. "See, you're going to have to take care of her."

"Oh, I plan to do just that."

"And we're going to be watching you, young-blood," Harry Jones said. "That girl has a place in our heart like she's our own

417

daughter." Harry downed his drink. "You better treat her right."

"The last thing you have to worry about is me not loving and cherishing this woman for the rest of her life." Clinton held up his glass and nodded at the men.

Leroy clapped his hands. "Then let's toast to Clinton and Nina. May God bless your union."

Now he was waiting for his future to walk down the aisle. As the chords of the wedding march began to play, the small crowd rose to their feet. Clinton smiled when he saw Nina being led down the aisle by her father and her sisters. When he locked eyes with his bride, it felt as if time stood still. She looked like an angel in her knee-length gown and her hair was wavy, just the way he loved it because it made you take notice of her beautiful eyes. His gaze dipped to the heart-shaped neckline of her dress. There was just enough cleavage showing to make him wish they could skip straight to the "I now pronounce you husband and wife" part.

She winked at him and Clinton licked his lips. Alex nudged Nina, then smiled. "Y'all are too much."

"Hush," Yolanda said. The music stopped and Clinton reached out for Nina's hand as she approached the altar. When their fingers touched, she felt a jolt of electricity.

"I love you so much," Clinton whispered as he brushed his fingers across her cheek.

"Me too."

Sheldon smiled at the couple, silently wishing them happiness for the rest of their lives. After the entire Richardson clan gave Nina away and then sweet vows were spoken, Clinton took Nina into his arms and kissed her with a passion that made her knees quake, and everyone cheered. Their lips parted and Nina looked into her husband's eyes.

"Promise me we're going to be this happy forever."

"Easiest promise I'll ever make."

ABOUT THE AUTHOR

Cheris Hodges was bitten by the writing bug at an early age and always knew she wanted to be a writer. She wrote her first romance novel, *Revelations,* after having a vivid dream about the characters. She hopped out of bed at 2 a.m. and started writing. A graduate of Johnson C. Smith University and a winner of the NC Press Association's community journalism award, Cheris lives in Charlotte, North Carolina, where she is a freelance journalist. She loves hearing from her readers. Follow Cheris on Twitter @cherishodges.